THE MASTER'S CHOICE

THE MASTER'S CHOICE

JOHN A NIX

Drombeg Books

ISBN: 978-0-9931143-9-7

Contents

FOREWORD

THE provenance of *The Master's Choice* is a story almost as fascinating as the novel itself. The book was written in 1931-32, apparently in exasperation at the author's failure to land a job in the nascent *Irish Press* newspaper. It appears in print now for the first time, more than eighty years later.

John Arthur Nix was one of the old-style gentleman journalist types, proficient in Latin and French as well as a scholar of the classics. His newspaper articles disclose an avid historian and devotee of English and European literature.

But he turns out to have been much more than that. He died in 1956, aged 72, but left behind a short resume of what he describes as his political and social background. It reveals him to have been active, as a journalist at least, in the nationalist cause. He edited the *Galway Express*, which he describes as "Ireland's greatest republican paper", during the absence in an English prison of its editor/proprietor, Galway solicitor and later TD (member of the Dáil, the Irish Parliament), George Nicholls. The *Express* was later destroyed by the notorious Black and Tans. And John Nix, with three others, was charged with sedition in September 1920.

During the Irish Civil War (June 1921 to May 1922), his house in New Ross was the Wexford county headquarters of the Anti-Treatyite party. It was searched on occasion and arrests ordered, which caused one fatality.

He bought the Nightingale Printing Works in nearby Adamstown with a view to running a county propagandist paper, but it incurred a considerable financial loss. Later as manager of the *Wicklow Newsletter*, he printed clandestinely election literature for a republican candidate in the 1923 general election. The imprint was illegally omitted and the type "pied" immediately afterwards. "We lost the County Council advertising over it," his resume says, "and I incurred the displeasure of my non-Catholic Unionist employers."

Later, as managing editor of the *Clare Record,* which was known as "the Bishop's Paper", he says he worked in devious ways for the Fianna Fáil cause in 1927-1929, but he "lost favour with His Lordship and had to sever my connection with the newspaper".

He became "a three-figure" shareholder in the Irish Press two years before the paper was launched in 1931. Whatever his enthusiasm for the new venture, his investment failed to attain him a coveted position as either a leader-writer or sub-editor with the paper. His own account records: "I was incontinently ignored in respect of a position in that paper on the mere *ipse dixit* of one man whom I had befriended, without a test of any kind. The

John A. Nix: a portrait of the author as a young man.

whole position was falsified before the controlling Director (Eamon de Valera). I expect to be vindicated even at this belated hour."

But the vindication never came. Which, as it turns out, may

have been our good fortune. Had he been exonerated, *The Master's Choice* would probably never been written, as we discover in the penultimate paragraph of the book, where we also find out that the "novel" contains some of John Nix's own personality. "Life up to the present has been an unbroken series of disappointment and inhibitions for me," its hero, Marley Swanton declares. And then, the author tells us, "For want of something better to do he jumped up, made a grab at a pen and a wad of paper and proceeded to write his first novel, making it partially autobiographical." What follows is the result of Marley Swanton/John Nix's labours. The manuscript came to light just recently, discovered among his papers on the death of his daughter, Rachel Nix, in New Ross, and it has been my great pleasure to prepare my grandfather's opus, almost a century later, for a wider audience.

The Master's Choice is set in rural Ireland circa 1930, a decade into Irish independence, as the populace assume a new confidence and begin to take their rightful place among the notions of the earth (to misquote a popular cliché). Its hero, Marley Swanton, becomes disillusioned with his school-teaching career and evolves into a journalist with the encouragement of a provincial newspaper editor who admires his facility with words. Swanton's joy is short-lived, however, as the newspaper is taken over by a malevolent proprietor who has already taken an inexplicable dislike to him and sets about making his position impossible.

The tale is told in an archaic Hiberno-English language redolent of the era in which it is set. Some readers may find the style difficult at the outset but the persistent reader will discover that it adds a richness and colourful authenticity to the depiction of a twilight age when entertaining discourse was treasured.

All the characters to be found in rural Ireland at the time are here – the small builder whose devotion to his craft is little appreciated by his justifiably impatient employer who has even less tolerance for the time the builder spends in the pub; the greedy publican who is up to every commercial trick to advance his social standing; the tenant farmer who lives on an economic knife-edge on the threshold of the Irish Economic War; the retired British army colonel and lord of the manor, the farming work hands, the young students. And, of course, the innocent but feisty *femme fatale*, Finola Macara, who steals Marley's heart and leads him a merry dance.

John Nix was born in Cartown House, Pallaskenry, Co Limerick, in April 1884, and partly reared there as well as on Deenish Island, Co Clare. He worked for a selection of newspapers other than those mentioned above, including *The Carlow Nationalist* and the (Wexford) *Free Press*. He wrote too for the *Irish Independent*, sometimes under the pseudonym Sean Sneachta (translated as John Snow, *nix* being the Latin word for snow).

Des Nix

Dublin 2015

desmondnix@gmail.com

CHAPTER I

A MODERN ORBILIUS

THE month of May was fast waning to a close in the far-flung parish of Menavia, and Marley Swanton, its cherished school-keeper, stood addorsed to a glowing turf fire. This was his inveterate posture during teaching hours for at least six months of the year. There the gerund-grinder would sit or stand, especially in the morning when a score or two of pupils would in standing postures describe a perfect semi-circle about him. In this way, he monopolised most of the heat that radiated from the fire, a fact which earned the silent resentment of some of the bigger and by no means uncritical boys. For this self-regarding reason, the pupils were compelled to stand a good deal more than at all necessary, and they would show the strain of it betimes.

Although Mr Swanton could supply the educational needs of his parish by imparting nothing much beyond a knowledge of the three Rs, he went beyond the strict curriculum in many ways. He was partial to Latin and other by-roads of learning, contending that up to the tenth century it was a universal language, and was moreover freely spoken in Ireland up to the coming of the National School system in 1831. Then, the English language steadily pushed out both Latin and Irish. Besides, the teaching of Latin helped to enhance his reputation enormously throughout Thomond. As the parent of the Romance tongues, he would tell all who cared to listen that it was the key that unlocked the door to at least half-a-dozen living languages, all mere dialects, he would affirm, of Latin.

He believed himself to be a descendant of some of the storm-tossed Spaniards who landed on the nearby shores over three hundred years before, when their well-intentioned foray on these hostile shores was fated to be futilised more by the raging elements than the force of arms. That was why he was intrigued into the teaching and preaching of a subject that could be of little use among the sons of farmers and labourers.

In aspect, Mr Swanton was a medium-sized, pale-faced, dark-haired, spare manner of man. His physical equipment tended to convince him that Spanish blood still coursed in his veins, and he derived a tincture of melancholy pleasure from this sentimental strain of reminiscence. He even maintained that his own name had been sadly altered from its original form in compliance with the inflectional demands of English, the most composite language of them all.

Arrived at his rectangular, one-roomed, oriel-windowed school, his first concern every morning was to see that each of his pupils came provided with one sod of turf, or its equivalent in cash or kind, during the fire-burning period of the year. Failure by any boy to contribute his quota towards his own and, above all, his teacher's creature comforts was regarded as a sin of omission of the first enormity. It was a lapse that seldom went without a lecture, followed by the application of the rod. This part of the teacher's work became a ritual. The delinquent, if he were a small boy, was almost invariably mounted on the back of a more bigly built school-fellow who romped round the room with his quivering freight while the preachy and ponderous pedagogue applied half-a-dozen strokes to a certain part of his anatomy with a flat, resilient, leather strop. In this way, the subduedly iracund teacher penally stimulated either careless or reckless boys to a timely sense of what he would call their "bounden duty".

His strokes descended with due deliberation and studied restraint. The onlooker got the impression somehow he was wielding the rod of castigation more in sorrow than in anger. With most boys, it was the modus rather than the measure of the punishment that mattered most. The more sensitive boys felt abashed. For all his simulation of regret, many nourished the suspicion that he only welcomed these occasions of manifesting his power and authority. His method was as effective as if he externalised more show of anger. Each stroke of the leather as it reached its destination would be punctuated with some such remark as: "If you forget to warm your poor perished master, he won't forget to warm your little tails. However do you think that patience personified can teach such an addle-pated crew without a spark of fire to warm his poor benumbed frame?"

At such times he would seem to be dripping with pity for himself.

A very substantial pyramid of pupil-provided peat in an outside shed, if it could be seen, would entirely controvert this assertion of a fuel famine, however. As far as the didactic part of his life was concerned, he caused one to think that he preferred to be feared by all than loved by any. He would make the failure of a pupil in any respect the peg upon which to hang a horta-tive discourse of ten minutes duration. He would, as it were, mounted stiltwise upon phrases tall and well-barbed, pour out a litany of real or imaginary ills that he was obliged to suffer in his quality of teacher. At such times he contrived to convey that nearly every sentient thing in the universe contributed somehow to his frustrated desires and demands. It is said that the minds of some teachers from too much contact with juveniles sometimes fail to grow up; he was not one of these, however. He was in his element among his pupils, however much he pretended to the contrary.

On this particular morning, Wilfred Macara was the delin-quent in the matter of the fuel supply. He was peremptorily ordered to mount the back of his much taller brother Fergus, a lad of about sixteen summers. Fergus was a newcomer to the school as he had spent most of his youth so far with an uncle near Limerick. The result was that his faculties had burgeoned earlier; he was more critical and less disposed to accept the teacher and all that he said at his own valuation. So far, they had not clashed.

Fergus Macara made no move to comply, and fixed the teacher with a prolonged, defiant stare. Revolt, resentment, scorn, showed clearly in every lineament of his countenance.

Marley Swanton glowered surprise at his recalcitrant pupil. As he seemed to be in some danger of being put out of countenance, a species of defeat in itself, he hastened to add in a crescendo of anger: "Who are you looking at, you curmudgeon?"

"Oh, the cat can look at the king, sir," replied Fergus.

"Indeed. I did not know he had that privilege," ejaculated the teacher, rather taken by surprise.

He was never yet so openly defied in his own school. And he would have flung himself at any other boy at once but he recollected that he had not yet broken down the studied reserve of this unique-mannered boy during their short contact with each other.

"Do you mean to vegetate there and by your arrant disobedience thus set a bad example to the rest of the school?" he thundered with well-simulated anger.

Yet, he clearly perceived that he was up against a strange and strong-willed boy and he did not relish this posture of affairs. In the matter of learning, he was easily the most advanced and apt pupil in the school and this enhanced his respect for him. Was the barrier of aloofness that had subsisted so far between them to be so rudely broken down at last? The boy's sense of awareness told him that if this once happened it simply meant the end of that subtle form of prestige that he had so far enjoyed in the school, a possession that was very dear to him. He felt that if the barrier was once broken, he would have to forfeit what he had so carefully built up. Then he would be the daily victim of his teacher's mordant wit – and worse.

Marley Swanton also realising, alas too late for his sense of self-respect to draw back, that he was up against an unprecedented situation, assumed an additional air of gravity and deliberation. He slowly reached towards his leathern ruler, his long-cherished symbol of authority. He, too, felt that he was crossing the Rubicon and he would have given much to be able just then to vision its *denouement*. It struck him as odd that he had never yet come to closer grips with this enigmatic boy, and he blamed himself for not forcing the issue before. Now there was no retreat for him and he must screw his courage to the punishing point, come what may. He knew what was expected from him by the other boys, a convincing assertion of his authority as usual. If he shirked the now-inevitable collision with this coltish youth, he quickly reasoned that he would shed in a moment that sense of awe that he had so calculatedly built up. Ever concerned to prove that he was a man of cast-iron resolution in the event of certain contingencies, he could show no vacillation now. If he were to abate a shred of his hard-won authority when such a glaring case for condign punishment had arisen, it would be the beginning of the end for him. Boys, and especially boys reaching out towards manhood, are quick to take advantage of every evidence of weakness on the part of their parents or teachers and turn it to their own suistic account. Yes, he quickly reasoned, this was clearly a case for an exhibition of granite-like inflexibility. Now he decided to dispense with the smug complacent lecture that so often preceded his punitive processes. Instead he made a sudden grab at his quarry but Macara handed him off the same as he would hand off an opponent in a game of rugby, a game which he used to play in the city during his sojourn with his uncle. Before the teacher had time to follow up his elusive pupil, he had vaulted over a desk, seized a slate as a possible weapon of defence and stood at bay, defiant, alert, challenging.

"You won't blackguard me in my own school, you little clod-hopper," shrilled the teacher.

Macara made no reply and even the teacher's accustomed volubility momentarily deserted him. Real anger or fixed resolution is economic of speech. "Up 'til now, you are what I would call an unlicked cub," said he, "but I will make an example of you."

They stood glaring at each other. The man of a thousand victories over even bigger and older boys was in a strange dilemma. He knew that he must nip revolt of this kind in its incipient stages or not at all. But how? To surrender now would be to cause revolt to become infectious. He must face the situation that he had so thoughtlessly provoked and see it through somehow. With all the solemnity that he could assume, he proceeded to divest himself of his coat and turn up his shirt sleeves in preparation for the great physical effort that he was about to make. If the boy, he thought, would only lay down that skull-splitting slate or, better still, make a dive for the door, it would tide him over this strange contretemps and save his face. He conjured up a vision of having to dodge an edged slate should he renew the attack. Aside from this, there was the possibility of defeat in a conflict of physical force with such an unknown quantity. He knew that public opinion – or at least that immature species of it contained in the school – was entirely against him.

Just then, a trinity of sharp authoritative raps resounded on the door in a crescendo of sound, thus seeming to herald the presence of somebody of more than paravail account. He felt it as a welcome interruption. He flung a further threat at Fergus Macara, composed his distorted features as best he could and hurried towards the door. Unbolting it hastily, he was confronted by the school manager himself in the person of Canon Lavelle. The teacher, although he still betrayed some symptoms of emotion, made a brave attempt to pretend that everything was more-or-less normal. The reverend manager remarked that he must be feeling rather hot in his blood to be minus his coat on such a cool day. A searching east wind was blowing, the sort of wind that brings all sorts of throat afflictions in its wake.

The teacher said he was about to drive some nails in the walls in order to hang or to alter the position of some maps. He did not care about the cold, he averred. He was still looking passion-pale and he jerked out his sentences spasmodically.

The Canon continued to dilate on the prevailing wind. It absorbed the moisture in the air, he said, and dried up everything before it, unlike the south-easterly wind which always comes rain-laden. Still, the east wind was unhealthy and biting.

At this stage, Fergus Macara confronted the Canon and asked leave to be allowed home for the day as he was not, he said, feeling too well. Scrutinising the boy sharply, the Canon thought he saw something in his features confirmatory of his assertion. Then he noted his blond curly hair, his china blue eyes — a rare pigmentation only found along parts of the western littoral — and his freckled, cream-coloured, wistful appealing face. He won his sympathy, and he felt that he was regarding an out-of-the-ordinary type of boy. After a nicely calculated show of hesitation, during which he so keenly noted the boy's features, he at last assented to his request.

"I hope your feeling of malaise, or whatever it is, will be of short duration, heh, heh. I do not think, having regard to your appearance that you are at all malingering."

"No, indeed, sir," replied the boy, and the other forty-odd pupils wondered what such a sesquipedalian word as applied to Fergus might mean.

The Canon came to enquire about the new residence now

a–building for the teacher; and when he left, the small boy who was the cause of all the trouble went unpunished, as the teacher pretended to forget all about the matter. Though baulked of what he considered was an overripe candidate for the cane in the person of his brother, he felt relieved at the unexpected turn the situation had taken. It came to him that Fergus Macara was possessed of a strong superiority complex, while the rest of the pupils seemed to suffer in the opposite direction.

At the same time, he declared aloud for the benefit of the other boys that Fergus Macara's escape today was only the postponement of the inevitable, which was a good thrashing. This young limb from Limerick must, he declared, conform to the rules of the school and the manners of Menavia. Given an inch, he would take a furlong. "When the goat goes to the door it doesn't stop 'til it reaches the altar," he declared emphatically.

His listeners were duly impressed, except a few in whom the seeds of revolt were already sown as a result of what had happened.

Then the teacher thought anew about this boy's aptitude at his books, his aloofness and reserve. There was that indefinable something about him which he had not realised until today.

CHAPTER II

SCHOOLMASTER AND MASON

A S a new residence was in course of erection for Marley Swanton within close proximity to the school, a thing which was long desiderated yet often postponed, he was obliged to go into lodgings as the old structure that had stood for so long was now demolished in order to make way for the new. That old shieling, composed as it was of clay, and lime-washed in such a way as to give it the appearance of something more substantial, had now been pulled down and the debris spread over the adjoining fields as manure.

These mud houses, as they are called, were rapidly disappearing and yet they subserved a useful purpose in their time. They were small but when well thatched they were warm in winter and cool in summer and, although hastily thrown up, they long outlasted their builders, as most works of man do. They were cheaper and more easily thrown together than the wooden houses that preceded them. When well kept, they were less unsightly in the eyes of the discerning few than those monotonous and standardised artisans' dwellings which now stud the countryside with their rectangular acre of land at the rere so clearly proclaiming the occupation of their occupants. A farmer or teacher may live in a mud house, a labourer or loafer must live in one of those cottages. Knowing the laws under which they were built, they leave nothing to the imagination of the passer-by.

Peadar Blanche, a big, bony, supple-sinewed young man, had recently blossomed out as a contractor in a small way. He had earned a local reputation as a worker in wood and stone and as such he was entrusted with the erection of the teacher's new residence. Blanche enjoyed a justly-earned prestige as a tradesman of more than ordinary ability. The fact that he had garnered some experience in England, where he served his apprenticeship, enhanced his reputation considerably. His services would be in greater request, however, were it not for his bar-lounging habits betimes. Then, owing to his Fabian tactics, he would have too many odds and ends of jobs on hands at the same time to make rapid progress anywhere. This was the modus which some of his critical neighbours used to describe as "going from Billy to Jack".

As a wit and joker, Blanche was seen at his best leaning over the little ill-kept sloppy bar of Quinburn's public house. Here, he simply exuded an exuberant kind of drollery all his own and often caused others to drink more than was good for them. Still, he was what might be called a regular man with irregular lapses. During his intervals of abstention from drink he could be morose and silent enough at times; a mood which seemed to indicate that he missed something which only a visit to the seductive drink shop could really supply. While gazing into a creamy potation, as he would call a pint of beer, he would bubble over with the milk of human kindness and show up the doings and misdoings of his neighbours in a lively and attractive manner. That was what he called "putting things to and fro". Whatever Blanche took in hands he did it well, but his besetting sin was bar-lounging.

After school hours, Marley Swanton would stroll forth to survey his new house and note the progress that was being made from week to week. He was not averse from engaging the contractor in conversation at times, provided that he felt satisfied with what he saw. Though still a young man, Blanche had a keen sense of the past and this caused him to express contempt for many aspects of modern life. He regarded Menavia as a microcosm.

Just as he was contemplating a cessation of work for the day, the teacher hailed him with a well-simulated show of heartiness.

"God bless the work, Peadar, avick."

"And you too, sir," replied the craftsman.

"You seem to be delving away in the debris to good purpose of late. I always like to look at a master of his trade at work."

Blanche, who had been fitting a tenon into a mortise, laid aside his work. He saw that the teacher was in a friendly mood, despite the snail's progress he was making with the house of late. He responded all the more readily on that account.

"Indeed then, I'm no great shakes of a tradesman, aroon. Still and all, such as I am, I'd be thinking I'm as good as the lazy loons in my own line and a bit to spare."

"Yes, Peadar, I seem to think you're no square peg in a round hole. I like the way that mullioned window is shaping, for instance."

"Did it ever strike you, sir, that the more you know about any given subject the more you realise your limitations?"

"Well, you know enough and to spare to be able to provide me with a tolerably good house, if you'd only hurry up with it."

"Maybe I do and maybe I don't. As regards the quality of my work, I am my own greatest critic. I'm never out and out satisfied with what I do."

"Qualitatively or quantitatively – which? You certainly take your time and there's a lot of room for improvement there, you'll admit."

"I'm slow but sure, like a mule on a mountain top. I hate to be bustled in my business and even the canker or hustle is beginning to invade this sleepy hollow of a place. I am still dissatisfied with that window sill and I have a mind to undo it."

"You ought to leave well enough alone. If every man waits 'til he can do a thing so well that nobody could find fault with it, hardly anything at all would ever get done. The use of cement has besides cheapened, accelerated and simplified the art of building."

"Well, I wouldn't say that. We have forgotten a power and all about building in recent times, not to talk at all about architecture, which is building touched with emotion. Everything is too slap-dash and hurried to be either pleasing to the eye or proof against that devastating hand of time."

"Then you favour that creeping paralysis form of endeavour in everything. The ca'canny method, as it is called, isn't it, Peadar?"

"Well, I do and I don't. There's a happy medium, so to speak. Nowadays, everybody wants everything done in next to no time. No man worth his salt can be a real artist in either wood or stone or in any medium that really matters who has got to work against time always. Work done at a gallop is as transient as man himself, just here today and away tomorrow. The wooden houses of Ireland used to last two and three-quarter centuries, just because they were built by dabsters. The stone and cement houses of today don't last half that time because they are built by botches in a hurry."

"Well, there is no express hurry about this house of mine anyway, you will admit, Peadar. At the rate at which it is going up in accordance with your own slowed-down plan of work, it ought to last down to the last syllable of recorded time, long enough to usher in the day of General Judgment. For my own part, I'm convinced that we must go with the times in which we live. You seem to be a man who has just stepped out of the sixteenth century. What's the use of doing too much for posterity anyway? It might decide not to live in houses at all."

"Oh, we are doing that, sir, more or less in spite of ourselves. If everybody took your view and acted on it, it would be a sorry world entirely. A photograph that can be taken in a jiffy and lasts only for a generation would supplant the painting that requires the experience of a lifetime to execute but lasts forever. If the people of the past took your view, there would be no great castles, churches or round towers to look at today. The greatest enemy of our old buildings up 'til recently was the stone-hungry road-mender and the builders of cottages and cowsheds. They were worse than Cromwell himself."

"The mention of Cromwell reminds me, Peadar, of an interesting fact. Spenser, the poet who wrote his greatest masterpiece with materials borrowed from Irish mythology while he was living in a stolen castle in Cork, set down on two thousand acres, wrote to his patron Queen Elizabeth that the best way to destroy the Irish and solve the Irish problem forever, was to kill off all the livestock and burn the then-growing corn crops."

"Those were devilish sentiments for a poet, sir, for a man who is supposed to be as tender-hearted as a chicken, if he is to excel in his art. Given Cromwell's power, he would be ten times worse than Cromwell."

"Yes, but see where the poetic justice of it all comes in. Cromwell came along fifty years later and drove Spenser's grandson out of his fine, confiscated castle as one of the Old English and a supporter of King Charley, and sent him packing into Hell or Connacht. There, the Spenser family sunk down to the level of peasants and beggars and never cut a figure in Ireland ever since."

"I knew a builder's labourer and by the same token he was from the County Mayo. The Spensers got a touch of their own remedy and they simply got their desserts. But I think we are rambling away from the subject. Did you ever throw any kind of a critical eye at that round tower over there in Ravensdale in Colonel Gloster's estate?"

"Not particularly, Peadar. I did notice that the year we took the field on which it stands for a sports meeting I painted a notice on a board warning *al fresco* diners and winers not to scatter empty bottles about. I proceeded to nail the notice on the outer wall of this blinking round tower but it defied my best efforts. The nails would buckle up, go anywhere but into the wall. You should hear my malisons on that day."

"Well, if you knew a little more, it's your blessing and utmost admiration you'd be bestowing upon it."

"But the crowd cursed it, and so would you in the same set of circumstances."

"But I thought I heard you saying one day that the mob is always more morose and stupid than any single member of society. Our ancestors knew how to build, we only know how to curse their masterpieces."

"Well, there may be something in what you say, Peadar, as such a praiser of past times. On thinking over my futile assault on the tower afterwards, it somewhat raised my respect for it. I sometimes wonder since, what causes these old buildings to defy so successfully the ravages of time. It proves after all that something has gone out of the builder's art which the cement makers are not putting into it."

"Even if the secret wasn't lost, they wouldn't practice that mode of building today, Mr Swanton."

"That is to say that they preferred to forego before they forgot, old chap. Have you any idea how they were able to build such enduring structures?"

"Well, the secret is well-nigh lost, but at the same time I know more than a little about it. 'Twas nearly all in the mixing of the mortar; it wasn't the big stones as did it because they were not much used as they couldn't be blasted, like nowadays. Not alone does nobody know anything about the ancient secrets of building so as to last for all time but, what is worse, they don't want to know."

"However did they happen so heedlessly, as it were, to lose their architectural cunning?"

"Faith, at the rate they are going on now it's losing the plumb line they'll be next, the same as they must have done when the Tower of Pisa was a-building. Well, to begin with, they used to wash the sand in a sieve, so as to deprive it of all foreign bodies, over a running stream. All earthy matter was thus carried off, do you see. Then they would mix dry lime with the wet sand and beat the two mixtures together for hours. They believed in a thorough mixing and in that way they anticipated the mechanical mixers of today. The preparation of sand, sir, in those far-off days was a matter of great moment."

"And now it is only a matter of moments. I can see, old chap, that time was not of the essence of the matter at all, provided that the work came up to the then-prevailing norm, whatever that was."

"In a manner of speaking, yes, sir. What people won't take their time to do won't stand the test of time. You cannot cheat time in that way."

"Well stated, old chap. You deserve a pull of the pipe for that."

Marley Swanton then extended a well-filled pipe towards the mason-carpenter who regarded it solemnly before conveying it to his mouth. Then he avidly sucked at it.

Offering a man your own pipe in Menavia was ever regarded as a gesture of peace and amity. For the nonce, it cemented the friendship of these twain, a friendship which was not unseldom strained to breaking point.

Blanche then subsided into a nearby wheelbarrow and declared that while spending the pipe, as he called it, all his worries seemed to vanish like the arabesque clouds he was wafting skywards. In Menavia, the character of a man may seem to be so hard that you could break stones on it, yet if he accepts the pipe of peace from his neighbour it shows that he is at least accessible through one amiable weakness. Some of the most inveterate

15

smokers in the parish could smoke an ounce of strong twist tobacco daily, and Blanche was one of them. Tobacco was no longer a luxury; it had become a necessity.

After an interval of silence, during which he seemed to enjoy the teacher's meerschaum pipe, Blanche again took up the thread of the conversation.

"While I'm having a well-earned smoke of this new-fangled pipe of yours, as many-coloured almost as Joseph's coat, I may as well tell you that there was another method of building. It's practised it was in places where stones were no bigger nor your clenched fist. The walls were dry-built between wooden boards in layers, near a foot deep at a time. The mortar, treated as before, was boiled in big boilers mixed with one or two other things of the nature of which we are not too sure now. When about as thick as liquid tar, this molten stuff was poured down into the pebbly layer. It was a searching brew, I declare."

"You mean, I suppose, that it found its way into all the interstices and bound the whole mass together," supplemented the teacher, a trifle pedantically.

"Just so, sir. It's grouting, that kind of building was called. They used to mix bullocks' blood and new milk with the lime and sand and the product of such a mixture would defy the ravages of a thousand years. The country was strewn with lime kilns then, now alas all abandoned and grass grown in favour of foreign building materials."

"Well, I'm fairly jiggered with admiration for the doings of the great dead now that I've got an inkling into their uncanny methods. Theirs was what one could truly call an integrating process that truly defied the blighting hand of time."

The teacher's lips parted in a smile, showing that he was preening himself as a commentator.

"Now you've put the coping stone on my attempt at a reconstruction of the past. That's the kind of work you couldn't drive a nail into at Ravensdale. Even if Mickey the Mowler himself were to try it, it would be a case of Kenn Barry's kingship with him. Building has decayed more nor any other art with us in recent times."

"Wages are too high, Peadar, to admit to such elaborate methods nowadays. It's not right to build such time-defying structures and, besides, we must leave something for posterity to do or it would die of ennui and sloth."

"Yes, but posterity doesn't ask to be born, does it – therefore it should be well housed when it comes into the world."

"Oh, yes it does, Peadar. When two people fall into what is called love, it is at the bidding of a *tertium quid*, a third something clamouring for a separate existence. The love-lorn pair don't know it. They think they are the authors of the next generation when they are merely its slaves."

"I'm afraid you're becoming too metaphysical for me this evening, sir. I'm blowed if I'm going to listen to that kind of woolly nonsense much longer. What do we know about love anyway, a pair of confirmed bachelors, and likely to remain so?"

"You never can tell, Peadar, you never can tell."

The teacher then retrieved his remarkable pipe and bade adieu to the contractor who in turn called after him: "Safe home!"

The irony of this remark was that he had no home, largely due to Peadar's own slowed down method of working at the new house.

CHAPTER III

WON BY A MILE

PENDING the completion of his residence, a work already of nearly two years duration, Marley Swanton decided that he had no option but to live with, and partially on, the well-to-do farmers throughout the parish who were possessed of children of a school-going age. There was some justification for this. Was he not, he reasoned, in the tradition to some extent of the ancient poets and bards who enjoyed all manner of rights and privileges down to about a century ago when they were welcomed, housed and fed in every big house throughout Ireland. Accordingly, he decided that he would stay a week or two at a time with each farmer. He never omitted to tender money at the rate of a pound a week in respect of his maintenance but it was not accepted except in the case of small, struggling farmers. Although not a paying guest yet, he made it appear in his selective visits to these people that he was somehow conferring upon them a subtle sort of compliment. At school he would occasionally refer to the way he was knocked about like a billiard ball due to his want of a house. Yet for all that it was not, he would aver on every pillow in the parish that he would lay his head o' nights. His artfully-worded confidences were, whether he so intended it or not, duly conveyed by the pupils to their parents' ears. Henceforth, they in turn began to take a much greater interest in the pedagogue's parochial peregrinations.

The result was that in no long time the status of a farmer came to be assayed by a new rough and ready rule. Did the homeless homiletic Mr Swanton think it worth his while to raise So-and-So to the dignity of a host? The fact that he sojourned in any house and continued to do so seemed to prove beyond a peradventure that the standard of living was high in such a place, the beds good and the family in question really refined. After all, do not most people spend more than a third of their lives in bed, so that sleeping comfort deserved more than passing attention. It came to pass that every farmer's prestige was raised by recurring visits from the teacher. Yet, this is not to say that his hosts always liked or welcomed him for his own sake. They didn't. He was in request among them simply because they hankered after a reputation for hospitality and a decent standard of living, and all that it connoted in Menavia. It was a comparatively cheap and easy way to pick up a reputation. In time it came to pass that visits from him which were at first considered partially intrusive were soon welcomed and later actively sought after. The wives of two small farmers were detected in the act of waiting on him clandestinely and warmly pressing him to stay at their farmsteads if only for a week on his rounds. Even servant boys and girls about to enter service throughout the parish would first drop a few discreet enquiries as to whether the teacher was in the habit of staying with that particular farmer? If the answer were in the negative then that family's reputation as a purveyor of the alimentary wants of human nature suffered accordingly. Formerly, the mistress used to engage the maid; now the process is reversed, the maid engages the mistress. The farmer who was eschewed by the teacher was also given a wide berth by both man and maid. Of course, the teacher never intended that this should be so; he was a secretive man and kept his confidences very much to himself but, for all that, Menavia was very much of a whispering gallery and everything seemed to be known to everybody else.

The arrival of the summer holidays was welcomed by the school-going part of the population. Marley Swanton was once more spending a few weeks with the Macara family. The Macaras, who were considered big farmers in the parish, a fact of which they were duly proud, tenanted just over a hundred acres of pasture and arable land. James Macara, the head of the house, although a farmer's son, was not a signal success as a farmer. As a boy he was apprenticed to a grocer and publican and a fee of thirty pounds was even exacted in respect of his apprenticeship which had to be paid in advance. After about three months service the prospective publican was given a month's holidays, a most unusual and generous action on the part of his master at the time. He returned in due course to find the shop shuttered up. After waiting on the doorstep for an hour, he was told by a passing policeman on beat duty, who was beginning to suspect that the boy was loitering for an unlawful purpose, that his boss had levanted to America. A moonlight flitting he said it was, leaving a pile of debts after him all over the place.

Nothing daunted, the boy's father brought him to another grocer to be bound. The latter agreed to accept four quarterly instalments of five pounds. His father tendered a ten pound note, half of which was to cover the first quarter. The grocer said he hadn't the change and the other man said he would get the change of it elsewhere and bring back the boy and the balance. The promise was never fulfilled.

What caused him to change his mind instead of the money regarding his son's avocation he never disclosed. James used to ponder over this matter fairly often in after years but he could find no clue to the mystery. He would speculate engagingly about the altered mode of life he would be living now had the trader changed the note in time or at all.

As a young hopeful he would relate how he was next bundled off to America where he remained for two years. During that time he worked for the most part with farmers in the virgin lands and did a lot of tree-felling work at which he became very expert.

Returning home at the insistence of his father who had a

few farms of land to divide among his sons, he continued to pine after the Californian manner of life. Although a man of elementary education, he cultivated the habit of opsimathy and, as his children grew up he simply devoured their schoolbooks too. He became an authority on the Bible, Shakespeare and astronomy. He would also revel in the verbal felicities of Pope who, despite his shortcomings as a poet, did more to make the English language a plastic mode of expression than anybody else since or before his time. Strange to relate, he only read one novel, but he could quote these poets whose works he pored over at all times, from cover to cover. This, in addition to his ability to name the major and many of the minor stars in their courses. The result of his concentrated, though restricted course of study was that he soon acquired the reputation of being a famous and formidable debater. He had the knack of giving an argument a certain twist and then appositely unleashing passages from the Bible or Shakespeare on his unhappy opponent who was at once confuted as much by the novelty as by the force of his polemics. He had a semi-risorial way of pressing home an argument that conveyed an impression of being all over his opponent. He was a phrasemaker, too, of no mean order. Although an unremitting worker on the farm, he failed to prosper in the same degree as his more bucolic brothers.

Macara's ancestors came from England soon after the Reformation. The first of the name to come to Ireland was a Protestant churchman. He found the prospect so pleasing that he sent for his brother Charles, a mulierose man by all accounts. He was at once put in possession of an extensive tract of land. Then he fell violently in love with a knight's daughter named Rachel McCutcheon, but there was parental opposition. After bribing her servants, he gained access to her room early one morning. Then he stole over to the window which looked out on the street, donned a sleeping cap, craned his head over the window sill and began to salute the passers-by while the object of his love remained rapt in profound slumber. In this way, he compromised the young lady in the eyes of her acquaintances, declaring that all was fair in love and war. With this undeserved stigma on her fair name in her native city, she capitulated, and they were duly married. Charles Macara thus became the founder of the family in that part of the country. He was only twenty years of age at the time but when nature makes us ripe for love it seldom happens that the Fates are unfavourable or unwilling to furnish us with a temple for the flame.

His wife too, it has been affirmed – an easy thing to do at this distance – was at the time an artistic pleasure to look at and an intellectual repose to talk to. Endowed as she was with so many pleasing attributes of womanhood and a fair share of the world's wealth, it was conceded that she had been sacrificed on the altar of the Saxon adventurer's ambitions.

Although endowed with every circumstance of prosperity and opportunity, the Macara family gradually shed their wealth and influence with the efflux of time. They lost their status and fell down from the position of landed proprietors to tenant farmers. James Macara's grandfather led a drink-sodden life, and in a moment of alcoholic dementia he sold a large farm of land to a boon companion for a quart of malt. Then he lost the price of another farm in an attempt to retrieve it at law. The tenour of his life are best summed up in his own words – "I live only by the dent of drams."

James Macara's father, who married a Catholic, became a Catholic in due course but only a Laodicean one. Macara was thinking over the ups and downs of his family when the teacher arrived.

He was glad to have somebody to confide in and he went over the whole history of his family for the teacher's benefit.

"The declension of the Macaras," said Swanton, "goes

to prove the ultimate superiority of the Celt over the invasive Saxons, especially the Saxon of the planter and placeman type. The Celt, although harried and harassed almost beyond endurance for a couple of centuries ultimately by pulling down, levels up with the alien, privileged element in his midst. Down the archway of the persecuted years, he accumulated deep latent reserves of cunning and strength and then, when the opportunity offered, he came back to the land once owned by his ancestors. Hope, no matter how hopeless the outlook appears to be, springs eternal in the Celtic breast. The love of the place of his nativity seems only to increase with the passage of the years and blossoms into a sort of second religion with him. Unless and until the foreigner in his midst is dragged down to his own level, entirely assimilated to his Celtic environment, he slowly but surely pines away. Then, when he assumes the Celtic religion and culture, he is assured of a new lease of life on a higher spiritual but on a lower material plane, however. There is a certain amount of loss but on the whole, there is much more gain."

"This fate has already overtaken the Macara family, don't you think, Mr Swanton?"

"I should think so. The transition stage is not very pleasant. It is nearly as Celticised as it can be. The Celt has qualities not unlike the camomile flower – the more it is trodden on, the more it grows. Else there would be no such being to write and talk about after all the centuries of oppression. He is not unlike the Jew in that respect. Despite successive plantations and evictions, he comes back like the aftermath that arises where the mowers have left the land bare. When the mowers, like Anteus of old, bestir themselves again, it is only to find it arrayed in a fresh increase of strength. Yes, the Celt has shed few of his ancient qualities."

Macara, who was well above the average in height, turned his mobile, bearded face towards the teacher. "Yes, I suppose there is something in that theory of yours," he asseverated. "However, at the moment I'm more concerned with present-day problems. The old world as we knew it came to an end in 1914 and a new world came into being four years later. As far as the ordinary farmer is concerned, the long dreaded landlord is, or soon will be, a thing of the past, but the joint stock banks are taking their place. During the war, and in fact till the great slump came in the May of 1921, the price of land quintupled because bank managers went about to sales and auctions pressing money on would-be purchasers. Many of them sold out their small places and bought big farms, making up the difference with money pressed upon them by the banks. As we are tied on to the English money system, we suffered tremendously when that country embarked on a policy of deflation. The prices of livestock and farming produce fell to less than half inside of a year and continued falling down to the present time. The result of all this is that the farmer who is stuck in a bank finds it two or three times more difficult to pay interest today than during the boom years. The position is really desperate at present for the vast majority of our farmers."

"It is said, sir, that the farmers lived up to their means and even beyond it during those boom years. They bought motors, spent tons of money on drink and abandoned themselves to a life of dissipation generally."

"Well, they did themselves pretty well, Mr Swanton, I must admit. They thought the boom years would last forever especially as they lasted for two and a half years after the Great War."

"Some of them have told me that they got into an expensive way of living that time and that they can't get back to the pre-war standard. It is like a bather who goes beyond his depth. I can imagine that it is a terrible plight to be in. During that time a certain farmer had two clever sons going to my school. I advised him to send them to college with a view to embracing some of the professions. He laughed at the idea and said they were actually beating cows with doctors and teachers they were such a drug in the market. One of those young fellows is a temporary road overseer today at about two pounds a week and glad to get it."

"They were all wassailing with that infernal publican Quinburn during those years and he seemed to have exercised great influence over them."

"Did it ever strike you that when there is a great boom in agriculture, the learned professions are at a discount? I felt my own position keenly during that boom because I was made to feel it. Every scraggy farmer having more money than he ever thought he would have looked out for the time when he would be a great territorial magnate. They began to ape the landlords – what was left of them – and the gentry."

"Sudden wealth is a dangerous thing. The farmers had seven glorious years. They lived in a sort of earthly paradise and now they are cast into the outer regions, pervaded as they are by doubt, debt, depression and disappointment."

"In fact, some of them go as far as to say now that it would be better that they never saw such boom years. They have unfitted them for the stern struggle of today."

"If the banks really wanted to do it they could put half the farmers of Ireland on the roadside nowadays, they owe them such a pile of money."

"Yes, Mr Macara, but has it ever struck you that when a man owes you too much money that he becomes, in a sense, your master. If you come down upon him like a load of bricks, you scotch him altogether and you get no more out of him. These creditors will have to wait and see and, in any case, a lot of their money will be irrecoverably lost in the long run."

"Oh, the banks, unlike private traders, never die, and debts owing to them never grow stale. They are continued in their books from one generation to another. Many an ambitious man has tied a millstone of debt around the necks of his children as won't be paid to the banks for the next fifty years."

"Paddy Quinburn says that the farmer's real friend is the shopkeeper. He says that he gives him several years' credit in respect of goods, that he is really a money-lender who charges no interest."

"Oh, that fellow is becoming a great authority upon everything and anything lately. Nobody says anything now without giving this bally publican as his authority."

"There must be something in the fellow, right enough. Once a very poor man, whatever he made during the boom years stayed with him. When a man of money talks nowadays it doubles the weight of his words. The fellow is certainly coming out of his shell latterly and he used not have a word to throw to a dog."

"Oh, poverty is a great silencer in this country. I wouldn't be talking to a man for a minute 'til I could tell whether he is in debt or not. There is that indefinable something about a man who is financially embarrassed that gives him away. It is the old story – money, like murder, will out."

At this stage, Fergus Macara burst into the parlour and felt somewhat abashed on seeing the teacher, whom he did not expect. Their meeting was characterised by a certain measure of formality which was lost, however, upon the boy's father, who knew nothing about the school episode, or whatever caused the boy on one pretext or another to remain away from school since it happened. Both, however, forebore to advert to the cause which so violently separated them just two months before that. The teacher now felt that he should make it up. For weal or woe, people have notoriously long memories in rural districts because deep layers of learning do not have to jostle with the commonplaces of their sedate, slow-moving lives and crowd them out.

Some exciting verbal sword-play used to be expected between the teacher and his poetic host but these clashes of intellect seldom came off, however. Marley Swanton, although a man of intellectual attainments far beyond the requirements of Menavia, was economic of speech except during school hours. There were reasons for this. Swanton felt that in some ways he was becoming stereotyped and hidebound. He reasoned that much of his life was passed among the very young and mentally undeveloped who could not talk to him on level terms. It was, he thought, a great and growing disability and one against which every primary teacher has to contend. In time, this constant intercourse with undeveloped minds would generate a certain amount of diffidence in him in the presence of adults.

Over the tea cups, the speculative farmer would sometimes try to allure his visitor into controversy on all manner of subjects, but he would evade the issue by pretending to agree with him. "Thoughts, and especially unprofitable thoughts, can annoy us more that unruly school urchins if we do not keep them under due control," he would say.

He often felt that James Macara was speculating beyond his depth.

CHAPTER IV

THE HEROINE MAKES HER DEBUT

BESIDE the Macara farmstead, a somewhat large tidal tribu-tary of the lordly Shannon meandered rather sluggishly. It invited the unremitting attention of Marley Swanton who, although unable to swim, was much addicted to bathing when he found himself set down where this passion could be easily indulged. He never pushed his enthusiasm far enough to learn the noble art of swimming but this was because he thought about it too late in life, and then he did not always live near tidal waters. In his matutinal wantonings with the waters, he would insist on being accompanied by either Fergus or Wilfred Macara, much against their wishes, which they strove, however, to subordinate to higher considerations. They were too bored with this river from daily contact with it to want to swim in it, and whatever thrill boating originally contained for them had now been exhausted.

Fergus would be sometimes told by his parents to concern himself more with the wishes of his teacher. In a farm, however, there is ever a round of minor tasks to be performed by children and, besides, they always felt ill at ease in the presence of their teacher and preferred the most exacting tasks to his company.

Just now, Fergus was under a cloud. A fortnight before, he had put down a dose of rat poison about the piggeries. It was great fun watching the results and seeing the sleek long-tailed pests lying dead in all directions. He had caught them dining with the pigs a few times lately as a result of which he would not eat any more bacon because pigs were the daily compan-ions of the most abhorred form of farm life. Then, he returned home from town early one day with four calves, bought by his father who stayed behind him in town, to find that a fine store pig had partaken of the poison and lay dead beside its trough. It was now a fine purple colour and his elder sister Finola had told him with tears in her eyes that the poor pig had died in great agony. It had suffered as much as any person and seemed to think, she said, that she should be able to cure it. The rats must have suspected baited food and tried it on the poor, portly porker. "You know," she said, "rats know everything; they are not right."

Fergus's father did not return home from town that day 'til the fall of night and, in the meantime, the promising pig was buried out of sight. Nothing more was said of it and all silently speculated how long it would be before his father would miss the animal from among the five others. This misadventure depressed Fergus, as he knew that his parents, though farming on a big scale, could ill afford such a loss.

In addition to counting the livestock and making sure that none of the sheep was stuck in the bushes or briars or suffered from maggots or lameness, Fergus had to milk six cows every morning before he set out for school. Parents lost no time in Menavia in convincing their children that work was their inevitable heritage; their *raison d'être* in the cosmic scheme of things.

In order to whet his flagging appetite, Marley Swanton announced to the household that he would "have a dip in the briny" first and added that he would be a bit late for breakfast perhaps. Mrs Sephora Macara assured him that it would be all right and warned him not to go in where there were a few deep creeks and crompauns. She had a certain regard for the teacher because she had gone to a convent school with an aunt of his for a few months. She even invited Miss Swanton to spend part of the summer holidays with her parents' people in the County Limerick. She now took occasion to enquire about her college companion. Then she proceeded to relate the

Parnell Split which was sundering the country. One evening while they were preparing to go for a drive in a little ass-and-trap they saw three tatterdemalion men coming up the avenue in the company of her father. On closer inspection they were found to be covered with mud and blood and some ochre-hued stain. They looked frightened and footsore. Then her mother met them at the hall door and asked them what kind of a meeting they had in the local village? Either Tim Harrington or Sheehy replied by saying in their best Dublin drawl. "I'm afraid it wasn't a very enthusiastic meeting, Mrs Dix." The fact was that they were rotten-egg pelted and hooted from the hustings by the anti-Parnellite faction, who were in an overwhelming majority. These poor lapidated men were then put to bed where they had to remain 'til their clothes were washed and dried. There were only four supporters of Parnell in the parish and her brothers had to remain away from school for some months as the other boys made life unbearable for them on that account.

"They were fearful times by all accounts," assented the teacher. "I was too young to remember it but those who lived through it say it was the greatest battle of tongues was ever waged in Ireland in the absence of guns, which were so treacherously used in the last great split. The Irish people simply adore their political leaders for a while and for no solid reasons as far as one can see in the light of their achievements, which are little enough. Then, for little or no reason, they turn upon them and cast them on the scrap heap. They were a bit premature, however, in the case of Parnell; he was the greatest political leader of them all."

Fergus Macara and his younger brother then ran in to look for their teacher. They piloted him to a deep creek that jutted into the river at right angles. As a spring tide was running, it covered and concealed these inequalities of the riverbed. Here he was told he could bathe with perfect safety and he eagerly proceeded to undress.

Up 'til now cold and formal enough with his pupils, his clothes and his hauteur came off together. A civilised man sheds much of his pride and dignity with his clothes. Even his courage dies down.

Marley Swanton was in what might be called a fey-like state of good humour, a mood which is said to come upon people when they are on the eve of passing from time into eternity. He suddenly thawed towards his somewhat brazen-faced pupils and twitted them on their unnatural and unmanly dislike of swimming. They were, he assured them, missing one of the major joys of life. As an exercise, it brought every muscle of the body into play as no other form of physical effort could do. He would pay Peadar Blanche next week to teach him the breaststroke, then the truncheon and finally the crawl. He would insist upon them being present when they could learn *gratis*. It was a positive scandal that few country-bred fellows could swim. It should be taught in the schools, at least in theory.

This sudden burst of friendship surprised his hearers, and Fergus reflected that it was scarcely worth his while making plans for the future. Wilfred, too, had formed a certain impression of a dour despotical man making life miserable daily for him and he did not desire any show of friendship now lest it may cause him to change his mind. He simply did not want his hostile feeling towards his teacher removed. A puckish spirit of mischief dominated these boys for the nonce and they failed to contemplate the awful consequences of their falsely-given advice.

Then, while standing on the brink ready to give himself to the sea, he still lingered to perpetrate what they confidently considered was to be his last joke on earth. He asked why the serpentine, silvery, ribbon of water before them was so like a clock?

Of course, they could see no resemblance. They were ready to condone anything he might want to say just now but they were unwilling to rack their brains in an effort to satisfy his final and futile whim.

The old josser will go on schoolmastering us to the end, thought Fergus, but he only replied quite mildly that the answer was beyond him.

Then the teacher triumphantly told them that neither the river nor the clock would go without winding He was a simple soul, off duty. Still he lingered, looking gleefully on the shimmering sheet of water to tell them that man was not by nature an aquatic animal, that he first learned the idea from that loathed animal, the rat. A pig though would swim 'til it cut its own throat with its forelegs. Yes, he was a veritable mine of information this morning. Then he regarded the landscape, the skyscape and the waterscape while the onlookers waited for the tragical *denouement* with feelings of ill-suppressed amusement. As a non-swimmer, they reckoned that he wouldn't have even a sporting chance where he was going to plunge in now in ten feet of water.

This forked radish of a man − for that was what he really looked like in his present posture − at last projected himself sideways into the semi-saline water. He lost no time in protruding a leg in one direction and an arm in another in a frantic reaching out for footing. It was, he thought, high time to establish contact with something solid. He frantically grabbed at a boulder which beetled over the bank; and to this he anchored himself for some seconds which really seemed an eternity. He threw a swift glance towards where he last saw the Macara boys standing in order to enunciate an appeal for help, only to find alas that the place knew them no more. They, too, felt unable to screw their courage to the point of witnessing such a sad event as the passing of their teacher and bugbear as they really imagined him to be; so they fled partially panic-stricken from the scene, their consciences already beginning to upbraid them. Like most boys at that age who have a severe earnest teacher, they were convinced that he was the enduring blight of their lives. That if he only ceased to be, happiness in plenary measure awaited them.

Realising at last that he was a human derelict on the very brink of eternity, Marley Swanton began to emit a series of "hellos" almost loud enough to do justice to the bull of Bashin itself. The vibration set up by his stentorian voice unfortunately loosened the life-sustaining stone which, coming undone, sank with a dull splash to the muddy bottom, carrying its human appendage with its head foremost. He swallowed a quantity of water in the suddenness of the immersion and all his past life flashed before him, especially his sins of commission and omission, in kaleidoscopic form. How crystal-clear and comprehensive it all was, as if it had happened only yesterday; the sins of a lifetime seen in a second in all their enormity and horror. Things that lay buried away for years because he wished them forgotten flashed to the surface of his mind; a certain sign of approaching dissolution. He felt that it was a terrible thing to be going before the living God thus unprepared.

He rose to the surface more or less mechanically but he could no longer rely on his lung power to call attention to his pitiable plight. But the help of God is nearer than the door, as an old Irish proverb has it. His crescendo of cries had not rent the air unheard. Finola Macara, who was in the act of retrieving a truant turkey, felt her ears assailed by the plaintive wails of woe and hurried to the place whence they seemed to emanate. It suddenly came to her that their visitor was dangerously addicted to wantoning with the water although unable to swim. This was surely, she thought, the very apex of folly but then he was a law unto himself in many ways. He was, by reason of his learning, so different from the plain people.

Finola, bounding to the river bank, saw just a head convulsing an otherwise serene silver-sheened body of water. She pulled off her pepper-and-salt coloured scarf to throw to him, but it was too short. Looking about, she saw the dosed oar of a derelict boat cast high and dry up on the land. Grabbing it, she reached out the end of it towards the fast-drowning man. He clutched at it in utter desperation and she pulled him to the edge of the bank. Then, she extended her hand and, with her face as much averted as such heroic physical effort would allow, she by the exertion of a great effort pulled him ashore. Before he could normalise his breathing apparatus in order to thank her for his life, she had as speedily quit the scene. She then ran to tell her father but was intercepted by Peadar Blanche on the way, to whom she confided the news instead. He sped to the scene, assisted the exhausted teacher into his share of clothes and shepherded him back to Rahora House, the residence of the Macara family.

The household was becomingly agitated by the alarming news. Marley Swanton was met halfway home by James Macara bringing a decanter of whiskey and a glass, still the antidote against all ills in many parts of the country. The teacher was given a tumbler of malt but after looking askance at it for a moment, he passed it on to Peadar Blanche by whom it was avidly dispatched in one gulp. Macara, who was also of an optative mood where a drop of drink was in question, helped himself to the remnant of the decanter in order to commemorate the teacher's timely rescue from a watery grave.

During this time the Macara boys, the joint authors of all this commotion, were nowhere to be seen; they had run off to confide in their colleague, Murty Linnane. With feelings of relief, not however unmixed with anxiety, they told that they thought that the bane of all their lives had "shuffled off this mortal coil". This irresponsible trio, in the first flush of their newly-won emancipation, poured out their feelings in such songful snatches as:

So he kicked the bucket when he couldn't kick the pan
And we're not sorry for the poor old man.

But a reaction speedily set in. Soon they were only singing in order to keep their courage up. After all, they tried to console themselves that they did not drown him but only told him where he might bathe in safety. Still, the fact remained that by their advice, given with malice prepense about safe footing, they trepanned him to his doom. Fergus, who was by way of being a casuist, finally reasoned himself into the role of a murderer.

Now that he had time to reflect, he wondered what tempted him to give such treacherous advice. He would have to confess the part he had played in the fatality, sooner or later. Open confession, he reasoned, was good for the soul. As for Wilfred, aged about twelve, well he was too young and innocent to grasp the moral and retributory consequences of such a deed before God and man.

When he returned home later, his heart bowed down with weight of woe only to find that his sister had played the marplot, he felt immensely relieved. His gratitude towards Finola knew no bounds. He ran up to her and by way of relieving his emotions imparted a kiss on her cheek. Shocked beyond measure at this strange conduct on his part, she gave him a resounding slap in the face and peremptorily told him to conduct himself. For the first time, he had felt how terrible it was to be in the toils of remordency. After all, it was God gave life and took it away. Nobody had any rights against their Creator. This experience had aged him mentally and suddenly caused him to pass from boyhood into manhood although not yet aged quite sixteen.

His younger brother lingered behind to ask Linnane was there any harm in what they had done? He assured him that they had only seconded the teacher's wish that he should bathe somewhere. Wasn't it safer, he said, to direct him into a creek a few yards wide than into a river a hundred yards in width. Besides, when a sin – if it were a sin – was shared by two, then it was only half a sin.

CHAPTER V

SOME LINGERING SUPERSTITIONS

THE river ordeal put an end to a keen source of enjoyment for Marley Swanton. As a form of physical exercise to be any longer indulged in, the element of danger in it was too great; and besides, the Macara family would, he knew, resent such foolhardy conduct. Nobody, he noted, bothered about bathing about there; familiarity with the tide had bred too much contempt for it. He refrained from divulging the part that the Macara brothers had played in his horrific experience. He did not, on mature consideration, think that they meant to drown him and finally referred it to their juvenile exuberance of spirits. How were they to know for certain that he couldn't swim even a stroke to save his life? For this reason the whole episode was entitled to the charity of his silence. Then his interest in their sister, Finola, was keenly aroused and for that reason alone the less said to the detriment of her brothers the better. It was a trifle humiliating to be saved by a mere girl yet in her teens. Still, he flushed with pleasure and he did not stop to consider why, in the thought that she was a rather tall, lissome, blue-eyed, flaxen-haired lass. He noted for the first time how elusive in her manner she was.

Dinner was at midday to the minute in the Macara ménage. After the midday meal of home-cured bacon, white cabbage and potatoes followed by an apple tart, the day, which gave such indications of being lastingly fair, falsified all expectations. A heavy downpour of rain ensued soon after dinner. James Macara, his sons and their pair of workmen were caught in the hayfield under a sudden deluge and fairly saturated. Their only alternative was to spend what remained of the day in the house speculating about a clearance. They need not be entirely idle, however, as a farmer's work is never done. They could, they said, twist some soogauns or hay ropes, fix the beam of the mowing machine and put a theeveen or two on their worn-out shoes in the shelter of the house, and so on and so forth. Tommy Cooley was told off by Mrs Macara, alias the vanithee, for this latter offence. In a well-managed farmstead it is possible to improve the raining as well as the shining hour.

This evening, however, both master and men felt averse from tackling these odds and ends of work and, besides, too many wet days recently left little arrears of work to be done. The event of the morning, that is to say, Marley Swanton's almost fatal tussle with the tide and the providential manner of his rescue, filled their thoughts. The news, highly embroidered, had already been bruited from end to end of the news-hungry parish. It was a tit-bit well calculated to call for comment and generate sagacious remarks at the teacher's expense. Blanche had brought the news to the local pub where he was treated to three pints of porter on the strength of it. The publican tossed the news over the counter to everybody who came into his shop for several days after, glad to have such a piquant conversational morsel for the delectation of his customers. The story grew in savour and sensationalism every time it was told.

The incident caused the Macara household to reflect on death and Cooley remarked that it was ever lurking round the corner. These reflections weaned them from their more mundane interests.

The vanithee, who never liked the sight of men about the house except at meal times, intimated to her spouse that he should find something to do for the men in the barn. He said she could give them their four o'clock tea a bit earlier than usual and then if it didn't clear they would see what could be done in the out-houses.

While men are engaged in an important job of work such as

the haysel, they are loath to leave it; yet, once such a stoppage is forced upon them they are just as slow to resume work. The sense of continuity is snapped. They resent the coming of rain, but having come they seem to wish that it might continue for the rest of the day.

A feeling of frustration pervaded the household; its daily routine was disturbed.

They were all seated in the kitchen and Macara, who was otherwise known as the fearanthee, or man of the house, remarked that farming in Ireland was one long battle with the elements; it wasn't that it rained so much, but it kept spitting a bit every day. There was a lot to be said after all for turning the country into one huge grass ranch. Just then, Finola Macara interrupted the train of his thoughts by letting fall one of her secondary school books as she was passing into the parlour. Her father picked it up and, peering into the open page, it fixed his attention and he read aloud:

> Death is here and death is there
> Death is busy everywhere,
> All around, within, beneath,
> Above is death and we are death.
> Death has set her mark and seal
> On all we are and all we feel.
> All things that we know or cherish
> Like ourselves must fade and perish.

These lines, read with much pathos, caught the prevailing mood and the reader's only regret was that the poem wasn't penned by one of his two favourite poets.

Then Marley Swanton, who had been down trying to measure the progress, if any, of his new house, entered with Peadar Blanche, rather gladly struck idle by the rain.

Tommy Cooley, the doyen labourer of the parish, hastened to congratulate the teacher on his recent escape. Swanton thought to deny that anything had happened and he felt piqued, but he was assured that the news was known far and wide.

The fearanthee read the poetic lines on death anew, which he now felt to be more timeous and topical, and Cooley capped it by reciting the history of three drownings in that very creek, the first of which, he said, occurred when he was a nipper of six or so. He maintained that that offshoot of a river, innocent as it looked, claimed a human sacrifice every seven years.

"Be me solemn oath, now that I think of it," said he, "such a victim is now a year overdue. It wouldn't be safe for anybody to go on that river till the debt is paid. The creek is only a small part of the river, but it always did its bit 'til today. Me father who did a lot of trucking on that river was a provider of seaweed and me grandfather afore him again always said that they saw the dacent river taking its due. Then, as if it were to make up for lost time, it would sweep off two or three together. That's the reason that me son gave up trucking and fishing this year. Still, I'm glad you have escaped Mr Swanton sir, in a way – as yet."

All eyes were now turned upon the pallid teacher and he felt that they were asking him how did he so meanly sneak out of his just debt to the sentient, moving, tossing river? He felt riled but only added that he did not give any credence to old men's tales. "Why should I who have only flirted with that river for the first time be singled out for destruction?" he asked.

"And why shouldn't you, as well as anybody else?" replied the fearanthee. "The elements, nymphs, or whatever spirits animate rivers, are no respecters of persons. A prince is no more than a peasant to them."

"In fact you'd be rather small fry, all things considered, sir," assured Peadar Blanche.

Then the light of bygone days came back to Cooley's eyes and he went on to say that rivers were peopled with legions of unseen things. They had a baleful, but no blind or blundering way of their own of collecting their debts and dues and over-dues.

"Yes, man cannot lord it over earth, air, fire and water all the time," agreed Blanche with impunity. "There must be a bit of give and take in this matter and man must pay his way to increased knowledge with his life. It is only just and equitable."

"Thems me sentiments too," replied Cooley. "Ever since I was a gorsoon the big of your knee, this blinking river always did its drowning duty 'til this year. There's something wrong somewhere."

"Surely it's not a bounden duty with this blasted river," protested Marley Swanton, shuddering inly at the role he was expected by the yokels of the parish to have played that morning. Then he reflected that it was absurd that the best in-tellect in the whole parish should be hurried like a raffish dog out of existence merely to verify such an asinine legend.

"I would have gone for a dip the other day," added Blanche, "but for this cloud that is hanging over us all with regard to these alarming river dues. It is not right either to deprive the waters of their pound of human flesh, and those who do by saving other people are just incurring the wrath of the rivers or the river gods."

"They are, so they are," concurred Cooley. "I wouldn't like to be the man as would save a mouse in Menavia, because then surely the vengeful river would get me or mine instead. It's not that I begrudge any man his life, not a bit of it, but I value me own too much to take any risks."

"Such as it is, Tommy Rot Cooley," sneered the teacher.

"Faith if I saw you going down today, I'd walk away and lay a leg on your shouts for help and, what's more, it wouldn't be the first time as I did it and that's why I'm the oldest man in Menavia this day."

"Life purchased on these insanely faint-hearted craven terms

41

isn't worth much," said the teacher. "You may as well be dead as to live under such fantastic delusions."

"Yerra, what's on you at all this day, Cooley, to be giving such lip to your betters?" ejaculated the good vanithee. "You must be surely doting in your old age. Much better for you to be cleaning out the piggery outside, you pishogy spalpeen."

"Och now, I don't wish that a ha'porth of harm would come to the Ildana, Mrs Macara, as we call the teacher among ourselves, but facts are facts. Anybody as goes between the river and its due is taken himself some time, somehow, somewhere. Look at Potch White as could swim like a duck and saved a power and all of people from drowning in his day. The last time ever he saved a pair of loons as couldn't swim and then went down himself and was never seen nor heard of more. The little boat turned turtle in a sudden airy squall within a foot of the shore under a press of sail. Potch – the Lord have mercy on him all the same – was going out for his third man if you wouldn't mind when he was taken himself, and that's that."

"Stuff and nonsense, man alive," snapped Mrs Macara, rocking herself to and fro in her soogaun chair, as was her wont when she was displeased with her surroundings. "I never saw you so full of strange fancies as you are today, me old gamboy. You must be near your end. Pishogues, I call them."

"Whatever might pishogues mean, mother?" asked Finola, who was passing out with a fiddle under her arm.

"Oh, that's Irish for superstition," said the irrepressible yarner. "A queer thing entirely that you don't know the language of your own country. If your ancestors ever came back from the grave to tell you where to find a hidden crock of gold in the farm as part of your fortune, be me oath you couldn't take the message, and you would maybe have to go without a man for the rest of your life because of your ignorance."

"They must be turning in their graves as it is at the two-

42

fold way that they are cut off from their kith and kin," agreed Blanche.

Cooley nourished a grudge against the teacher. The grandson of a hedge schoolmaster himself, he thought that he was somehow usurping the position that rightfully belonged to him and his. He considered that he was getting some satisfaction now.

During a lull in the conversation they stared very hard at each other. Whoever out-stared the other in Menavia was assumed to have won the victory. It was also an article of belief that the person who could not look you straight in the face while speaking to you has a moral twist, an oblique line tucked away somewhere in his composition. They have their own rough and ready methods of judging character in Menavia and the clash of the eyes between man and man was not unseldom resorted to in reaching out after the truth. It was also taken for granted that anybody who was perennially posing as an honest man simply wasn't.

Marley Swanton, who felt that he was being ogled out of countenance, suddenly asked by way of a diversion "Do you think you have the eye of Balor?"

"And who might he be now pray," queried Cooley, shifting his eyes on to his pipe and deliberately conveying it to his mouth.

"He was the warrior in ancient Ireland who used to wither up his foes with a glance of his evil optic."

The teacher was ponderous rather than penetrating in verbal swordplay. Besides, he did not think it *comme il faut* for a mere farmhand to treat him so. He felt a consuming desire to crush his opponent with a few venom-barbed words but then he was an old man and entitled to much respect on that account. He felt that Cooley was a tongue-valiant man. He could not, he found, talk in the same preachy way to adults as to his schoolchildren without getting as good as he gave. He was up against the intellect of the parish here.

As it continued to rain without intermission the company felt resigned to the prospect. Besides, a steaming kettle heralded the approach of teatime. In some respects they felt that this is the most pleasant meal of the day. Breakfast is a rather hurried affair and people have a long day's work before them. Dinner is only a break but at teatime they could look forward to a stimulating cup of tea and backward on a good deal of work well and truly done and a surcease from work for the day. Then everybody is in better humour and the difficulties of the day have resolved themselves.

Although there was an entire absence of cold, the prosy company described a distant semi-circle around the peat fire looking into it very occasionally for inspiration. They saw all sorts of images in the live embers betimes.

An apple cake in an oven over the blaze gave off an appetising aroma. The patter of the rain against the windowpanes added zest to the half-holiday thrust upon them by the sum total of everything that we call the weather. In order to the perfect enjoyment of some creature comforts they must be sharply contrasted with discomforts close at hand to overwhelm one. Then they loaded their pipes and regarded the azure-tinted smoke as it wafted its way towards the rafters with complacency. Up there among the rafters it was additionally serviceable as it helped to flavour and season about a dozen flitches of bacon that depended therefrom.

The yarning mood was now upon them in plenary measure and although Peadar Blanche would bestow an occasional malison upon the rain he would be the crestfallen man if it cleared up just now.

The housewife and her maid-of-all-work, who chafed under this invasion of the kitchen by such a multitude of futile fellows, kept a sharp lookout in vain for any sign of a clearance.

The conversation next turned on the weather and James Macara, fresh from a short siesta in the parlour sofa, said that Ireland was a pastoral rather than an arable country. The weather was as uncertain at harvest time as an inland lake on a March day and rain at the wrong time precluded the possibility of a return to tillage on a large scale. The saving of hay and corn resolved itself into a hurried panicky dogfight between the farmer and the elements. It was a yearly gamble and this annual stress and strain had generated a choleric nation of farmers. The months were no longer seasonal. May was well christened because it may be anything in the way of weather samples. Harvesting here, compared with where he had lived in California, was simply a form of crop snatching. There were only two seasons in the year nowadays, namely winter and summer, with no gradations. Winter, which lasts half the year at least, is one long siege against the farmer and harvest time was the practical preparation for that siege, during which the creative forces of nature are locked in silence and death.

"Yes," said Marley Swanton, "the climate is as changeable as a woman in love."

Then he shot a swift glance at Finola, but it was lost upon her as she was telling the maid to lay the table both in the dining room and in the kitchen for tea.

"The farmer isn't a really good judge in his own case," pursued the teacher. "There are as many terminological inexactitudes…"

Just then, a Kerry Blue terrier howled in the yard and Cooley asserted that one of Mr Swanton's big words had fallen on him and broken his back.

The latter ignored this quip and added that life for all simply resolved itself into a food-snaring expedition. It was the incentive to almost everything in this nether word. "The secret of good farming is," he said, "possessed by few. Woman is nature's greatest secret, the profoundest mystery of them all."

"What's the good of being a secret anyway?" enquired Finola, smiling coldly upon him. "Only that and nothing more."

"There's one that's a great life saver anyway," butted in Cooley.

"You're a garrulous old man and no mistake," retorted the teacher.

The company then divided for tea, the Macara family and the teacher retiring to the parlour while the three men and the maid partook of it in the kitchen.

As a rule, small farmers dine at the same table as their servants when they happen to have any, but the Macara family were much more highly laminated in the social scale. During the Great War years, when labour was very scarce and highly paid, labourers became very sensitive on this point of etiquette and the male members of the family, or at least some of them, compromised by dining with them at the kitchen table.

CHAPTER VI

SOME ELDRITCH TALES

OVER the tea cups the flagging spirits of all were revived. The teacher sampled the three kinds of home-made bread and ventured to presume that Miss Finola had a hand in the baking. The town bakers, he said, used make fairly eatable bread from barm before the Great War but now yeast is used and the results are deplorable. There was nothing nicer than homemade bread made with milk and spiced with caraway seeds. Then he praised the marmalade and Finola said it was homemade too, but it had to be made in April at latest as the oranges go dry and out of season after that. "I made it over the Easter holidays," she said, "and stored it away; over a hundred pots of it."

"Precious little use in storing it away in this house," said her mother, "because it goes at the rate of a crock a day. 'Tis cheaper and better than shop stuff. Finola has been introducing a lot of new gadgets into the house since she's been to Kylemore to school. She has too many ideas for an old-fashioned place like this."

"I wouldn't say that at all now, ma'am, if I were you. You know people grow old-fashioned rapidly and they are kept young and up to date only by the rising generation. Your daughter is a great credit to you." Then he regarded admiratively at the young girl.

"Oh, we are supposed to show something for the little smattering of education that we get, sir," said Finola. "That is about all there is to it. If I didn't do something out of the ordinary when I came back, mother would have another story."

"You'll have to get married, Mr Swanton," said his hostess, "when you get your new house. A house is nothing much minus a housekeeper, although it isn't for me to sing the praises of my own profession."

"Devil a house you'll have, sir, till you're too old for anything," said Fergus, who came into the room just then. There's Blanche abroad there in the kitchen and he splitting lies as fast as a horse would trot when he could be lifting your house for you."

"Apart from your uncalled-for opinion, my boy, I feel it my bounden duty as your teacher in the presence of your parents to correct your flagrant breach of bad grammar. Then the teacher looked gravely at the boy. "Bad language from you is a grave reflection on me as your teacher."

"Mo naire thu, Fergy," protested his mother. "You are too flighty and flippant with your superiors."

The boy flushed but said that English wasn't their native language and they were not supposed to be able to speak it like a Londoner. Then, in the trepidation of the moment, he let some jam fall on the diaper tablecloth, an act which drew forth a sharp admonition from his mother.

"You are supposed to be perfect at anything that I teach you, my boy," continued the teacher. "You used the word 'abroad' a moment ago when you should have said 'outside'. When you say a person is abroad you mean that he is on the continent, whereas the subject of your discourse is only outside there in the kitchen."

"Thank you for the correction, sir," said Fergus, feeling abashed.

"Every county has its own strange turns of speech," said Finola. "I was a bit pally with a cailin from the Model county and she used to say 'I bees' and 'I beesn't' when she meant 'I do be' and 'I do not be' and 'I'll see you in short' for 'I'll see you soon' and 'have a care' for 'au revoir' Instead of saying 'I did not go', she used to say 'I didn't get to go'. If you do not notice these strange turns of speech in time you don't notice them at all.

"That's a great stave out of Finola," said her mother complacently. "I'm thinking it's a school teacher she would make."

"And married to a school master," added Fergus.

"Boys become very unruly during holiday time," palliated his mother. "Boys aren't what they used to be."

"They never were, ma'am," assented the teacher.

The boy's pert remark started a fresh train of thought in Swanton. Was he too time-stricken as a mate for Finola? Surely she was not above falling a victim to the amiable weakness, but not just yet. Then he silently pondered on the composition of love and concluded that it was a biological impulse, honied and sicklied over with sentiment. At that moment, he felt his blood tingling with the joy of life and looking across the table at Finola he somehow felt that she was in similar case.

Tea over, the teacher was left alone in the parlour to peruse the *Weekly Recorder*, the local paper in which he took a keen interest. As a prospective house furnisher, he took especial stock of everything in the room in the hope that he could borrow an idea or two. For such a large rambling room, it was, he thought, rather sparsely furnished but perhaps that was the fashion. He noted the green Connemara marble mantelpiece over the fireplace, a massive and ornamental sort of thing in its way. Then he recollected that the house was built by an old landlord who lived for the alliterative cognates wine and women, and buried his dead near the hall door.

The centre of the floor was laid with tarpaulin while the border was painted a chocolate brown. The table was on the massive side and so also was the two-headed mahogany sofa which needed to be upholstered. The rest of the furniture was modern and cheap.

"Is it that outcast of a sofa you're looking at?" queried the vanithee, returning to the room.

"Not particularly, ma'am."

"Well, my dear, an interesting history attaches to that there sofa. That belonged to hubby's grandmother and, naturally, we have a great regard for it. A few years ago, his cousin Willie married his own servant girl, all the way from the wilds of Kerry she was, but a great worker otherwise. The first thing the poor ignorant angashore did was to fling out all the fine old furniture that had been in the house, most of it for the best part of a century, and replace it by new cheap, rubbishy stuff. The doctor came along when her first child was born and his horse was tied to the outcast sofa leg out in the yard. He made some enquiries about it and was told that he could take it away if it was any good to him. It was through him that we got this much out of the wreck. We were not speaking to Willie at the time for making such a low-down match. We must get this sofa covered in leather. A Jew who walked the way lately offered twenty pounds for it as it stands which shows that it must be worth two or three times that much."

"Yes, any man would make a fool of himself sometimes over a pretty wench but he must be a blinking ass to allow her to fling out the family heirlooms. One would think that marriage would sober and disillusion him and put a period to his further folly."

"You're a bad judge of matrimony as a mere bachelor. You know nothing about it."

"Except what the novelists tell me and they're supposed to be real dabsters on the subject. Sentiment alone for the belongings of her betters should have saved her from committing this last folly."

The men continued to enjoy themselves in the kitchen. Finola plied them with apple cake towards the end of the meal while her father, who sat in an armchair near the fire, intimated that he would have just one cup of tea where he sat.

Cooley, who was still in a yarning mood, said that over forty years ago when he was breaking into a man, he used to double and even treble his earnings playing cards at night. The only thing wanted to be a good card player was a good memory. He could, he averred, remember what was played three games back and nobody could renege on him.

"A great gambler tends to become a great nuisance," said the fearanthee. "If he invariably rooks everybody he causes an all-round feeling of loss, dismay and disappointment and in due course everybody fights shy of him as a kind of amateur swindler. His mere presence calls up ugly feelings as to future losses."

"Sound talk there, sir," said Cooley. "I used to be out often gambling till two o'clock in the morning though I had to be about me master's business at seven. At last my name as a great gambler was on every man's lips. Then, as time went on, I had to go farther afield in order to get a game where I wasn't so well known. I bought a horse and saddle out of my winnings, and so well I could. Then, I could ride away ten or twelve miles for a gamble and double that distance on a Sunday."

"A great luxury for a mere workman, wasn't it?" queried his master.

"Not if you could afford it, sir. It enabled me to find fresh victims to teach and rook almost at will. With me coal black mare I was really respected at a distance and I used to get in among the farmers and well-to-do shopkeepers and their sons and even some of the wasteful gentry. Far from me own little bailiwick, I used to let on that I was a man of consequence and titivate myself out like the best of them. I often relieved a malt-muddled buckeen of a fiver of a night and I was thinking of giving up being a farm hand once and for all. Returning home much earlier than usual one fine bright moonlight night, a tall man stepped out from Mogue Nowlan's forge and bid me the time of night. Then he proposed a game of cards. Late and all as it was, I could never resist a game and here was a chance of increasing my store. We settled down to work and some light showed from the forge as I thought, but that did not strike me as strange at the time. We played a shilling a fifteen and I won the first half- dozen rubbers. Then, he proposed the doubling-up of the stakes every game, one of my own tricks when I would be losing by which I used to win tons of money. The luck turned at once and in next to no time the stakes were up to a pound and then two and then four and so on and so forth. I was stony broke before I fully realised it. Then he proposed to play for me mare as my stake and he laid down what appeared in the moonshine to be three ten pound notes against it. I lost the finest mare in Menavia and it broke me heart. I felt I was only a tyro and a fool at the game after all, when I met a real gambler. A grim, silent, compelling kind of man, he was. He jumped suddenly to his feet, did this poker-faced man, and said he'd call for the mare in the morning and went through the forge. I mounted my steed for our last gallop home together, a beggar to the world, me who had been a rich man half-an-hour before. The mare whinnied, a thing as I never knew it to do before, and we covered the four miles that lay before us in as many minutes almost, the mare for some reason or other in a lather of sweat beneath me. Slowing down to open your father's lodge gate, who strode past it at the other side but the accursed man who had made a pauper of me ten minutes afore that. I got such a start that I nearly fell off and the mare even trembled violently. How did he get there before me, considering the way I galloped and the hurry the mare itself was in to get home? There was a longer way around which, if he took, would mean a mile more. That was the last I ever saw of me gambling master. I wept over the mare, kissed it good night, and so well I may, for it was found dead in the morning. It cured me of gambling anyway. The devil himself, I believe it was."

"Queer things do sometimes happen," said Blanche. "I'd be disinclined to believe that yarn but for something that happened to myself when I was a boy. Bill Lanigan used to bring me to a card school to keep him company as he was timid at night. One night, the cowardly ass asked me to see him into this own house half-a-mile past my own place. I called him a hen-hearted man but I did as he bid me all the same. I felt proud to be called upon to play such a part at such an early age. Suddenly he gripped me by the arm like a vice. 'Do you see the black dog?' said he. I could see nothing at all and I laughed at him for a fool born ass and told him to give over this codraulin'. He complained that the hair was standing up on his head and knocking his hat off. Arrived home at last, faith he looked a sorry sight and even fell on the floor. His mother wanted me to stay the night but I said I wouldn't be daunted by man or devil; so I set out and saw nothing. I arose next morning with a maddening pain in my finger. The next night it was so great that I attempted to drown myself but the tide was out. Then Bessy Lanigan, the boy's mother, said I should put certain herbs to it. She told me how to concoct them, pointed them out to me in the field but said that I must pull them myself. She said she wouldn't do as much for me only that I came by the pain because of her son. I got well but not before two bones came out of my finger."

"Tis hard to believe all that we hear," said the fearanthee, "but for all that, only fools defy mystery and try to set it at nought. There's no explanation for these things or they would fail to be ghost stories."

"Well, Lanigan, as you all know, never did much good after that. He was a good athlete and won a few foot races but he died down into a public house loafer."

"Now," said Cooley, "I'm not the kind of a fellow who goes in for slaving day and dark, but I think the one thing that's keeping the country most down hereabouts is laziness. These lazy loons should be rounded up and compelled to build banks and reclaim the square miles of mud flats that are going to waste for want of a few feet of a wall. Then we'd have a rich country with plenty of eating and drinking for all. Then there would be no idlers lying up against the village walls all the day and half the night to keep them from falling on a mouse or a duck that might be picking up a living."

"Look at that fellow over there at Coolnawinna," said Blanche, "that let the gable end fall out of his house, and I wanting a job at the time, because he was too lazy to replace a stone that a passing lorry took out of it. He'd lie in bed all day smoking and talking; the passing showers used to refresh him where he lay. Then he got up one evening to give a hand in the meadow because he heard there was a gallon of porter going. The rain came down and the thunder came on and a flash of lightning killed the temporary toiler. That's the fatal reward he got for getting up from his safe snug bed of down to look after an old sop of hay. You see that work doesn't always pay, me man."

"Yerra, do you remember the day long ago, Blanche, that yourself and that bed-pressing codger Lanigan went in for the bag race at the land and water sports. You broke your toe on a stone as was sticking up covered by a bit of paper. Lanigan took a cramp in his femoral bone and the Coolnawinna man shuffled past the winning post first. 'Twas the first and the last time he ever won and 'Bejannies', said he, "I'm first at last. I was always behind before.'"

"I'm afraid you'll be all behind with the harvest the way you're getting on," said Mrs Macara, rebukingly emerging from the parlour. "You ought to have enough of backbiting done now, Cooley, for a month of Sundays. Bring up the cows from the corcass and give the women a hand at the milking of them."

"Oh, sure we were only putting a few of our neighbours to and fro in our spare time, ma'am."

CHAPTER VII

ROMANCE AND REALITY

THE summer months, like everything that is sensuous and pleasing, sped all too quickly and the countryside was once again in the relentless grip of winter. The dark, dreary November days had arrived, bringing with them that feeling of resignation to which both urbanist and ruralist alike has to deadness and decay in the vegetable world. A dull monotony became all-pervasive of country life 'til the coming of Christmas which is eagerly anticipated as a period of welcome change and uplift. The last swallow had flown to more congenial climes, and the raucous rankling cry of the wild geese is heard overhead flying high in V-shaped formation. This bird is very fearful of man but then so is nearly every denizen of the air. They live in a state of almost incessant fear, do the feathered tribe and the mortality among them from one cause and another is very high. Fowling as a winter sport or pastime provides fewer thrills with the flight of the years because of the growing paucity of game birds and the almost uncanny wariness of the few that remain to us. Unless bird sanctuaries are provided throughout the country, the time will inevitably come when there will be nothing to shoot. Birds have to work hard for a living and the ubiquitous fowler with his cheap fifty shilling gun, that so miraculously fails to burst and blow him up time and again, is rapidly denuding the land of its feathered phenomena.

Marley Swanton, suddenly realising the plight of the birds, decided that he would lay aside his gun. But then, somebody else might pick it up, use it and the slaughter of the innocents would be greater than before. He filled the top of the muzzle with soft oozy mud, loaded the gun, placed it on a wall steadied by a few heavy stones and pulled the trigger by means of a long cord at a safe distance. There was a loud explosion and the falling of the lethal weapon to pieces was a well-staged event designed to mark the passing of the teacher as an incontinent taker of bird life. The passing of all pernicious practices should, he thought, end in an elaborate form of ritual as a pledge in itself that it could not be lightly renewed. If he were ever tempted again to resume the practice, the means of satisfying his whim would not be to hand and before he could buy it his better nature would have once again prevailed.

It was a mild season so far but he was most hortative nevertheless on the subject of the fuel supply in respect of his school. On the failure of any boy to bring a sod of turf or a pebble of coal to school daily he was ever ready to wax both prosy and passional. There was no allowance from the Department of Education in respect of fuel or lighting and the teachers had to fend for themselves. He often provided books out of his own pocket for poor children but he would have to draw the line here. Many elementary schools were out of repair and the sanitary accommodation was also very deficient. The question was who really owned these schools? The Department, he reasoned, certainly did not, and the managers were only custodians during their pastoral charge of their respective parishes. The teachers only taught in them. The general public were, in the last analysis, the real owners of these antique buildings but if the roof fell in, it was impossible to prosecute everybody in the parish to compel them to repair it.

Murty Linnane, now the eldest and tallest lad in the school, was latterly beginning to copy the daring self-reliant ways of Fergus Macara. Several causes conspired to bring them together of late and they began to view their teacher's crotchets and caprices from the same angle of vision. They both felt that they were too big and important in the scheme of things to have the menial work of fire-lighting thrust upon them. Both agreed that they should bring no fuel next morning, to see what would happen. The punishment was that they were told off jointly to light the fire for the next week.

Linnane felt that Macara, although a newcomer and a younger boy, had somehow usurped the position of authority that he had held for the past year. He must do something outstanding to retrieve the position. Of course, he knew that Macara had seen a larger slice of the world than himself as he had been to another school. He could pick a quarrel with his rival but then he was not sure of being able to out-box such a spirited youth.

Now, however, these twain agreed to sink their juvenile differences in face of the common indignity that had been so wantonly bestowed upon them. Linnane reflected that he should do something striking and dramatic if he were either to regain or retain that sweet hegemony that he 'til so recently held among his school colleagues. But what could he do? He decided that something should be done to show that they were more than mere hewers of wood and drawers of water.

"We ought to light a fire for our master that he won't forget for the rest of his life," said he to Macara. "I am practicing on the wild geese these nights with an old gun and the day he blew up his own gun he gave me a lot of powder and shot to bring home to my father as he said he had given up fowling. We were flailing a few loads of wheat for thatching purposes last week in the byre when Paddy Lawton, all out of breath and a gun with him, ran in. He begged my father to hide him anywhere as the police were after him hot-foot for assaulting his landlord who recently decreed him in the court for his house rent or something. My old fellow – daddy, I mean – told him to lie down under the sheaves of corn and in a minute or so four police rushed in and said he must be there because they only lost sight of him a minute before. That he had even fired on them. They warned daddy that he would be charged too as an accomplice after the crime for harbouring a criminal and defeating the course of justice. He told them to search away and he continued to flail the sheaves on the floor and poor Lawton under them getting the father of a thrashing all the time. He was getting flogged to death under every lash of the flail but it was the only way to convince his angry pursuers that he wasn't there. I never saw me da work with greater gusto or strike with greater vim and vigour. At last, the limbs of the law left, and Lawton was pulled out, more dead than alive, and his clothes bound to him with his blood. The flogging that had to be given to him if he were to be saved simply cut rashers off him. He departed under cover of darkness and left me his gun. Now we can play a trick upon our teacher that he'll never forget and serve him right."

"Oh, the bally gun, is it? Cut that out," said Macara.

That evening they selected the largest sod of turf they could find, scooped a large hole in it and inserted a cupful of powder and covered it up again. They damped the surface of the sod that it would not ignite too soon.

Next morning they set the fire with great deliberation taking care to make a bigger fire than usual, putting the powder-filled sod well to the back of the hob grate. This precaution would ensure that nothing would happen while they were in the danger zone.

The teacher stood with his back to the fire facing the pupils as usual. As it was still in the kindling stage, he both covered and concealed it. Then he began to rally the fire lighters in a good-humoured way. Every boy should know how to light a fire as it was a liberal education in itself and a knowledge of it contributed to the sum of human happiness. When these fire lighters would be finished with him they could get a job in a train as stokers, in fact they could go anywhere and do anything as graduates in the art of stoking fires. Fire, he assured them, was worshipped as a god in ancient times and although people had outgrown that form of nonsense yet it was still a formidable factor in the life of man. Yes, fire was a fine servant but a murderous master.

The class that he had drawn about him were reading about the great fire of London in 1666.

Just then a deafening report rang out and Marley Swanton was catapulted forward, falling on a forum which fortunately broke the fall, but nothing else. Rolling over, he safely subsided on the floor.

His verbal flow was hushed for a minute or more 'til he realised what had happened. There was an additional explosion but this time it was only in the nature of an immoderate burst of laughter on the part of the pupils at the expense of the teacher. His momentarily fallen condition, sprawling as he was on the dusty floor, appealed to their risible faculties.

He quickly picked himself up, however, and took off his coat only to find that there had been some holes burned in it. It was partially alight and a strong sulphurous smell exhaled from it.

"Water, boys, water," he shouted, but they saw no ways or means of complying with his request.

Goaded by fire and fear, he raced out of the room with the smoking garment. At the door he was confronted by Peadar Blanche who, hearing the commotion, lost no time in hurrying to the scene in order to sate his curiosity, a quality always very much alive in him. In order to make sure that no sparks of fire lay concealed in his clothes, Blanche hurried him to a barrel of water and saturated him with its contents by immersing him in it.

" 'Tis from the frying pan into the fire with me I fear, said the teacher, feeling slightly abashed at the figure he was cutting in the presence of his pupils, most of whom felt concerned to follow him out in the interest of his safety for which they felt a real concern.

"'Twill be from the fire into a fever bed with you," said Blanche unless you change your clothes."

"I say, Linnane," said he, "where are you going with your master's coat?"

"I forgot to return it to him," said the boy who was in the act of sloping away in a fit of abstraction. This pointed query recalled him from his brown study.

"If a rich man steals, they say he forgets; if a poor man forgets they say that he steals," said the teacher. "I shall have much to say about this later on. I wonder where did he steal all the stuff he put in the fire? I was destroyed only for you, Blanche."

"I wouldn't say that, sir. Accidents will happen a cat."

The teacher, beyond a slight sense of shock and the violence that was done to his feelings, felt little the worse for being blown up. It is not everybody who escapes so well after contact with these elemental opposites. His dingy clothes suffered to some extent, but that was all.

He deputed the contractor to take charge in the school while he was effecting a change of clothing.

The pupils, but especially Macara and Linnane, were all delighted at the prospect of their teacher's absence from among them for an hour or two. With these two dare-devil boys he had become a kind of obsession for the past week. They felt that he could be very boring at times and that his heavy sense of humour could rankle and rub them the wrong way. Anyway they welcomed the protective presence of Blanche just now and their spirits readily rose in contact with the jovial contractor.

Blanche, already feeling that he was half a hero, readily reacted to his position of authority. He laid aside some of his bluff and breezy manner at first and became grave and authoritative. He gradually thawed, however, and the boys secretly admired his quiet, manly form. They reflected that if their teacher could only manage to be like that, how it would transform their whole outlook and make school-going a labour of love.

During the teacher's prolonged absence, his deputy sat on the high stool on an elevated dais. All he insisted on was comparative quiet so that he could regale the now exuberant pupils with yarns of his own school-going days. The best remembered schoolbook lines ever written were, he said, "Jack has got a cart and can draw sand and clay in it." Why it was that the minds of young and old were as wax to receive and marble to retain that simple line, to the oblivion of almost everything else, he could not imagine. His father, he said, was named Jack and he wondered for quite a long time why his simple household effects were noted and singled out for such universal mention. As one grew older, he said, he found that education was a process of unlearning much of what one learned and, alas, replacing sweet romance by stern reality.

A sudden crescendo of noise – the bane of so many teachers' lives – would cause him to assume all the mock gravity of a pedagogue, strike certain attitudes and utter minatory maxims as mimetic of Marley Swanton as if he incarnated him – almost. Then the pupils felt that their temporary teacher was a tonic and a treasure. Blanche also felt that he was in his element and that this day in his life should be marked with a white stone.

"It's not enough to fit up houses and school houses for you but I must fit you to live in the houses," he declared. "While I'm only moulding mortar, I'd prefer to be moulding minds like yours. The right men are doing the wrong sort of work and the wrong men are doing the right work; the tenon never seems quite to fit the mortise and the result is a creaking world."

"'Tis a croakin' world anyway," said Fergus Macara.

"And 'twill be a choking world as soon as Mr Swanton gets hold of us," added Murty Linnane.

"If I were a permanent pedagogue," proceeded Blanche, "how I'd fire your imaginations with patriotism. I'd have you running after grass ranchers, banks and bailiffs as fast as a politician after a job. As for all the alleged lambasting that goes on here, I'd cut out that. A man should be able to rule you with a leer of his eye; the rod is the last resource of a bad teacher. Oh, how I'd build you up, boys, if I had half a chance."

"Why don't you build up the teacher's house then and you have every sort of a chance?" asked Linnane. "It's not improving his temper to be houseless and homeless so long; so mother says."

At this stage there was half a pot of ink emptied upon the temporary teacher.

"My baptism as a schoolmaster," he cried. "If you can't stay aisy, stay as aisy as you can, boys."

CHAPTER VIII

HALF A HERO

A hush fell on the school as the door suddenly flew open and Marley Swanton entered looking very grim and determined, followed by the school manager Canon Lavelle wearing a very serious aspect.

The teacher, after donning some dry clothes, decided that he would be unable to deal out condign punishment to the two most clever and daring boys in the school single-handed. It was with a certain amount of reluctance that he appealed to the reverend manager; it was to a certain extent a confession of failure, yet he could not overlook such a facinorous act.

Blanche faded silently behind a blackboard raised on an easel where he was temporarily lost sight of and the teacher, ordering Macara and Linnane to stand out on the floor, said: "These are the pair of unmitigated incendiaries who so nearly blew up myself and the school this morning, sir. Nothing seems to be too hot or too heavy for them of late."

"Ha, by the way what is this good man doing here?" queried the Canon, looking at Blanche for the first time. "I seem to think, that he could be more usefully employed somewhere else."

Then he brandished a riding whip ominously.

"Maybe I could and maybe I couldn't, your reverence," retorted the degraded teacher.

Macara signalled an appealing glance at him not to budge and it was not lost upon him.

"Buzz off now, Blanche, like a good man," ordered the teacher. "You had a noisy job of work in my absence but sure when the cat is out the mice can play. Thank you for your time and trouble all the same but the Canon and myself will carry on now if you don't mind." This curt and peremptory dismissal of the contractor deepened the gloom of the pupils. They felt instinctively that his big burly presence shielded them from danger. His presence was the one redeeming feature in the untoward situation.

Blanche fumbled about for his hat, which he did not seem to be able to find, still reluctant to quit the scene.

He sloped slowly towards the door but lingered in the porch, determined not to miss the denouement.

The teacher then darted about the room for his rod of castigation but in vain as Blanche had carefully secreted same beneath his coat. It symbolised corporal punishment at that moment, and he knew it.

"These two boys are going from bad to worse every day, sir," complained the teacher. "As far as I can see, Macara is the ringleader and he simply seems to exude mischief at certain times. By their calculated policy of naughtiness they will in no long time infect the rest of the school."

"Ha, ha, and turn the whole place into a bedlam, I suppose," assented the Canon. "These wild wanton ways of theirs must be nipped in the bud."

"These are my sentiments too, sir. Macara is, so to say, a newcomer to this place and if I had the bending of that twig while it was young and teachable he'd be a docile boy today. I have no hesitation in saying that they are going blue mouldy for want of a beating and I will leave the rest to you, Canon."

"Desperate ailments require drastic remedies. I am profoundly shocked and alarmed, that is to say, alarmed for the welfare of the parish to learn on such irrefutable authority as that of our worthy teacher that we have such monsters of iniquity in our midst. They are, so to speak, the prime ministers of the devil himself in the parish and in a position to do his work better than he could do it himself."

"I wouldn't say that, your reverence; I wouldn't say that at all now," interpolated Blanche, who stood framed in the doorway. "That's a thunderin' charge to make agin two poor gossoons on the unsupported evidence of one man, even though he is the teacher itself. There is such a thing as corroboration even in a court of law and you, sir, stand for a higher form of law."

"What is this interloper doing here again? You have no right to be here at all, sir, and I must ask you with all the weight of my authority to quit our presence. I have an ugly yet a compelling duty to perform, and you are butting in where you have no rights."

Then he gripped his massive whip to show that his mind was made up in this matter; yet he no longer spoke with the same sense of conviction. He felt that there may be a snag after all in the teacher's story and he hoped for the morality of the parish that there was.

This interruption caused him to lose the thread of what he intended to be a sweeping rhetorical indictment rounded off in flowing periods. He could declaim but he could not debate; pulpit oratory did not lend itself to interruption of this kind.

"By what authority is this egregious man here at all, much less pleading a hopeless cause for lost-souled boys speeding to Hades and getting there?"

He was making yet another valiant effort to resume his pulpit-preaching stride.

"Don't provoke the Canon, like a good man," protested the teacher. "I asked you to keep an eye on the school while I was going for his reverence but that is no reason why you should vegetate in the place."

"This is no fair concern of yours, my good man, ha, ha. There's the door and let it show us your back. Your absence is very good company here."

The Canon then indicated the exponent of the builder's art with a determined sweep of the whip as the pupils, one and all, trembled like aspen leaves at the thought of Blanche's departure which they felt could not be very long delayed now. The situation seemed surcharged with menace, and Linnane went white with fear.

Blanche, who was craning stubbornly over the half-door, felt nettled by the teacher's taunts and the pastor's assentation; so he tautened himself against the doorway.

"Was it any concern of mine to cease work to save our precious teacher from being burned to a cinder," he vociferated. "Then I lose half a day minding and teaching school for him while he is jig-sawing about going from Billy to Jack yarning about these poor children and trying to get them the father of a batin'. I'm after saving him from death here and damnation hereafter this day and that isn't enough for him."

"Ha, ha. Judge not and thou shalt not be judged, my good man," warned the Canon.

"But, as I was saying…"

"Silence, sir, silence I say again, ha, ha," interjected the Canon, striking the rostrum with his whip as a restorative to relevance. "Proceed, Mr Swanton, ha, ha."

"Yessir. This pair of unlicked cubs are as full of mischief as an unsprung rat trap. You could rake Thomond in vain for their equals in evil, I think."

"Or superiors in virtue," added Blanche, "and besides, thinking is bad politics. You're not sure you know. I won't listen to such a thumping pack of lies."

"And who the Hades is asking you to listen to anything, ha, ha?" rejoined the Canon. "You were ordered to quit our presence long ago. We want no Nosy Parkers spying and prying about here. You'd be better employed raising that house outside, ha, ha."

"While you'd be raising blisters on the boys in the wrong. I tell you here and now, sir, I'll not stand for it as long as I have the use of my limbs. You'll beat those boys over my dead body, yourself and your tale-bearing teacher."

Suiting the action to the word, Blanche stepped into the centre of the room and struck a dogged and menacing attitude. The culprits breathed a sigh of relief at last as they felt that their saviour had crossed the Rubicon. It was clear that he would not be argued out of the room any longer come what would. His fine physique and youth would defy their united efforts at expulsion if it came to a test of strength.

"I was a welcome trespasser here when I snatched the brand from the burning, your reverence," said he, indicating the worried teacher with a backward tilt of his massive head. "You can say what you like to me but you cannot do what you like to innocent chaps."

"He could cling you to the ground if he wanted to," snapped the teacher. "Couldn't you, sir?"

Canon Lavelle pursed his lips prior to saying something both emphatic and final but ere he could vocalise his rising resentment or translate his volcanic thoughts into action the teacher broke in: "It's not enough that the average teacher should have the duties of a nursemaid at times, the mere pay of a policeman, and a life of carking care but he must be blown out of his school. It's not enough for me to be houseless and homeless and knocked about the parish like a billiard ball but I must be mined and murdered in the performance of my onerous and exacting duty. I cannot live at the mercy of a pair of scheming arsonites. Excuse this strong language, Canon, but that is the exact posture of affairs."

"Ha, ha. Honest indignation is the voice of God," palliated his pastor.

The teacher then looked at the Canon to see had he at last

screwed his resolution to the point of penology.

"Ha, ha, sir. You have said quite enough to convince me of the enormity of this crime against God and man. They must be taught a lesson that they won't forget as long as grass grows and water runs in Menavia. These boys seem to have bloomed and blossomed up to a certain point and then blighted. Before we proceed to deal out ample justice where it is long overdue you can all go to lunch now except these two imps of the perverse."

Mr Swanton darted to the door to make sure that his quarry would not escape and the other boys filed out almost dripping with pity for their two forlorn colleagues. As for Blanche, they heroised him in their hearts.

The latter once again retired behind the easel and the Canon who espied anew asked: "Ha, ha. Are you an aerophyte that you can abstain from your dinner this way?"

"As I was about to say before, sir, when I was interrupted, sir, I can throw some light on this burning question the same as I threw cold water on it at first."

"Ha, ha, and why didn't you say so before, my good man?"

"Sure you had such a terrible power and all of talk that I couldn't get a word in edgewise."

"We are no martinets, yet we will tolerate no marplots in our midst, ha, ha."

"Then there was that bathing incident at Rahora last summer," said the teacher but I will let bygones be bygones."

"Ha, ha. I've heard something about that already. You were saved by a lady," said the Canon quizzically.

"Oh, I daresay. Who doesn't hear of all the insults that are heaped upon me from time to time? I didn't beat the badness out of these fellows in time."

"Or at all, ha, ha. The lees of a too lenient folly have been drained in your case."

Meantime, the joint causes of all this to-do were now fully

convinced at last that they were the most sin-torn wretches on earth. Yet youth is very resilient and soon triumphs over its miseries. Just then they felt that a cabbage leaf would cover them.

"Where's my riding whip, ha, ha?" queried the Canon. "Who ever had the colossal audacity to spirit it away, what next, eh, ha, ha?"

"My explanation, may it please your reverence," proceeded Blanche, holding both his hands and the whip behind his back, "is quite simple. It's about time that we cut the cackle. I stepped in just to tell you an hour and more ago that I was the blinking cause of all the teacher's miseries. Just after the break of day and my fast, it dawned on me that I wanted a certain class of stone for a certain part of the house. I'm ruinated entirely, said I to myself."

"Whose house? Come to the point and stop at it, sir, if you don't mind."

"Yerrah, whose house but Mr Swanton's. Scholars must be housed like any class of men instead of wrapping themselves up in their learning."

"You're eternally talking and saying nothing, ha, ha. At least, nothing relevant to the would-be murder of the master. Whenever is this blessed house going to be built, by the way?"

"Well, I'm slaving at it all the day and half the night and then there are other odds and ends of jobs to be done for other people and a strike to be settled. In olden times when a fellow died all the people came and flung a boulder on his bier and thus raised a carn over him. In that way the depth of their grief measured the height of his popularity. It occurred to me that if every boy brought a stone under his arm every morning this house would be built in next to no time. Instead of stones, which we want, they bring turf, which we don't."

"Speak for yourself, Blanche," said the teacher.

"This morning I was bringing a blast of powder to the

quarry; the old battered half-gallon was missing so I scoops a hole in a sod of turf, sticks in the blasting powder and covers it up again. Then after a bit, some urchin comes along and craves a bit of turf off me to save him, as he said, from a terrible hiding from the teacher for forgetting it. I was cold as charity at first but the poor little beggar said it was worse to forget one lump of turf than a year's learning. Then I forget the pyramid of turf piled ever so high in the old shieling and, worse than all, I forgot to refuse him the sod as contained the blasting powder. I thought of it after a bit, however, and I was near knocked of a heap with the fright. I was just doing a hand gallop into the school to prevent the murder of the master when he just fell into my arms, tongues of flame hanging out of him and hugging him like a lover in a dark lane, so to speak. There's the truth of it all now and no lie, your reverence."

The two boys were amazed at Blanche's facile imagination and the air of verisimilitude that he gave to the story. Macara stepped out to confess his guilt but the Canon enjoined silence and the opportunity passed.

"Ha, ha, that puts a different complexion on it all, I am very glad to say," said the Canon, visibly relieved. Then he turned his pale ascetic face on the two boys and continued: "You are entirely exonerated from this hideous charge. There was what would seem to be strong *prima facie* evidence against you, as the lawyers would say. I am more than delighted that you are innocent and you may now go home for the day after this terrible ordeal. Our teacher was too hasty in his conclusions as a sleuth hound of crime."

"Blanche has built up a likely story anyway, whatever about the building of my house," said the teacher querulously.

"Come, come, one thing at a time, sir, ha, ha. Try to be generous some time or other. It seems to me that this thunderin' turf mania of yours has wrought all this mischief, ha, ha. That's an obsolete practice, this daily hodding of fuel to school and it must cease from this day. From this day, ha, ha. I will pay for all the fuel that you may require in future out of my own pocket as your school manager, ha, ha. I'd pay much more to know that his parish doesn't harbour such high-viced boys as I was led to believe."

He then patted the pair of culprits emotionally on the head, gave them half-a-crown each by way of compensation to their feelings and dismissed them for the day.

The Canon felt delighted beyond measure at the turn the crisis had taken as he shrank from the idea of having to inflict corporal punishment. He felt suddenly well affected towards the contractor, in fact towards everything and everybody, with the possible exception of the teacher. However, he felt constrained to deprecate his carelessness but this was only by way of a sop to the conventions in his judicial capacity. He felt that Blanche was the real hero of this tense and dramatic situation and his heart went out to him. Still, he reflected that it might spoil his character and his home-spun good nature to tell him so.

Tommy Cooley, who happened to be passing along the road with a load of beets as the Canon emerged from the school, said his face was lighted up with a glow of laughter and good humour.

CHAPTER IX

COUNTRY LIFE

PEADAR Blanche's well-embroidered version of how the teacher was blown up and his attempt to incriminate two of his most advanced pupils was readily credited throughout Menavia. The incident created a mild sensation and the comments thereon were not readily exhausted. The consensus of opinion was that it was a blessing in disguise as it had caused the abolition of the turf tribute. The adverse verdict too did much to lessen the popularity of the teacher and nobody ever doubted that he was in the wrong, in fact, grossly so.

The teacher himself, despite the manager's decision against him, nourished a deep-seated suspicion that Macara and Linnane had more than a little to do with the explosion; and he ever knew Blanche to be, among other things, a man of facile invention. Then he audited the contractor's character and satisfied himself that where his interests were concerned he could be a veritable monster of unveracity. He reviewed his inglorious mishap from every angle and felt dandered against everybody concerned. The Canon, of course, knew little about Blanche and that was all in his favour. He grudgingly admired the man's bluff plausible manner of stating a case and getting away with it. He was, he thought, turned into a subject for burlesque because his pupils had related every detail of what had happened to their parents.

The school stood upon a slight rise of ground; its white-washed walls looked dingy while a yellow distemper did duty for paper inside, bare except for four maps that could be slided up and down. The well-worn desks were free alike from either elegance or ease while the sanitary arrangements were of the most primitive kind. The one redeeming feature about the school was its fine fuchsia hedge, which glowed with colour in season. As the teacher looked out upon the scene his face seemed as grave as a clown off duty. He would, he thought, have to seek a change of either school or employment.

Menavia, he reasoned, held nothing much for him in any case, except Finola, in whom he was beginning to take a growing interest. But how was he to begin to make any progress in her affections? She was even more shy and aloof ever since she had pulled him out of the pill. In grace and ease of movement, she was at least the equal of the fawn; and the boarding school with which she was now finished had made her fit to be the mate of any man. Her elusive wayward ways were in his eyes an additional charm. He must begin at once to externalise his feelings towards her – but how? Did he expect that mere telepathy alone would operate in his favour? If his house even was finished he would be in a position to give a house-warmer and he could invite the Macara family, and a few more so that it would not look too pointed. The Fabian tactics of Blanche would not permit of any strategy along those lines for the present. Then there was that lumpish lady in the female school paying increasing attention to him of late and her father, who was also a teacher six miles away, hinting to him that he should seek a mate. She was, he knew, a perpetual fountain of good sense and all that it implied, but her sheep's-eye advances left him cold. He knew that teachers were expected nowadays to marry teachers and so double their incomes and halve their responsibilities.

He would have to be careful with those two coltish youths in future, try and draw out the best that was in them and, as far as possible, let bygones be bygones.

Alas for the futility of human resolutions, he was to see no more of them, at least as pupils in his own school. Canon Lavelle, who was a very learned man, had been president of the diocesan college before he came to Menavia and still took a perfervid interest in its welfare. Ever on the look-out for eligible recruits for it, it occurred to him that these boys should be sent there as soon as possible. To that end he called on their parents on leaving the school and expatiated on the advantages of a secondary education in their case, especially if they did not intend to be farmers.

This remark opened up a new train of thought in James Macara. "It's no wonder, Canon," he said, "that farming is in such a backward and hopeless condition in this country. Every farmer is told to educate his brightest sons and send them into the professions or something in the towns and cities. The dullard is kept at home to carry on the farm and raise the next generation from a dull stock, and so on, generation after generation. Although farming is our seventy-five per cent industry, and there is every prospect that it will remain so despite the £12 million Shannon Scheme designed to light up the poverty of the country, yet the fool of the family is thought to be good enough to carry on our greatest industry. It's a perfect scandal to my mind and here are you doing your best to perpetuate it."

"That's a plausible argument, ha, ha, James, but there happens, nevertheless, to be a snag in it. Children for the most part inherit whatever brains they have from their mother. The mental qualities are supplied from the maternal side and our physical contours from the paternal side. You will, I daresay, notice that all great men had remarkable mothers, ha, ha. It is a case of brawn versus brain and the balance is fairly preserved in that way. Besides, the law of primogeniture is still fairly respected and the eldest boy is not necessarily the most wan-witted of the family, ha, ha."

"But you forget, Canon, that the same bad tendency is operating on a growing scale among farmers' daughters. The bright lasses are kept at school to be turned into teachers, typists and nurses and thus placed out of the reach of the marrying farmer.

Teachers will only mate with teachers and so on; so that when the professional and clerical classes are supplied by the brains-carriers on both sides, only a low form of mentality is left for our biggest industry. That is why farming is the Cinderella of the trades, occupations, or whatever you like to call it. Everybody looks down on the bally worm-cutting old farmer, more especially in times of financial depression such as at present. He is belectured from pulpit, press and platform; everyone seems to know his business better than himself."

"Ha, ha, you were never intended for farming yourself, James. When men are too clever they can be a misfit at farming and the professions turn in handy to prevent that in the interest of our biggest industry. Farming can be, of course, a most diversified, many-sided business but then, most of them only practice a few lines of it to suit local conditions and that makes for simplification and stupidity."

"We are very particular about how we mate our livestock and very careless about the mating of our farming stock. The scrub bull is eliminated but the scrub farmer is perpetuated."

"You are trenching on the subject of eugenics, James, ha, ha, and that is preserved ground, except for those specially trained to deal with it. That subject has too many implications for casual discussion. I am convinced, though, that we are not getting full value for the four millions that we are spending on education in this country. Only five per cent of our children go to secondary schools and only a tithe of college boys go to the university. There are six thousand primary schools in the country, the teachers are paid and some would say overpaid. The schools are too small and unsanitary. The salaries are paid by the State but we, the local managers, must equip, repair and maintain the schools."

"Teachers should help you out, Canon. I see in the *Recorder* that fifty years ago they had only fifty pounds a year."

"So they do, ha, ha. The community for which they are caring are not getting that service that is commensurate with their salaries, but that is the fault of our muddling State. It has not cost the older teachers very much in the way of preparation to secure all this status and security and then with their pensions they are secured from all anxiety as regards the future. In Germany, teachers take charge of rural libraries, help in rural co-operative banks and cultivate horticultural plots. We can blame the State if our teachers are not what they should be, ha, ha."

"Our teachers think very egotistically about themselves and very spasmodically about the rising generation. We want a change."

"Oh, we will always have change, ha, ha. Education is verily a Penelope's web which has to be unwound and spun anew every generation or so."

Canon Lavelle then left to see the Linnane family. The result was that soon after this Murty Linnane and Fergus Macara were bundled off to college only ten miles away. They were delighted to be rid of Mr Swanton as their relations with him were becoming rather strained.

When he heard a few days later of their hegira in pursuit of a higher form of culture, he felt temporarily annoyed. The boys had wormed themselves into his thoughts more than he would care to admit. He somehow felt that their departure was a slur on his capabilities as a teacher and he was tempted to give vent to his feelings. A decadent moralist had said that the best way to get rid of a temptation was to indulge it, and so he refrained.

The matter was keenly debated in the local public house in due course. Blanche was seated on an upturned beer barrel in the little dug-out of a bar. His eyes wandered lovingly at frequent intervals towards a foaming pint of black porter that stood on the counter before him. The bar was so short and narrow that much of the drinking was done in the kitchen and outhouses. As it was a league from the most proximate police station, supervision was purely spasmodic.

Mrs Belinda Mary Anne Quinburn, although innocent of any pretensions to culture – or perhaps because of it – was an excellent business woman and bar-tender. She knew the exact earnings of her clientele and how much credit she might risk between one weekend and another in respect of drink consumed both on and off the premises. On Sundays, both farmers and labourers would slouch into barns and outhouses within easy reach of liquid refreshment and wile away the time playing cards for porter. Paddy Quinburn himself would act as the connecting link between the gamesters and their source of supply. The game was so regulated that even an hour's strenuous play among men of arid throats scarce sufficed to win or lose the drink stakes. Those more flush of money had shorter games. Then Quinburn, eagerly picking up the stakes, would potter along aimlessly as it were towards his pub, swinging what would appear to be a slop pail in his soft red hands. On Sunday, he was emerging with a gallon of drink when he saw two police hurrying up to raid the place. Pretending not to see them yet awhile, he called as if talking to somebody: "Them pigs didn't get a bit, bite, nor sup today. Such lazy trollops of women as I have about the house. Only for me, they'd starve entirely. They would, so they would."

Then he heard a noise in the gambler-haunted den and addressing the two representatives of the law who now confronted him he half-angrily exclaims: "Do ye hear the way, gentlemen, these bally pigs is chrustin' the dhure from the dint of the hunger this day. It's destroyed they are."

"You know we can prosecute nowadays under the Cruelty to Animals Act for starving anything," said the sergeant, and the publican's knees knocked together with the fear that he had overdone it.

The police passed on and Paddy passed in to the barn. The noise referred to was made by somebody trumping the game.

Blanche, who overheard the conversation through the closed public house door, drained his glass to the dregs, shut the door, flung off his hat and coat and proceeded to open the kitchen door for the police with a pot hook in one hand and a whisk in the other. He was at once mistaken for the publican's factotum and they hurried away convinced that it was a waste of time to be visiting such sequestered God-forsaken places.

Then the dozen barn stormers entered the pub knowing that they were free from police inspection for another month of Sundays. Blanche had resumed his place on the porter barrel, silently preening himself on his histrionic display. He was being rallied and congratulated by five cronies who were able to crowd into the bar. Mrs Quinburn, realising that he had saved her from the cost and stigma of a prosecution, decided to stand a round of drink, a thing she had never been known to do before.

This was the drink they were now enjoying when the cultural aspirations of the Macaras and the Linnanes came on for consideration.

The publican, who was a sturdy, smug, complacent, red-faced man of about fifty, said it would be fitter for young Macara and Linnane to remain at home carting manure to their parents' potato patches. Bad and all as Swanton was, he had, he said, forgotten more than they would ever learn and that wasn't a lot. The idea of sending such wooden-headed fellows to college.

"In fact, now that I think of it," said Blanche, "if they would only put their pair of heads together they'd help to floor that new house for me."

"'Tis well known," added the publican, "that the Macaras, although they have a big spread of bad land, are only struggling and striving. The postman told me over a free pint lately that he was carrying more bankers' letters to Jimmy Macara than to the rest of the parish. Surely 'tisn't the compliments of the season they do be wishing James and the wife so often if you ask me. Putting two and two together, all this extra work on the poor lame postman can have only one meaning as far as I can see. What do you say, Peadar Blanche?"

"Begobs, you were always a cute shrewd butt of a man, Paddy, and I wouldn't say agin you. What you don't know about the neighbours isn't worth knowing. If you didn't go to school itself, you met the scholars, as the saying goes, and as a publican you are in a position to pick up a lot of reach-me-down second-hand information. A good pub is as good as a bad school as a font of information. At the same time, if these people can buy a bit of superior learning for their boys, they owe an apology to nobody."

"That's the point I'm coming to, Peadar. It's a case of borrowed plumes with borrowed money. That's the kind of co-draulin' that I'm all out agin, high notions and low stations like Bradley's gander. I'm a league away from wishing harm to anybody but I can see that some of us are riding for a fall. You should cut your cloth according to your measure."

"Hang it, man, you're not a tailor, Paddy, needles and all. These people never darken your door for a drink so they can't owe you much to growl about."

"That's the trouble, Blanche. Macara would run up a long bill here only he makes out he's too grand in himself to come under my roof, himself and that teacher fellow. Pride takes the worst forms and pride always goes before a fall."

"Faith, I wish I could borrow some of their qualities, I'd be the rich man this day. I'm a slave to drink, a fool, and you know it, Paddy, but still I can't keep away from here and I'll drink to the end of the chapter. I suppose you'd call me a proud man too if I took a leaf out of Swanton's book and kept away from your frothy swill. I hate to hear louts backbiting their betters."

"And who might they be, now. You don't refer to me, do you?"

"If the cap fits, you can wear it."

"You made a tailor of me a minute ago and now I'm to be a hatter and, I suppose, as mad as any hatter."

This sally caused a gust of laughter and the heavy-witted, mocking publican, who was beginning to feel nettled, felt gratified that the company was laughing with, rather than at him.

Quinburn, who had been very poor before the Great War, was waxing wealthy of late due to the never-ending efforts of his wife, a dour, silent, close-fisted woman. When drink was scarce and could not be had for love or money, they used to brew shell cocoa in the dead of night and mix it with porter in order to eke it out. His wealth had now the effect of unleashing his tongue and he was fast developing unbecoming facets in his character which, as a struggling trader, he would take care to tuck away. His more recent philosophy of shop-keeping was that there should be no credit given in respect of drink. He reasoned that once a man became a debtor in a place he was inclined to go elsewhere.

As for his wife, many of her customers felt that she had the gift of words in an unfortunate way. Once the few days credit that she gave was up, she had a chronic way of reminding them in the presence of all about their "long overdue little bill, do you know".

On fair days or pay nights her memory was a marvel, or at least so it was said by those who had reason to know. Her outlook was severely and soundly practical, so much so as to be quite colourless and at times almost depressing. To get money and to rear her children, if and when they would come, was her only aim and object in life. Anything that did not relate to these practical objectives was ruled out as irrelevant or nearly so. However, if she did not radiate very much cheeriness and happiness, she ruled a turbulent and morose spouse and a credit-running debt-eschewing clientele fairly effectively. Paddy was inclined of late to drink himself into a state of insensibility beneath a beer barrel because he was not founding a family and she had to guard against this creeping form of extravagance. She succeeded where a more cultured woman would fail and fail miserably, did this woman, with her notoriously spiky character and exterior.

CHAPTER X

MARLEY SWANTON'S DILEMMA

HAVING decided, largely in compliance with the wishes of their pastor, to send their sons to college, the parents of both boys found that rather elaborate preparations had to be made before they would look presentable in their new surroundings. The college prospectus showed that each entrant would require at least two suits of clothes, a dozen pairs of socks, half a dozen shirts, shoes, boots, sports boots and a rug and so on. It was found that they would have to discard almost everything that they were presently wearing, including shorts for long trousers. The new change of raiment marked an epoch in their lives and they felt pleasantly excited.

These identical aspirations brought the Macara and the Linnane families into closer touch with each other than they had ever been before and an exchange of visits took place between them in order to cement this newly-born friendship.

Finola Macara did not return to her conventional school the previous September as intended and it was assumed that she would be allowed to return after Christmas. Her mother got a cold and gave it out as an excuse for not letting her back. At the fair the previous week her father sold only some of his cattle and even then at a discount owing to an outbreak of foot-and-mouth disease. Then the question of the translation of her brother to a more costly seat of learning loomed up and her interests were sacrificed, at least for the present. So far, she had received an excellent training in lacework and domestic economy at the convent. This enabled her to make all the underwear for her brother, which was a big saving in the family budget. The Linnanes had a sewing machine which they seldom used and she decided to pocket her pride and borrow this. Strange, she reflected, that her mother had never bought such an indispensable household adjunct, but then she had noticed since her return from school that she was already old-fashioned in many respects and all unknown to herself. She did not immediately refer the omission to straitened circumstances in the home. Her mother, who never worked what she called any of these new-fangled things, reluctantly gave her consent to the borrowing, remarking however that she who goes a-borrowing goes a-sorrowing. Mrs Macara had long ago got into a rut and she did not want to make the acquaintance of anything that she did not learn in her youth. That was why she was so often seen up till midnight plying a common needle and thread with great dexterity.

Murty Linnane brought over the sewing machine and told Finola that she could keep it until he would call in person for it, and added: "There will be no hurry on me." She vaguely admired him. She had the advantage of him by reason of her more advanced education and, in any case, girls develop faster at that age. She was fashioning a laundry bag for her brother when it occurred to her that she could do a like service for his college colleague. Besides, was she not greatly beholden to him for the machine; and then he had come with it himself so as to pay her a greater compliment. Then she made two such bags for him and embroidered his initials on them elaborately in the national colours.

The recipient and his parents appreciated the gift very much, together with the forethought that inspired it. Besides, its utilitarian character was beyond question.

All feelings of enmity between the two collegians were long since dissolved.

Canon Lavelle resolved that no useful purpose could be served by visiting the teacher until the elapse of a few months in order to give him time to recover from his recent anti-climax. He was a deep-thinking manner of man and he knew that

Marley Swanton, though hasty in his judgments as he thought, was at least industrious and well-meaning. Of course, at the same time he reflected that half the world's mischief is done by well-meaning men and women. Anyway he would leave him to his own devices for the present.

On the other hand, the teacher was most anxious to see his manager in order to release himself of certain worries that clouded his life of late. The average attendance in his school was falling at an alarming rate. He must, he thought, have fallen into a certain degree of ill odour over the recent school incident. Then again, the neighbouring teacher whose daughter's advances he had recently definitely turned down since Finola swam into his life had canvassed and taken a number of borderline children from him. A very capable, in fact a learned teacher, he knew that he was considered too angular and rigid in his ways to be ever really popular. Quinburn had six relatives on the border who had left his school and he must, he reasoned, have had something to do with it, as he had been visiting their parents a good deal recently. If the school average fell by one more pupil he would lose his status and his school. Why did Quinburn nourish such an active dislike to him, this loutish man whose path he never crossed?

He differed from most teachers both lay and clerical inasmuch as that he was addicted to writing. For the past few years, partially to get rid of the *ennui* which would oppress him, he would write essays and short articles. Then, after reading them he would grow diffident of his powers and tear them up. Still, he was gaining confidence of late because he often saw thoughts to which he had given expression appearing in print couched in much worse language. Then, Menavia was no longer the self-contained microcosm that he would like it to be. It was, he thought, in a state of flux and transition greater than at any time since the twilight of fable. Children were even changing; they knew much more about life and sex at an earlier age. Motor and bus had also an unsettling effect on the plain people. It was idle, he thought, to bandage his eyes to certain crystal clear facts any longer. Then, he sat down and after much cogitation wrote the following letter to Canon Lavelle and duly posted it, as a stamped letter was more formal and business-like than one merely delivered by hand.

"Dear Canon Lavelle. While the temperament and characteristics of our people remain unaltered, the changes that I observe recently in their outlook on life and their reaction towards the social and economic problems of the day call for more than casual comment. Some of the evolutionary changes have been all to the good and others are such as to raise the utmost misgivings. That degraded form of pleasure only to be found in pubs and clubs is on the wane and we can obtain a modicum of comfort from the decreasing popularity of drunken brawls. Against this, however, is to be set the growing laxity in morals among both young and old. Formerly female immorality was confined to the towns and cities but now it is spreading to the country. There were two cases of it alone in the next parish this year when girls had to go away to hide their shame. In work and sport the female of the species is being brought into contact with the lord of creation, so to say, as never before. The barriers thrown up over 1931 years by the Redeemer himself are being broken down. Thrown together so much, they beget a contempt for the laws and conventions that formerly held them in leash. Liberty is rapidly degenerating into license and with all these new-fangled, space-annihilating inventions I wonder how long Menavia will remain untouched. The Linnanes have got a wireless set. Invited over to listen in, I was shocked to hear a lecture given by an atheist on a saint. I felt concerned for the faith of Finola Macara and others who were present. Just imagine an atheist as a spiritual engineer. If Ireland ever becomes an industrial country like England with a person to the acre, or over twenty-two millions, then it will be a case of hell let loose. Then again, we have a cinema newly set up in the village and with its lurid depictions of high life and its incessant harping on the sex appeal it is doing its share of the devil's work. Then we have dances and sitting out in covered motor cars where erring couples can hide their shameful carryings-on. In a country like ours, where even kissing was regarded in my youth as indecent and even sensual, the bacchanalian revelries and highly-spiced suggestive love scenes shown in the films imported from foreign cesspools of iniquity are bound to lower the moral tone of the people.

"The short-skirted, short-haired, short-mannered, short-educated Miss 1931 is now hovering like a dragonfly on the borders of Menavia. Then we have the long-haired pomade-scented Oxford bags of a boy now being turned out in scores by all our colleges. I was profoundly shocked in the sartorial change that has already taken place in young Macara and Linnane. Such perfectly appalling types. Old norms of morality, though perhaps in need of slight revision, are flung upon the scrap heap in their entirety by standards that will surely lead to perdition. Self-discipline, as shown by a recent incident in my own school, is being tossed to the winds. The revolt against discipline and the ever-spreading spirit of unrest and irreverence for parents, preachers and teachers is shown by the rising generation in a great variety of ways. The teacher, who came next to the pastor in the eyes of youth, is mocked and plotted against in his own school. The only serious crime now is to contradict a policeman. The world is gone sport mad at the moment.

"You will be surprised to learn that my two greatest school rebels, Linnane and Macara, are now gone to college. I hope they will try and live up to the best traditions of our little school."

As an amateur writer so far he revised parts of the foregoing half a dozen times before he could finally approve of it. It was, he knew, a very laboured effort but easy writing makes difficult reading. The manner of saying a thing was no less important than the message itself. Proper words in proper places could only be achieved by much revision and deletion.

Then he took up his favourite daily paper and as he was laying it down he noted the page specially preserved for literary freshness. There was a small paragraph in script type inviting original short articles from readers and promising a substantial money reward. Then it occurred to him that although he was a man of very wide reading yet he had never written anything more important than a correction and a comment in a child's copybook. He had read that sincerity and truth were the chief things to be aimed at in writing. But then, if one had nothing to say and, worse still, if he could not couch his meagre thoughts in happy compelling language. He had read a lot in his lifetime and reading should issue in writing. Could he cash any of his experiences? He had, he recollected, seen Blanche fitting a door on its hinges recently and he had to plane it forty times and try it many ways before he succeeded in fitting it. Yes, writing was something like that. Then he clawed his thick black mass of hair and exclaimed aloud:

"I have it. How it feels to be forty."

It occurred to him that forty was a magical number. Our Lord spent forty days fasting, Moses spent forty days in the mountain receiving the Decalogue, the Israelites spent forty years in the desert and the Redeemer spent forty days with his apostles after his resurrection. It was just his fortieth birthday but he knew that he passed for little more than thirty in Menavia. But then, if literature was to ring true to life, the truth must be told. It would never do to start off a new career with a lie in his lips, or rather, in his pen.

As a teacher of composition he should, he thought, be a

master of it but he knew that most teachers weren't. He reached out for a wad of paper and after about four hours work during which he tore up and revised what he wrote a score of times, this is what finally emerged for the approval of the editor of the Dublin daily paper.

"Was it not Hugo said that forty was the youth of old age and the old age of youth? The cycle of youth has been considerably prolonged since his time and since Thackeray thought that maidens who had not mated at five and twenty were henceforth in the sere and yellow leaf stage. Growing older is just like mountain climbing. When you set out from the level, even the foothills seem far away. Arrived at these, you look back like Lot's wife only to realise you have scarcely begun. Each stage of the journey while being approached seems a long way off – like the road to Tipperary – over the hills and far away. Yet, when you have done it you wonder that you have done it so speedily and come such a little way.

"At twenty you think that thirty is unattainably remote. Then you will be quite a different person, serious, sedate, semi-prosperous – anyway, different. Doctors tell us that physiologically we become another man – or woman – every seven years. Then what will our mental metamorphoses be like? Arrived at forty, it seems only a short time since you were thirty. To one in his teens, forty conjures up a vision of autumn leaves, of a fellow blown, fly-blown almost, bloated, bald and bulky.

"Yet at forty I find that I can smile at the fears and fancies of fifteen. In spirit you may be just as young as ever. Age is no longer the awful matter of chronology that it used to be, especially if we subscribe to the dictum that a man is only just as old as he feels, while a woman is as old as she looks, that is to say lipsticked, 'lifted', powdered, painted, perfumed and all. Yet they are discarding both clothes and cosmetics for work and sport and growing ever so much taller than their grandmothers. It is a sure sign of racial decay when the female outgrows the male.

"The writer is just gone over to the cemetery side of forty. Still he feels that yet awhile he will be able to defy the plaguey hints and suggestions of tonsorial artists of the hair-restoring variety.

"'Bad case of trichorrhea, sir. Can I sell you anything for your tonsured top storey, sir?' Yes, at forty a man should still be a tolerably good advertisement for his tailor. If he happens to be a gourmand, tosspot or the like, then he will have an inflated corpus, a sure index not alone of age but of degeneration.

"Recently a man who had arrived at this intriguing age was asked to release himself of his impressions? He said the first day that he had realised he had parted with his youth was when he saw half a dozen young policemen in a wayside town. The Force had youthfully altered. It used to consist of grave elderly men, not callow beardless boys. Then he realised that the change was in himself.

"Another clear proof that you are becoming year-stricken is the calculating way you skip up steps two at a time helter-skelter in order to convince yourself – and others – that you are as young as ever. There is a halo of heroism about such an act and he who shrinks from it is less than a man – of forty. Youth care-lessly conscious of its dynamic vigour lazily dreams and drifts along. When you begin to hear such suggestive nasty remarks as 'at your time of life' you should be convinced indeed of the fardel of your years.

"Youth expects a lot from life. Forty finds that the world is not unlike a bank, paying an exact interest on deposits made with it but nothing more. The lottery winners are negligibly few. Yet a man should be thriving rather than striving at forty. Forty is a searching and significant milestone in your career but it is not yet the period of sapless age and weak, unable limbs. The worst that can be said about a man arrived at that magical age is that he is like Coleridge's archangel, just a little damaged."

The teacher felt much relieved as he finished his maiden attempt at authorship. To make it more attractive, he had it typed, a decision that cost him a shilling in the county town. Then he posted it to the daily paper and awaited the result with a sort of nervous interest. A month elapsed and it did not appear and yet he felt it was the effort of an Apelles. Then he began to fear that it had been consigned to the waste paper basket and he blamed its rejection on the hebetated understating of the editor.

CHAPTER XI

THE PAROCHIAL OUTLOOK

THERE was only one Mass said at Menavia on Sundays because it was a succursal church. It stood in about six yards from the road. Weather permitting, most of the male population would gravitate towards the house of worship so as to arrive nearly an hour before Mass time and line up along the low-lying walls at both sides of the entrance gate. Here they would sort one another out according to the caprices that may rule them at the moment and earnestly canvass everything from the state of the crops to the latest happening of any note within a radius of ten miles. Everything was debated on centrifugal lines, events in the outer rims of their horizon receiving less attention than the happenings nearer home. Then the priest might be a quarter of an hour late and this would give them extra time for gossip. Lined up in knots along the walls at both sides, they swopped the latest stories and tidbits of scandal with great gusto and relish. Here the appetite for news and views grew upon what was fed to it.

Standing with their backs to the wall and given that kind of courage that comes from numbers, they would at the same time turn their optics on and relentlessly survey and outstare every woman, girl and child, as they would file in in front of them to their seats to prayerfully await the arrival of the priest. Stretched along the roadway for a considerable distance, their fixed gaze became a steady barrage before which the stoutest-hearted would quail at times, lower their eyes and look confused. Passing such a sea of human faces twice in the space of an hour was an ordeal which many tried to dismiss as if it did not exist. They knew they were ogled up and down and every bit of finery, or the want of it, duly noted. These gossiping, ogling men were the last into the church and the first out of it so that they could resume their accustomed coigns of vantage and feast their all-devouring eyes anew on the rest of the community as if they had hailed from another planet.

Visitors to the church would come in for the maximum amount of attention but in their absence they would visually feed on everything and anything that would present itself for inspection.

Under this severe, searching, audacious scrutiny the women-folk would make a brave attempt to wear an air of unconcern but silence among themselves would supervene; they would hang their heads and look both sheepish and bemused. Visitors to the parish would endeavour to look as unconcerned as possible and carry on a desultory conversation while passing this serried sea of surveyors, but even they would feel the terrible oppression of it all in no long time. The latest bit of female finery is mentally noted and often commented upon by this human phalanx. All are visually vetted as they file past. The bell is not rung till the priest actually appears on the altar and then there is a wild ravening rush for seats, the gregarious instinct prevailing to the end. Having seen and heard all that they can see or hear for one Sunday, they quit the walls *en masse*.

Should anybody be tempted to detach himself from this human herd he is treated as a traitor and subtle forms of punishment are meted out to him. He knows that his character or some aspect of it would be rent to pieces as a deserter. He would not have the moral courage to break away after a certain time. He lingers to the last.

There is a pleasant and persistent delusion among city people that the ruralist is a very simple, guileless sort of person, merely living the simple life among his flocks and herds. Rural folk take a certain interest in some aspects of national affairs, yet they remain the product of their environment. The great outer world, its breadth, its sanities and its tolerances, is something much beyond the parish pump and interest wanes accordingly. The major portion of his curiosity must be aroused and sated locally in small daily doses. From incessant practice most of the gossips become masters in the art of innuendo and can give a startling and sinister twist to the most innocuous story. All sorts of subtle meanings are read into the most unpremeditated actions of others. Real first-rate scandals are of rare occurrence yet they are often imagined for all that. Immunity from them would appear to show that many lack the moral courage to face the comment that they would arouse. The intensive, ever-prying interest and criticism that is concentrated on the merest germ of scandal in Menavia is too much for the most hardened potential sinner. There are certain conventions and those who do not conform to them must abide the consequences. Their corrosive causeries show that they must nurse unacted desires, and are self-revelatory in their way.

Quiet people who never do anything notorious are just as addicted to the spirit of unsleeping local enquiry. Every spicy bit of news that comes to them is given a more highly-flavoured twist and sent careering on its way.

The gossip saunters into the public house where he feels it his duty to talk and play up to the humour of the person behind the bar. Given the germ of a story, they can be relied upon between them to pad it out into something worthy of further comment. What a practiced yarner conceals yet manages to convey is the kernel of the story; the rest is only the husk. Nothing much ever seems to happen to the confirmed gossips themselves; they seem conventional, contemplative and, above all, craven-hearted. Ceasing to be an actor, he or she, as the case may be, becomes an expert critic and commentator.

The publican's wife, or daughter, leers the tidbit to the lass who turns in for a few odds and ends of groceries. She in turn shyly simpers it to her mother or her mistress who are, of course, profoundly interested and properly shocked. Having wallowed in all the details of the latest parochial scandal, they hurriedly tell their informant to hold their tongue, and forget to hold their own.

The tradesman or labourer, feeling ill at ease at home, decides to pay a visit to the abode of his betters. He knows that such a visit is intrusive and may be even sharply resented. How is he to dissipate his fears and render himself welcome? Merely by retailing all that he knows, and more than he suspects, about his neighbours, the man or woman who is either too rich or too self-respecting to go about cabin-hunting have their needs catered for in this way. News is scattered as thickly as sparks at a forge. The self-respecting farmer and the well-to-do old maid spread their nets for news without having to go pub-crawling for it.

In this way, the most amazing and incredible canards cover the countryside emanating nobody knows whence. In a dull rural district, when people are going *blasé* for want of a sensation of any kind the last thing they concern themselves about is the veracity of what comes their way. That can wait. Anybody who may venture to doubt a good story steaming hot from the gossip factory – whatever that may be – is silenced by the hoary reminder that there is no smoke without fire. That is a real sockdoliger.

The exclusive family driving to Mass or market may pass one of these humble gossips on the road unrecognised; he cuts no figure at social functions, yet he is a power in the parish but they pretend to ignore it. He is the creator of local gossip, the man who moulds local opinion and gives it that malign tendency so much relished or dreaded, as the case may be. Shunned by many, yet the professional gossip's lightest word percolates everywhere and causes many an uneasy flutter of wings.

If you want to be daily analysed and dissected, live in the country where you will ever be a puzzle and a pleasure to your neighbours.

Menavia is possessed of a sturdy mentally-alert population but culture and rudeness in certain forms prevail. The country may be best for the development of the body up to a certain age but the town is the only place for the growth and maturing of the mind.

Nine months had now sped since Fergus Macara and Murty Linnane had gone to college. Instead of lining the walls as heretofore, they defiantly filed past the ranks of the serried gapers going to Mass. They even further angered them by carrying on a laughing conversation as if they did not exist. Before going to college they felt that they were heroes on account of their daring escapade in Marley Swanton's school. Now they felt the prolonged hostile cold-as-charity kind of stare bestowed upon them. They knew that they had shed their popularity. The boys of their own age also fell away from them; they knew there was no longer the same identity of interest and yet they thought that the boycott need not be so pronounced. On the other hand, the home-keeping youths felt that they were being outrun and slighted in the race of life by their more highly-favoured collegians. The inferiority complex was already upon them and this was the only way they could combat it. The collegians would like to compare notes with them and hark back to old times, but they were not given the chance.

The Macara and Linnane families never lined up against the walls on Sundays but their sons used to do so before they went away.

Quinburn was as usual doing the wall-flower, smoking and taking in everything about him as the college boys passed in. He was always a rich centre of attraction and by reason of his calling wielded much influence of a certain kind in the parish.

"Begor, Peadar Blanche," said he, "when we were boys a national school was good enough for us and a hedge school was good enough for our ancestors. This part of the country is becoming just as full of goster and nonsense as if it was in the middle of Dublin."

"Oh, I suppose we must go with the times and get out of the rut. It is not for the likes of us to decide where and why we should put a period to the onward march of education."

"That's not the point, Peadar. Too much learning destroys a fellow unless he has a sound sober brain."

"We cannot be too conservative in educational matters."

"Isn't a conservative some kind of a politician or something?"

Á conservative is a man who will not look at the new year out of respect for the old. Even the new moon goes unseen."

"You're up in the clouds again, Peadar."

"And you're down among the clods as usual; a clodhopper and nothing else."

"Yes, I have ten acres of land with my little shop and I wish I had a few more to hop over. I'm a common-sensible near-the-ground kind of man as started from scratch. If we all paid our debts in Menavia, faith there wouldn't be much left to college educate our children. Education is simply a crime when you cannot afford it. This parish is simply stinkin' with pride lately. At one time only the gentry would send their children to the higher schools but now our upstart farmers are trying to be even better than their betters."

"You have nothing to educate so far but, of course, time enough. Who are the gentry that you have all the respect for anyway but Cromwell's looting soldiers who hunted the old stock out of their lands and took possession of them. There's many a small farmer and labourer today and kingly blood flows in his veins if he only knew it. The people who have the pelf nowadays have no pedigree and those who have the pedigree have no pelf. It is a case of money minus mentality, brains without bullion. As regards the Macaras, your hissings, spittings and devourings are, and always were, simply terrible."

"Oh no, Peadar. I've seen farmers' daughters go away to high-class schools. They come home knowing all about how to strum a piano and they can tell you that horse is *cheval* in French but they will dry up when you ask them the French for foal or ass, asses that they are. They have forgotten how to milk a cow or cook a potato, too proud to work and too poor to pay for it. The high-class schools are letting loose a host of hussies year after year with their high-falutin' ways on a country too poor to stand it. Education makes poor people cry out against their lot and call for that moon you were talking about a minute ago. Education is alright in England, an industrial country where millions of typers and clerks are wanted to keep accounts, but the devil a farmer ever kept a day book or a ledger. If you want to know the price of a few stone of oats when you want to sell it, well there are ready reckoners going for a penny. The curse of the country is educating anybody above his station in life. We are coming to the time when there won't be half enough collar-and-tie jobs to go round for our so-called educated lads and lasses. Of course, we educated for export but emigration is now stopped. Then in the attempt to make black-coated jobs for themselves they will create red ruin and revolution in this old worn-out country. You'll never get a BA or an MA out of a job to snag a drill of turnips. Look at the Macaras."

"Faith I'm thinking that a lot of your talk, sound as it seems, at the same time emanates from beer and badness, beer in your belly this day and badness in your mind against your neighbours. The nasty sources from which reason and rightness often flow, envy of our neighbours. You ought to stand on one of your own beer barrels and start a crusade against the evil tendencies of school and college life. The old College Green type of politicians always spoke from the top of beer barrels, and drank from the middle of them. I will preside at your meetings for a good draught of free beer and none of your dregs and rinsings either. Keep them for the pigs that you say the educated daughters of farmers won't feed."

This raised a hearty laugh against the publican. "Faith, I don't give a tinker's curse about all the farmers in Ireland," said he, "but that won't stop me from telling them how they are going astray."

"Faith, you don't, because you made your pile during the war, dishing out cocoa mixed with porter, and no blame to you when you got the fools to pay for it."

"And it kept them from getting drunk and fighting about the place giving it a bad name."

"Oh, you're a temperance advocate type of publican now, are you? 'Tis you can afford to laugh at culture and colleges this day. One yard of your sloppy counter is worth more to you than all Macara's big farm of land."

"I'm an old man," said Cooley, "and I never saw the third generation of publicans to prosper. They fail because they have the curses of the wives and mothers of the country falling down on them daily. A fat publican means a lean labourer. Look at myself. I'm near fifty years going to the one pub and I was refused a pint on tick last Friday and the tongue burning out of me with the druth. No names mentioned in present company."

"Well, wherever you spent your bit of money I daresay you got value for it," said Quinburn. "You raked in all the people's money while they had it and now we are all too poor to lean over your counter for long."

This kind of what is called half-joke and whole-earnest banter would have continued much longer as they were all wound up, but the bell tolled out at last and they disappeared into the chapel.

CHAPTER XII

A FATAL FIGHT

FINOLA Macara, now on the edge of nineteen years, had developed into a very comely girl of late; lissome willowy and curly-haired. She was determined that she would not stay on the land and was divided between being either a nun or a nurse. From what she had seen of farming she was convinced that it was a constant round of laborious work, an eternal drag. Even the wives of the most extensive farmers have to work hard and there was little for it owing to over-production and low prices. Pigs, which were six pounds some years ago, were now down to thirty shillings apiece. Salaried people and civil servants on the other hand were having a great time because food was very cheap and their wartime salaries still held. She continued to correspond with Murty Linnane and met him during his holidays but no love words had as yet passed between them. Their epistolary commerce was concerned with the sewing machine, which had not yet gone back, some handkerchiefs that she had since made for him with it, with his initials in the corner, and news about the teacher and his ever-building yet never-completed house.

The first intimation she had that Marley Swanton took a great and growing interest in herself was from Mrs Quinburn. She thought that the publican's wife was joking at first and paid little attention to her shrewd, penetrating remarks on a subject about which she had known so little. Seeing that she did not like it, Mrs Quinburn used to tease her on the subject more than a little and even invent little stories about Swanton's great admiration for her. In this way she was not allowed to forget him. Between visits to town, the Macaras would sometimes run out of odds and ends of groceries and this brought her into contact about once a week with the publican's wife. Latterly she felt that it was a bit beneath her to be seen in such a place even though she was always brought into the little room that did duty for a parlour. She liked the walk and, stranger still, the dour, dark, distant shopkeeper liked her and did her best to be amiable in her presence despite her spiky character.

The Quinburns, who were very poor and despised, did well during the war, and the boom years which helped to enrich them lasted till the middle of 1921. Even for four years after that, before the prices of agricultural produce went so low, they continued to do well in the little shop. Most farmers had financial reserves and they foolishly thought that, sooner or later, prices for their produce would rise. Instead, they continued progressively to slump. They had gotten into a costly mode of living during the years of inflation and they felt both unable and unwilling to get back to pre-war conditions.

Today, Mrs Quinburn bustled into the little cubicle of a parlour where Finola was waiting as usual and she was more voluble and vehement than ever before. She told Finola by way of a great secret that Paddy and herself were thinking of selling out the shop and ten-acre farm and going to live in the county town.

"The fact is, Miss Finola," she said, "that business is getting quieter every day. Between the fall in prices and the rise in everything the farmer has to buy and the fall in everything he has to sell they are cleaned out. We can do no more business here except on the Kathleen Mavourneen system and that would soon cause us to lose what we have."

"I've read of that as being one of the old poetic names of Ireland."

"Oh, that's a cock-and-bull story, alannah, It means giving out your precious goods on a mere promise to pay to the likes of Blanche and Cooley that would drink the cross off an ass's back, the Lord save us. The old country hereabouts is dried up in the way of ready money and it's dangerous to be living among needy people. We made our bit during all the wars – God bless 'em – and we don't give a thraneen for the big broad-acred farmers as used to be always looking down upon us. The likes of Blanche and Cooley calling the boss 'Paddy'. Wouldn't it sicken a dog? They got the bad habit when we were poor strugglin' publicans glad enough of their bit of money. Now we expect a power of respect due to money and we are not getting it hereabouts. Besides, we want to be near colleges and convents for the sake of the children."

"What children, ma'am? I didn't know you had any."

"Oh, the children that are still surely to come to us, alannah."

Finola would listen sympathetically to all these out-pourings but she would make very little comment. She had not yet acquired the art and practice of gossip which infected almost every adult in Menavia and if she had she would not hear half so much. Mrs Quinburn, though married quite a long time, still cherished the hope that she would have a goodly-sized family.

Finola did not think it worth her while to tell her mother about the shopkeeper's confidences because she did not believe her.

Marley Swanton, who was now staying in the village of Margadnua, a league away, as a paying guest, used to come to Rahora on one pretext or another about once a week. Ever since the day she saved him from drowning she occupied an uppermost place in his thoughts. During these visits to the home of her parents he would refer to the subject of a beseeming occupation for the object of his desire, now that she had arrived at woman's estate. Told by her mother one evening recently that she was flirting with the idea of becoming a nun, he heartily disapproved of what he called a cloistered life for such a fine, comely slip of a girl. The real profession of woman was, he

101

thought, marriage and motherhood. Every other career should be only in the nature of a passport to that.

"That's all very fine and large, Mr Swanton," replied the vanithee, now that she had suspected the clue to his remarks, "but there's not enough men to go round. Even if there were, the half of them are well missed."

"People tell me that I should be ready myself to go round if my new house was built. If and when I did select a mate, faith the lady of my choice would not be a hundred yards from here."

"Well, you're a pretty settled man now and if you married itself I suppose it would be to a teacher of your own age, like all the members of your profession. It's a settled girl you'd be wanting if you did decide to change your life." She knew that Murty Linnane and Finola were corresponding and that the former had made up his mind to be a doctor. She was favourably inclined towards him.

"Well, as men go, ma'am, I'm not too weather-beaten yet. Take a man and a woman each of forty. From a chronological point of view they are the same age but regarded from a physiological viewpoint the woman is at least ten and possibly fifteen years older than the man. Conversely, the man is that much younger than the woman."

"Tut, tut, man-alive, that's very rambling talk. How lucky men can juggle with the years as if they were so many gob stones – cast them aside, and pelt them on to women and weigh them down with years before their time. I don't believe it at all, at all. There should be no mating between Spring and Autumn. It would be too unnatural."

"Oh, persuade a woman against her will, she's of the same opinion still. Women fulfill their highest ideals only through marriage, and those who shirk that great and noble responsibility are not doing their manifest duty. Withdrawal into a convent means a certain amount of moral cowardice. Finola could train for a teacher or even marry one that I know without going to that expense or trouble."

Mrs Macara did not pretend to understand the drift of this remark and while she was formulating an evasive reply a blend of noises violently assailed her ears. Shortly excusing herself, she bustled out of the parlour and, stepping out into the yard at the back of the house, found everything in a state of chaos. On opening the back door, Biddy Ward, the maid-of-all-work, swooned into her arms. Looking beyond the limp and lifeless lass whom she gently yet speedily deposited on the doormat, she saw the big three-year-old blood-red bull rushing wildly round the spacious yard, in and out among the cows after something that appeared to be dodging from and eluding him. Lo and behold, the quarry was none other than Finola. The vanithee gave vent to an alarming scream, which brought Marley Swanton to the scene followed by his pet bulldog.

"The bull, the bull. Jesus save my child," she vociferated again and again.

The teacher, picking up the maid's shawl that she dropped outside the door in her frantic race for safety, with great presence of mind threw it over the head of the infuriated animal. This device blindfolded him for a minute or two and he shook it off but not before Marley Swanton had grabbed up the exhausted girl just in the nick of time and raced into the house with her. Meanwhile, the bull, coming towards Mrs Macara, who forgot her own in her daughter's danger, stood as if transfixed and was met by the bulldog who hurled himself upon him not a moment too soon. With true canine instinct, he got the nose of the ravening bull between his teeth at the first bound in the air and a fearful struggle for supremacy ensued. The bull made desperate efforts to shake off the faithful animal, but in vain. He held on to its nose with grim determination. The bull continued to bellow like a lion, raise its head on high and dash the dog against the ground time and again in a frantic series of efforts to shake it off. The score of great lumbering cows were huddled in a corner of the yard, panic-stricken and bellowing with a mixture of fear and anger. The deep rumbling noises that they emitted were heard at a great distance and those within earshot began to hurry to the scene.

At length, James Macara and others arrived, followed by Blanche who was working about a mile away.

Worsted and cowed at length, the bleeding bull knelt down in order to lessen the weight on its nose. It was an act of surrender on its part but the dog would not relax its leech-like hold. The men crowded round armed with pitchforks, and the teacher grasped his dog by the hind legs and tried to pull him off but to no purpose.

Blanche suggested pouring hot or cold water on its head and this was done. While two men held hayforks horizontally towards the bull ready for any emergency, others poured water on the head of the relentless animal, which caused it to relax its grasp as it had caused him to smother. The humiliated, much chastened bull bounded away but the dog lay limp on the ground. It was soon found, alas, that the noble animal's back had been broken as a result of being hurled against the ground so often. It had saved two lives and Blanche said the only cure now was to shoot him in order to put him out of intense pain. Marley Swanton was seen putting his handkerchief to his eyes and Finola, who now appeared on the scene, burst into a flood of tears at the sight of the poor animal quietly moaning on the ground. Then she fetched a bone of cold mutton, an inviting morsel at all times for either dog or man, but he refused to touch it. This was taken as evidence that it was done indeed. Finola continued to pat the writhing animal who regarded both herself and the bone wistfully but that was all. Then she tried to insert a piece of the meat between its teeth but its succulence no longer appealed to him and she wept anew.

"I can assure you, Miss," said Blanche, "that it is all over with, the poor fellow. A dog as refuses a bone is as good as a dead dog."

Then her father returned with a double-barrelled breach loader and said the animal should be kept alive if there were any hope of its ultimate recovery.

"Devil a bit, sir," replied Blanche. "He could only dander about at best at a snail's pace and he would be good for nothing. When a dog refuses his bone it's as bad as when a toper refuses his beer. My own uncle, who used to drink thirty pints of porter in the good old times, fell sick at last when I was a nipper. He refused whiskey one day and his unfortunate wife was delighted to see him going temperate, like all wives. Then the doctor told her it was a fatal sign and that she could be ordering his coffin for him any day. Inside of a month, the champion trencherman of Thomond was dead.

The tear-stained women were then ordered into the house and the dog was shot by Blanche as James Macara, who was a tenderhearted man, shirked this office at the last moment.

Then Biddy Ward explained that when she went to drive in the cows as usual that evening the bull began to bellow and paw and puck the ground. As she was milking a cow the bull came towards her and she in her alarm shot out her stool, which struck the animal in the eye, delayed its onset but further maddened it. She ran towards the house but was tripped up in her trepidation and hurry by her shawl and flung on the ground at the mercy of the bull. She felt temporarily dazed. Then Mrs Macara, followed by the grim and grinning canine, appeared.

"All's well that ends well," said James Macara, quoting his favourite poet, "but we must be very thankful to Mr Swanton and his dog for the way they saved so many lives. Finola went to the assistance of the maid and her mother swung to her help but they would be all done to death only for our beloved teacher and his brave bulldog."

"I'd give more than a mere dog although I'll miss it greatly," said Swanton, "to save any member of your family and I owed that much above all to Finola."

Then he glanced upon her endearingly, and the look was not lost upon her this time.

The vanithee did not like that events had transpired in such a way as to bring her daughter and the teacher so close together and thus forge a link between them that she was determined should remain sundered.

"But as I was saying a minute ago when I was interrupted," said Blanche, "my uncle was a journeyman harness maker and a champion eater, before he took to the drink."

"Stop your story telling this hour of the day, Blanche, and let us return to our work," said the vanithee.

"Oh, you can buzz off, ma'am, if you like."

"You are a champion, too, in your way, Peadar," said the teacher.

"A champion of what?"

"A champion time-waster and yarner."

"Thank you, sir."

"Do tell us all about your uncle, Peadar," entreated Finola. "Tell Mr Swanton and myself."

"Yes, Miss. He was a long, lean, platter-faced, ivory-coloured man. He used to go from house to house mending harness and making it for the farmers for half nothing in the way of pay. He was a great tradesman entirely but no farmer would take him on a second time on account of his great stroke at the table. Two griddle cakes for breakfast, half-a-dozen eggs and half-a-dozen cups of tea were no trouble to him. He used to work for half wages on account of his great consuming capabilities but still he wasn't considered worth it. The poor fellow used to be ashamed of his appetite at times but sure eating is one of the three primary passions and it must be done. He used to gulp down his food and his shame together."

"And what are the other two primary passions, Peadar?" asked Finola.

"Drinking and sex, Miss. You are too young to know anything about some of these passions and may you always remain so. Well, everything else after these are only mere desires or optatives. My uncle was working one time at the other side of the Shannon, not above a dozen miles away as the crow would wing his non-winding way. It was in the depth of Winter and Lord Massey was entertaining a shooting party of English gentlemen and noblemen. At dinner one day the talk turned on the subject of eating and drinking, subjects very dear to the hearts of Englishmen always. One great lord said that in order to be a great eater or drinker one must have plenty of practice at it and have lashings and leavings of food on his table every day. As the Irish peasantry lived only on potatoes and sour milk, they couldn't eat much meat even though they got it itself. Lord Massey who, as luck should have it, was giving a month's work at the time to my uncle, made a bet of a hundred pounds with the Britisher that he could find a native peasant who could eat a leg of mutton. The stakes were laid and others also wanted a like bet with the native lord but he wasn't such a rich man that way so he only took on two more on like terms. Next morning, a nine-pound leg of mutton was weighed and put down to cook. Luke Blanche was told that he was wanted to eat it at noon and to come as hungry as ever he could. Although he was well watched by the butler, yet he got down a loaf of bread and a mug of tea extra while his back was turned. Sharp to the hour, he was ushered into the large dining room and planted down to the great feed in the presence of the exalted company. The dish was garnished with loaf bread, white turnips, five potatoes, and he was given an hour to do his duty like a man. All the nobility sat around sipping sherry and bitters as an appetiser for their own lunch later. The task was a labour of love to Luke. He polished the great knucklebone at a quarter to the hour and washed it down with a pint of sharp beer. There was a great stir when he won the bet for his master and made the rich fellows from England fork out. They all put their hands in their pockets all the same and gave him a fiver apiece and he had near fifty pounds coming away with him. Every Christmas after that, Lord Massey would make him a present of a pig but he would have it eaten out of the tub before it was time to hang it. He fell into bad health from the dint of eating and drinking and died a young man, so he did."

"As the poet says, 'those heads and stomachs are not the best who nauseate all and nothing can digest,'" said the teacher. "Besides, it was probably a disease rather than a passion with your poor uncle. There is such a disease as limosis, but I daresay that you have never heard of it. It is a morbid disease and the symptoms of it are a ravening desire for food and, to a lesser extent, for drink. Even strength can be a disease at times if some glands develop too rapidly and at the expense of other things in the human body. That is about all there is to it, I think."

"I don't believe a word of it," said Blanche.

CHAPTER XIII

MARLEY SWANTON AT FORTY

SEVERAL weeks had elapsed since the teacher had sent in his confession of age to the Dublin daily paper and, as it had not appeared, he concluded that it had been consigned to the waste paper basket as being really too raffish and silly for publication. At first, he was inclined to execrate the editor for treating him with such scant courtesy. He might, he thought, have dropped him a line telling him what was radically wrong with his maiden literary effort so that he could profit by it in the light of which he could perhaps make a second attempt. He did not know that not only do most editors write very little themselves but that their chief function would appear to be to keep others from ever getting into print on one pretext or another. Their work is of a negative and destructive character. They only pass about a tithe of what is sent into them for publication. They are just like the postage stamp without which a letter cannot go through.

With the lapse of time, however, Marley Swanton began to feel relieved that his self-revelatory article had been suppressed. Its publication would have made an old man and a laughing stock of him wherever he was known. Such an article was too personal and intimate. What obligation was he under to society to confess that he was a decade or so older than he looked. He was not born in Menavia or everybody there would have known his age to the minute and debated the matter at regular intervals. Why not hold on to such an advantage, especially as he yearned towards a girl of half that age or less. It would have been intelligible enough for a married man to make such a wanton and gratuitous avowal but for a bachelor in pursuit of a girl still in her teens it was well calculated to blight his marital prospects in that direction. Besides, was he not making some headway in his love quest of late? The incident of the bull was all in his favour. It had enabled him to repay the debt of his life to the person with whom he was most concerned for weal or woe. Her parents, although they were proud and broad-acred, could give her no fortune but he did not mind that. Beyond a year or two at a boarding school, that was about all they could afford to give their three children. Their fiscal embarrassment was all in his favour. James Macara, he knew, thought that none of his children should ever get married, but why did he not abstain from it himself? There were a lot of contradictions like this in life to be sure. Did Macara sample marriage only in order to arrive at this strange conclusion? Yet his own connubial venture was not unhappy as far as one could see. Then he indulged in more self-analysis. What possessed him to write such an article at such a crucial stage in his career, putting himself definitely among the ranks of the senescent? Such an article, had it appeared, would have been the dearly purchased fame – notoriety rather. He now felt very grateful to the newspaper in question. Editors were, after all, very wise men and prevented fellows like himself from making perfect asses of themselves. Had such a confession appeared, then women who could be Finola's mother in point of age would be setting their caps at him. In fact, his age would not stop at forty at all in the further estimation of his neighbours; it would be moved on yet another lustrum or two. Then he would soon be told that he was as old as his prospective father-in-law. Oh, if he could by hook or crook attain that precious relationship with the poor yet proud, well-descended Macaras. After all, writing was, he felt, a fatal if fascinating business, because a person could not say anything worth saying without giving himself away miserably.

The teacher was above the middle height, slenderly built and ever so slightly stooped. He had keen, not unkindly, blue eyes flashing through large unrimmed spectacles. His mouth, owing to his vocation, was moulded to sternness. His pale face gave him an ascetic appearance. He held certain theories regarding his personal appearance. He believed that it was a certain sign of degeneration to grow fat or stout and he prided himself on his wasp-waist, his well-cut, pin-striped clothes, striated diagonal tie, black bowler hat and clocked socks. He would give himself a weigh at regular intervals and if he found his weight going up he would puncture his bicycle and go in for ten- and even twenty-mile walks so as to scale himself down. Whatever about growing bald or grey, everybody, he reasoned, could save himself from excessive adipose tissue. Once a man, no matter how young, has lost his waist line and allowed it to come near the breadth of his shoulders, then he has indeed shed his youth in earnest. As for early baldness, he thought it was a matter of keeping dandruff at bay by the application of essential oils; and bodily excess, in any way, made for early greyness. He always walked at the rate of four miles an hour as merely ambling along only induced fatigue. He was a hiker always but he did not suspect it. He wore boots instead of shoes for ankle support. Of course, he could get nobody to accompany him on such walks; nobody believes in walking merely for walking sake in the country. It takes a townsman to grow enthusiastic about such a form of endeavour but he walked for reasons only known to himself – antiphonic reasons.

The basic principle of walking as a means to health is so sound that it should never fall into desuetude despite the ever-growing tendency towards mechanised modes of progression; not forgetting the eighty pound motor car. Walking is certainly a revolt against the tyrannical conventions of black coats, white collars, toothpick-shaped shoes and a machined life generally. It is a reaction to all the things that are in a conspiracy to kill individuality. Man, he realised, has a natural instinct for the open spaces that will be always with us with their concomitants, the sights and sounds of the countryside. A good brisk walk suffuses the cheeks with a glow of colour, muscles the bones and brings a rush of pure air to the lungs. Besides, it is not alone the most healthy but the cheapest mode of locomotion; and the roads and the countryside are free. The elements will harden your body and temper your spirit. A good brisk walk is the best antidote to a rutted routine way of life.

A bright boy at school in West Cork, Swanton wanted to linger in the University and pick up various degrees, but his practical parents willed it otherwise and compelled him to pick up his own living at the earliest possible age. Thus early, he began knocking into the heads of boys truths he did not as yet fully subscribe to himself. At first very shy, he gradually mastered his diffidence. Daily contact with forty urchins always ready for mischief gave him an irritated distraught look at times. Ten years ago a lady had attracted his attention but he had to support an aged mother, then she would not procrastinate even for a year, married another and was now a mother of six children. This more than anything else served to remind him that he was getting on in years. It was high time, he thought, that he spoke wooingly and winningly to the lady of his choice but she seemed so elusive and young. Better wait perhaps till she became more mature; then he might be more to her mind. Girls were so capricious at her age and it may be better for him to allow another year to elapse before he would proceed to lay serious siege to her heart; whereas an early rebuff might spoil all, and he knew himself to be a sensitive easily-wounded soul.

He preened himself on the fact that he still looked an extremely young man. But then again, it sometimes happens that those who cheat the years for a long time are quite suddenly made by a fit of illness to look older than their actual age. His position was precarious enough from that point of view. Then the thought of his predecessor in office occurred to him. He used to say that by the time a man can afford to place a leg of mutton on his table he hasn't the teeth to eat it. How true. He could only do justice to it now with the aid of the dentist. Yet another sign, if signs were wanting, that he was fairly time-stricken. He once again rejoiced that he had escaped from making a Methuselah of himself – in spite of himself.

That night, Paddy Quinburn and his wife, Tommy Cooley and a few others were playing a game of cards in the kitchen when the inevitable Peadar Blanche entered. As he could not interrupt the serious game, he sat down in the hob seat near the fire, feeling ill at ease. He wanted to talk but nobody would listen to him. In order to beguile the time somehow, he picked up the daily paper and began to engross himself in the news. His eyes roamed restlessly over it. He contrived to keep one eye on the paper and the other on the players to see when would they give it over. Even the Rathmore murder case in Cork did not fix his attention. He was just about to fling the paper aside when the words 'Marley Swanton' caught his roving eye. Every fibre in his being was at once aroused. Looking just above the signature, he saw a slab of type and, above that again, a line of bold type: "How it Feels to be Forty".

He could not credit his eyes, so he read and actually re-read the article in silence to himself before venturing to make any comment upon it.

The gamblers were morose and silent, a sign that they invited no interruption, least of all from the prosy Peadar with whom the publican felt he was already on too-familiar terms.

"Who'd ever have thought, boys, that our dandy of a teacher was forty years of age?" he ejaculated at last.

"Dry up like a good fellow," shrilled Belinda Mary Anne Quinburn. "And keep your breath to cool your porridge," said her spouse.

113

"And let me win the fall of me life," vociferated Cooley.

"He'll be forty by the time you have his house ready for him, old cock in the corner," added Quinburn.

This ought to silence him, they thought, once and for all.

"Sure 'tis here in the paper for all to see. Sure he says it himself in the public newspaper," persisted Blanche.

"I'm robbing," added Cooley, putting down a card and taking up another. He was not averse at any time from siding with the majority and taking his cue at present from the publican.

"But I'm not robbing Marley Swanton of his youth; he's doing it here in the paper so that all who run may read," persisted Blanche. "Begor, ma'am, I'd never suspect it but sure he ought to know," thus making a direct appeal to the woman's curiosity. He was simply bursting to share his great discovery and to rend the subject of it to pieces in the light of such a strange confession.

"I was reading about the great pig-feeding food value of fish when my optics fell on something too funny entirely to keep to myself so I thought I'd make you smile awhile. Even that codraulin' old codger Cooley will have to believe what he sees in the paper."

"You were always a bit of a codfish," retorted Cooley. "What is it, Blanche?" demanded Mrs Quinburn. "Read out what's in the paper if it is in the paper and let us get on with the game."

Blanche cleared his throat and emitted a few well-calculated coughs as a sign that he enjoined both silence and attention. Then, in his deep bass voice, he droned out the contents of the paper on the flight of a certain measure of time with special reference to its devastating effects on a person who signed himself Marley Swanton.

The company was amazed but the cross-grained Cooley, who pretended not to understand, said: "I thought it was all about fish. I have an old three-inch mesh net out there and you might do a bit of poaching with me the night?"

"Yes, if you will eat enough to give your brains enough to understand what I'm after reading. It's a great brain-giving food, you know."

"That's a bargain anyway. How much must I eat to get your free labour?"

"A whale on toast every morning for a month."

Even Belinda Mary Anne's features wrinkled with laughter at this sally and Blanche read the article anew without any more interruption.

The cards were incontinently tossed aside in order to discuss the latest orientation of the teacher who was no mean provider of minor sensations of one kind or another lately.

Cooley, who was winning at the cards and speculated on being able to drink a pint at the expense of the others, resented the turn things had taken, but in silence, however.

"Well, all jokes aside, it's a mighty clever well-mounted stave to put in the paper, true or false," commented the reader.

"It's only too true and, what is more, I always suspected it," replied Belinda Mary Anne. "It's a very foolish confession for a fellow to make who is all out for a wife and a young wan into the bargain. When the fellow titivates himself out on a Sunday and swaggers into the church, he only looks about as old as the present century. It's destroyed he is as a wife-getter now and no mistake. He could have picked up wan in the parish if he would hold his tongue."

"That's what nobody can do hereabouts, that is, to hold his tongue," added Cooley sardonically.

"Faith he is very sweet on old Jimmy Macara's daughter," said the publican, "and he thinks nobody knows it. That will put a stop to his gallop now, I hope."

"You need not let on that I was telling you, Paddy," enjoined Cooley.

Blanche, who was never a high priest of flattery, then turned on Cooley. "A moment ago, we were all a parcel of idle gossips and now you are telling mean Nosy Parker tales on your boss, and women listenin' in."

"Well, women are better able to keep a secret, if it goes to that, than most of the porter-muddled blokes as come into my bar," retorted Mrs Quinburn. "Such sloppy, sentimental tale-bearing, secret-blabbing old golliwogs as men become under the influence of drink. You could worm anything out of them with an extra free pint. Drink loosens their tongues."

"And liberates the controls like the works of a motor," said Blanche. "But you should be the last to give the game away ma'am. That sort of talk coming from you who have made most out of our infirmities is enough to make a fellow take the pledge."

"Oh, you'll never do that, Peadar, and even if you did, it won't matter very much to me before long."

This was the first obscure hint this managing, strict, exacting woman gave so far of her intention to quit her pub, but it was lost upon her hearers.

"I think you could pleasure us with a pint now, Ma'am, all the same."

She rose, looking vital and efficient, to comply with this overdue demand after which she ordered them out and locked up for the night.

Then the publican told his wife to keep Blanche in good humour for the present as they may want him to do an important job of work before long, after which they could ignore him forever. He was, he said, a necessary nuisance about the place for the present.

Then they seemed to finally decide that they would sell out the little place very soon and go to live in the county town about ten miles away. Paddy said they had made money in recent years but it had not raised their status in the parish. The big farmers, such as the Macaras, Linnanes and others, still affected to look down on them the same as before. There were only tradesmen and labourers left to wile away the time with. People would only rate them as they were before the recent series of wars when they had no money and less pretensions. They felt that the old families who set the tone of the place were crusted in their conservatism, learned little and forgot less. Some of these old families over the fire at night would trace their ancestry and give themselves handsome pedigrees. Ground down by wars and confiscations for centuries, yet they managed to save something from the wreck. It was hard for the Quinburns, who had great social aspirations themselves, to make much headway against this ingrained amalgam of rude pride and dourness.

Next day, Paddy Blanche, in consideration of a free pint or rather the slops and dregs that were kept tucked away in a bucket near the barrel, was induced to part with the paper containing the teacher's confession. Formerly, these slops used to be fed to the pigs which slept and fattened well on them. Now that they had given up pig feeding, these dregs did not go to waste either. Stooping under the little counter and bulking their bodies between their customers and their casks, they contrived to insert a modicum of these lees and rinsings into every pint that they filled out.

They regaled their customers by reading the Swanton article for them over the counter for the next two weeks, at the end of which they could almost recite it from memory. Trading on the curiosity of the public, they increased their profits as people could not walk in and, apropos of nothing, ask them to read to them without buying something. The preliminary to due satisfaction of their literary needs was a drink or two. In this way, the place became a source of literary as well as liquid refreshment. They knew how to turn the morbid curiosity of their neighbours into a source of profit.

"I always suspected that Swanton was a purty hardy old codger," said Blanche in the pub one night as the two-week sensation was dying out.

Quinburn concurred. "Those gents," said he, "who never take off their coats to do an honest day's work in field or factory never grow old looking. Never."

In the matter of criticism in Menavia there was no *via media*. A person's character was either black or white; there were no intervening tones. When praise was bestowed, it was laid on with a trowel and, when he was adversely criticised, there was nothing left unsaid that could be thought of at the moment to his detriment. Black never shaded into any suspicion of any other colour and colour scheme for the nonce; superlatives were lavishly exhausted.

The man who would be lauded up to the skies today would be painted black as Erebus tomorrow by the same set of critics. The reason for this was that listeners taking their cue from the originator of the debate seconded his vehement mood of the moment. With a "be me oath 'tis true for you", they urged him on to the utmost limit of slander or the reverse, according to his humour.

Everybody's character issues in behaviour. Everybody's actions and inactions were freely commented upon in an exaggerated twisted kind of way. Yet, people could do and say the maddest things without being in any way considered abnormal. Colourful actions were relished because they provided scope for a flowing measure to talk and criticism so dear to the heart of the true Menavian. He was always going more-or-less *blasé* for want of a sensation so as to whet his dominating passion for never-ending talk. Those who would attempt to live a drab life and never rise to the daring of an out-of-the-ordinary act very occasionally would cease to be popular because they would not purvey in the way of action a certain amount of comment and spicy criticism. This seldom happened, however, owing to the lively imaginations of every bar lounger, forge frequenter and cross-roads politician.

CHAPTER XIV

THE OLD ARISTOCRACY

TEN minutes after the postman's knock, James Macara ruminated rather ruefully and then announced that he would have to go to the city. The arrival of the post of late caused him on balance more worry than otherwise because it was well interspersed with reminders from banks and traders of overdue accounts. He was peremptorily asked on opening one letter to come to an immediate accommodation about a matter involving upwards of three figures else the law would be invoked against him. He worried more than a little over money matters of late but he did not infect his family with his fears. They should remain care-free as long as possible; they would be initiated into the worries of the world soon enough. Youth, he reflected, has its own hidden anxieties and phobias without piling on the agony, especially when nothing was to be gained by it. For this very reason his children were possessed of a double dose of daring, amounting in some ways to a species of recklessness and *hauteur*. Yet, he would not chasten their spirits; they should live dangerously yet awhile and their reserves of these things were an essential part of their equipment for the oncoming stern battle of life.

Since the return of Fergus from college, he abstained from the rough labour of the farm such as weeding and the carting of manure, but there was plenty work of a fancy character to engage his attention. He broke in and trained a fine, well-bred three-year-old mare and thus dispensed with the services of a professional horse trainer. He boasted that this mare was sired by a horse that had won three races in Limerick.

This was the mare which Finola, who took a great interest in its career, was now asked to drive to Limerick with her father. She had a notion of riding it to the hounds later – and why not. Although only a farmer's daughter, her parents had already convinced her that the bluest of blue blood coursed in her veins.

The fearanthee decided that his daughter would drive him to town; or rather she cleverly caused him to make the announcement as his own decision well and truly arrived at. Then he had to face the irksome task of donning his Sunday raiment. Ever a hard-working man, yet he found it of late years a more labourious task to shave, fix on a collar and cravat and a change of clothes than to face half-a-day's work. A townsman has to do this every day and it becomes second nature to him, but not so the ruralist who goes about unshaved for a week, collarless and hatless. Macara would spend a few hours making up his toilet if left to his own slow motion devices, so his wife or daughter would lend a hand in the metamorphosis. He never seemed to know where to find any of his personal belongings since he used them before. Only for the growing particularity of Finola it is to be feared that he would venture forth to Mass or market looking very much like a struggling small farmer.

"An odd day's outing is much to my mind," he would say, "only for all this dolling up business. The fellow who invented collars and studs should be hanged, drawn and quartered. The fellow who invented the first razor should have slit his own throat with it before he inflicted it on a long-suffering world. It's flying in the face of nature to be forever scraping and mutilating our faces with such atrocities. Why can't we stay as nature made us?"

"We must go with the times, papa," Finola would assure him. "Nobody can flout the fashions or they would look loutish and ill-bred."

"And if fashion, that tyrant that has the world destroyed, decreed that we should wear two hats?"

"I would wear two hats too, papa. I would wear two hats too."

"Oh, the tyranny of collars and ties that won't stay put. It beats Banagher and Banagher, you know, beats the devil. Those city jackeens have nothing else to do but to be dolling themselves up morning, noon and night, but farming is a whole-time job. They are all parasiting on the old farmer the same as the warbles I picked out of the cow's back this day and yet they are all lecturing and hectoring him."

"Brostaig ort, dad, the gig is at the door."

"Wherever did I put me pipe now? High up or low down, it's not to be found. Bad scran to all this chopping and changing of clothes."

"Of course it's in your old cast-off coat as usual. We'd be in town while you're looking for everything and failing to find it. Your pipe is a horrible tyranny that you could discard, papa."

"Oh, that's different, my child, that's different."

"I daresay. Everything as you say is different. There are no two blades of grass alike but what you like is different and what you don't is devilish. So like a man."

"Buzz off now and get the written list of messages from your ma. Tell her to cut out everything except what is absolutely necessary."

Then when the ordeal of dressing would be over he would burst into a snatch of song:

Then where is the use of repining
For where there's a will there's a way
Tomorrow the sun may be shining
Although it is cloudy today!

Beginning the process of personal renovation in a bad temper, he would sing himself into a cheery mood. He always seemed to lay not only his clothes but his memory aside. Making a collar go round an eighteen-inch neck without including some of his chins would call forth some expletives. When dressed, however, he was a fine figure of a man and he was not unaware of the fact, despite his age. Broad-shouldered as a door almost, blue-eyed and aquiline nosed, his wife when finished with him would tell him that he was worth dolling out, after all. Yes, a country man's toilet is a tedious affair, especially as he advances in years.

As he was just ready to step into a gig, the arrival of his neighbour, Sedna Linnane, was announced. He was ushered into the parlour and subsided rather wearily on the sofa. When Linnane entered to meet him he said he was returning from the fair and was feeling the effects of an early rising at his time of life. As Linnane seldom paid a visit to his friend, he ran no risk of out-wearing his welcome. His host knew he had something important to say, so he produced the decanter which contained a remnant of whiskey. This he divided into two glasses, remarking that drink was a great social lubricant which mellows the friendship between man and man.

"A man of my time of life," said Linnane, "is not able to get up so early as of yore and drive eight miles to a fair and back again without feeling all knocked of a heap. The day is over when old fogeys like us could get up with the lark or the nightingale."

"But sure there are no nightingales in this country to compare notes with and, if they are such early risers as you say, they should be called morningales."

"I'm compelled to work as hard as ever though," went on Linnane, ignoring his friend's bird lore. "I should be taking things easy from this on. I had a brace of the finest sons in Ireland up till ten or twelve years ago but since they took to the blinking game of politics, patriotism and the pistol and all that kind of tommy-rot, I can't get a decent day's work out of them. They're either too grand or too lazy, or both, to go to a fair or a market. One of them has a bit of a pension for gadding about the country in 1923 and, like every man on the dole, he will lie up like a ferret in his burrow. He was too crawsick to go anywhere today especially as his pension came yesterday. The publicans are getting all this gun money."

"Ill got, ill gone, they say. The poachers of 1916 are now turned gamekeepers and grinding down their own people; but let us get away from the cursed subject of politics. It will be all the same to us in a few years what happens. I hear that bally publican is selling out and going to live in the county town."

"Oh, the sooner the better, but sure somebody else will carry on the evil tradition. By the way, that's one of the things I came here to warn you about. He made an offer of the pub to my ex-soldier son for three hundred pounds or six hundred with the bit of land thrown in. If he can get two or three men to back a bill for him in the bank, the poor loon will spring to it. He would be his own best customer and he would be dead in no time at all. Quinburn suggested that you would do the needful for him, although ye differ in yer political outlook. This move would be from the frying pan into the fire with him."

"I'm glad you warned me in time. That so-called fight for freedom played the very devil with the youth of the country. My own lads would be just as bad only that they missed the movement by being too young at the time."

"Murty, who went to school with your son, is now worth the two eldest fellows put together. The great bulk of the people were caught up in that devil of a movement and they all, except the very cute boys, lost more than they gained by it. My pair of brigadiers were degraded down bit by bit and finally pensioned off and they are now more disappointed than ever and waiting for the next round either with Ireland or England."

"Between Mick and Dick and Dev and Bill and old Timsy in the grave resting away for himself, they have the old country in a horrible urey yarey."

"But posterity will surely benefit, James, posterity will surely benefit. We have paid a big price in blood and treasure for what we had been looking for for 750 years."

"Posterity indeed. What has posterity done for us that we should be fighting their battles for them? Let every pig dig for itself."

"Well, it would be better surely if we got more of the fruits of victory in our own time considering that we delivered the goods."

"And let them slip through our hands again. The land annuities were handed back in 1925, four million a year which were to be a set-off against all the over-taxation that existed for one hundred and twenty years. We were told that Ireland got a big nought in respect of the Great War debt, but she gave away six big noughts preceded by the figure four. O'Connell, the biggest humbug in history up till lately, got us a religious measure, and the price that had to be paid for that was the disfranchisement of the forty shilling free-holders and all the subsequent evictions and clearances."

"And who has wrested the palm for humbuggery from Daniel O'Connell?"

"Oh, time will tell, my friend, time will tell. Dan was a man of gross passions and appetites. As my friend Dan MacParland says, you could not throw up a stone in many parts of Kerry today but it would fall down on one of Dan's gets. Parnell was a great man but Tim, whom he raised up from the ranks, threw him to the wolves. Redmond was a perfect gentleman but a weakling. Sinn Fein erected itself on the ruins of Redmondism. Most of what we fought and bled for in the name of Sinn Fein has turned to dust and ashes in our hands. Few are satisfied now but the paid politicians and highly paid civil servants; and, of course, a host of pensioners. Ireland loves to be betrayed on a large scale about every second decade or so. Then she lets loose her pent-up emotions when she wakens up. She is dozing at present but, my word, she will waken up one of these days and then there will be wigs on the green."

"This is a strange country, James. Did you see what happened at the Dublin horse show the other day? When the British jumping team came on the grounds, the people on the grandstands who represent the cream of the country roared themselves into a frenzy of homage, as it were, for a quarter of an hour. Our own fellows went unnoticed, and the French and German jumpers said we were a queer, inexplicable people. That shows that this country is still very unsettled. If the British came back they would be more welcome than ever. We are fed up with politics. As Colonel Gloster's agent, I want to speak to you about another unpleasant matter today. You know, James, that most of your big farm is part of his estate and I have warned you in a friendly way about all the tree-cutting you were doing. He was absent that time and during the fight for freedom you thought that that was your own pet way of achieving it. You took umbrage at the time as a hot-headed man, but the Colonel is sitting up now and taking stock of all the tree stumps that dot the place. You can see the moat in Bill Cosgrave's eye but you cannot see the beam in your own. You are a simple man in many ways, James, for all your love of books and poetry and that kind of piffle. As a body, our people possess the mentality of children and the half of them never grow up at all."

"A nation of Peter Pans, you mean."

"They take the devil's own delight in wanton destruction. You are a man of peace but among the Colonel's trees you were a terrible vandal. Ireland has less than two per cent of trees while France has twenty. With all the trees gone, the country becomes a rain-sodden, wind-swept wilderness and colder than ever. Grapes once grew on the well-sheltered hillsides of Wicklow, now they can only be grown in glass houses. Up till the sixteenth century, vast wolf-infested forests stretched from Limerick to Galway, fringing this place. Many of the landlords were greedy and grasping in their way, but now they are going, going, gone, like a stick of furniture under an auctioneer's hammer. Yet in their heyday, they built fine houses and preserved the forestine character of the country – what was left of it."

"They built big houses to overawe the plain people by their huge size in the reign of the Georges. Labour was only four pence a day and many tenants had to work for less."

"Half a mo', James, please. They built what I would call the house beautiful; they preserved beauty spots and enhanced their natural charms by every known art and artifice. But for them with all their faults greatly exaggerated, there would be no beauty spots left now and nothing to attract people from foreign parts."

"Faith there's a lot of them very sorry, Sedna, that they ever scuttled away to England with themselves. The British have too much to trouble about themselves without throwing away sympathy where it isn't wanted. This landed class could have identified themselves much more with the people's interests for the past few centuries, but they preferred to live as a caste apart from the native untouchables. England was their spiritual home all the time; they took English wives, newspapers and education."

"That may be true, James, to some extent, but even in their decadence they rarely cut down the woods and groves which their ancestors planted and promoted. I knew a decayed gentleman who used to stir his punch with a poker rather than pull a bramble off any of the trees. They were great lovers of art and conservers of the beautiful. Look at Larry Smullen, that rude upstart farmer and county councilor. He bought that decayed gentleman's place and, before a month was out, he was carting dung up the front avenue and tethering his horses to the halldoor knocker. Then, he turned the lodge into a piggery. He seemed to take a devilish delight in his desecration, like yourself and the trees, James. The majority of our mansions are now derelict, or going to be, and the worst of it is that there is no class with the requisite culture even if they had the cash to carry on the old traditions of the old aristocracy. No sooner is a demesne vacated than it is parcelled out among land-hungry lousers who hack away every tree and gate, and the big house is locked to moulder away in time. This is a mistaken policy because with the rise of a new aristocracy they would be taken over some day."

"But wherever is this precious new aristocracy to come from?"

"Nature hates a vacuum and something would turn up in time to fill the gap."

"As a matter of scientific fact, there is no such thing as a vacuum in nature. You cannot have culture without wealth and it takes three generations to make a gentleman. The poor fellow who has to start from scratch, or even behind it, hasn't time to think about culture."

"Even if he had, he would want to be educated up to it. Regretting what he never got himself, that is to say a good education, he sends his children to college and they return with the first glimmerings of culture. It is a thing of slow and uncertain growth and once uprooted will take a long time to return."

"But you forget, Sedna, that there is no room in Ireland for an aristocracy any more. These old chaps, in order to be able to keep their places in such apple pie order, levied tolls in the form of heavy rents from half a parish apiece. The State is the landlord now; the Cabinet lives in Dublin, thinks in terms of Dublin and forgets all about the country except at general elections, just one month every lustrum."

"That may be so, but no country is normal without a leisured aristocracy. A land without them is like a lamp without oil."

"Those lamps are antique furniture too; you forget the Shannon Scheme."

"No, indeed. There is nothing more calculated to kindle a traveller's interest than the sight of a big house. Trees enrich the land, lower the rain fall, temper the climate. Trees shelter livestock from the winds of winter and the flies and sultriness of summer."

"You mean, if and when summer comes. I have not seen much of it this year."

"That's all because of your bally tree cutting propensities. If the people realised the real result of your vandalism they'd tear you limb from limb. Only four fine days last July to save a sop of hay."

"But grazers consider trees waste."

"They are the real curse of the country, are grazers. Grattan, when asked to cut down a fine tree in his home at Tinnahinch because it grew too near to his house and made it unhealthy, proceeded to remove the house. You have cut down scores of fine ash and beech trees for firewood even when firewood was cheap. Where did you learn the art of tree- felling?"

"You know I spent two years in America. With axes only two inches wide across the edge we used to have tree-felling competitions. I even brought back one of these things with me as I never saw their likes here."

"Oh, mavrone, mavrone. What may have been a virtue in America, a virgin country, is a vice here. These countries are polar opposites. The old Colonel has been speaking to me about your tree-cutting habits lately, more than once, and he seems to be getting up that kind of edge against you that you get up against the trees. He means to do something about it and he told me to go over the ninety acres that you hold from him and to count all the tree stumps. You have levelled five fine thickly-planted groves while he was absent in England since the outbreak of the Great War. I have reckoned up 314. He was half afraid to remonstrate with you at one time, but the sheriff and bailiff rule the country once more. Some of these people look at trees as live things and they regard the cutting down of them as a crime bordering on murder."

"You can tell him that there is no tree-felling going on now. What can he do about it now when he did not protest at the time? To the devil I pitch him and everybody like him."

"No thanks to you, because you must get a permit from the police now. At the same time, they cannot keep their eyes glued to every tree and there is a certain amount of it going on. 'Tis a great pity for your own sake that such an otherwise brainy man as you are said to be should have given way to yourself in that way."

James Macara moved uneasily in his chair under the sting of these words and finally stood up and began to pace the floor. He was about to reply when Finola burst into the parlour and somewhat petulantly asked him was he going to town today or tomorrow? The horse was pawing the gravel outside the hall door, she said, mad for a gallop. Then she curtsied sweetly to the visitor, excused the interruption and disappeared.

Turning to her father, Linnane said: "By Jove, but that's a fine pullet of a girl of yours. She'll cut a great copy in the world yet and I admire her fine temper too. Temper is as necessary in females as the edge in a knife. It's a great protective shield. Me son, Murty, up there at St Flannan's is always talking of her. Who knows what the future may have in store for them? I don't want any harm to come to you, James avick, over this tree cutting business and I'll cut down that figure to half if I can."

"Oh indeed, I know you wouldn't injure a hair in my head, Sedna, I do indeed."

"Well, God prosper you in your journey now. I must be off to get a bit of sleep for a few hours."

CHAPTER XV

A CLASSIC RACE

"**A**M I expected to be a paragon of patience?" shouted Fergus Macara who was engaged in holding the spirited mare all this time. "It's just as hard to get father and daughter out of the house as to get a silkworm out of a cocoon."

"Half a jiffy, Fergy," shrilled Finola from the stair head. This final delay was caused by the good vanithee who had forgotten some item in the household budget. She always insisted on committing the catalogue of her needs to paper so as to "make assurance doubly sure" as she would say herself. During the lapse of time caused by the conference in the parlour, she found that she wanted to add to the list of groceries. The omissions made good, Mrs Macara then descended the semi-circular steps that lead to the hall door, holy water in hand and sprinkled some on all present, paying special attention to the prancing horse.

The high-wheeled gig had recently been varnished and the harness oiled and polished so as to match the elaborately wrought vehicle and the colour of the mare. The jaunting car once so racy of the soil had now fallen almost into desuetude. The gig was copied from England in or about 1870 where it was all the rage among the 'upper ten'. Just then in England the gig was being discarded for the Croydon which in its turn was again discarded for the ralli-trap or dog cart, all antiques now. Nowadays the roundabout or tub trap is most favoured by those who cannot afford a motor car. Gone are the days of the mid-nineteenth century and later when the women would use the bed quilt as a rug with a bed of straw to their feet. What would the mild-mannered, soft-spoken women of those not so far-off days think of their short-frocked, short-haired, short-mannered grand-daughters of today?

It was early in June and the advent of the sun after a cold, wet May was all the more welcome. The day was such as to give promise of better things in store after a dreary, drooping, long winter. It was already near midday and vegetation which was held in check all along by such backward conditions was looking its best because it had shed none of its early freshness. Every sentient thing seemed to luxuriate in the temperate glow of the sunshine. Even the cawing crows overhead in the double rookery seemed to distil a more joyous and soporific kind of cacophony than usual. The air was subtly scented by the blooming lilacs and other flowers which grew in fair abundance near the house. The carelessly-cultivated roses, which fringed the sparsely-gravelled front where the mare stood drawn up in readiness for the road, were already beginning to look their best. They were extracting all that they previously pined for today from the sun in full measure.

The high-spirited mare was restlessly pawing the ground and champing the bit between its teeth anxious for exercise, and these bulbous flowers seemed to be nodding in unison looking shy in their virgin loveliness. The swallows were flying and shrilling higher than usual and this was said to be a sign by those versed in weather lore that it was going to be fine and sunny for a few days at least. As father and daughter stepped into the high gig they heard the melodic note of the cuckoo for the first time, away at their sinistral side. They would have preferred to have heard it in their right ear but there was no cure for it now. Finola, who took the reins, surveyed the equipment with a certain amount of pleasure not unmixed with well-concealed excitement. This was mostly all the work of Fergus and she felt it was indeed his greatest masterpiece so far. The vanithee seemed vaguely apprehensive but said nothing beyond warning them to be home as early as they could. Did a young girl, she wondered, ever show off to better advantage than when driving a high-spirited young horse? The high gig looked fragile, almost spectral, under her pensive gaze. Its occupants, at last cosily fitted in with a rug across their knees, somehow looked to her like a pair of large spiders precariously poised in a framework or web that was rather insubstantial to bear their united weight.

The avenue that gave to the public road was bordered by a brook at one side whose limpid, scintillating waters murmured its meandering way towards the all-absorbing Shannon. All felt moved by the mood of the moment; there seemed to be something fateful about it all. There are few finer thrills than a drive under such circumstances.

Fergus at last released his hold on the horse which curvetted and caracoled rather alarmingly at first. Then it was feared that such a high-spirited display would cause something to snap or that the car would be backed into some remora. However, Finola lilted lyrically to the mare soothing its nerves and causing it to move forward with great celerity. The travellers were soon lost to view as the avenue faded into the public road.

Tommy Cooley, who was coming in to dinner, turned his sunken old face and red-lidded eyes after them and remarked that it would have been better if they had heard the cuckoo in their right ears. Then the cock crew, the dog barked and a foal that he was leading by the halter whinnied.

As the town-going pair were passing the somewhat dilapidated lodge, a lone magpie slanted slowly away right in front of them but they pretended not to see it at first and then scanned the horizon anxiously for its companion.

Macara silently regretted that he had not been looking the other way at the time. Finola was too wrapped up in the motions of the mare to think much about what is regarded as a bird of ill-omen when seen alone. A little farther on they met a Titian-haired woman and Macara wished that they had met a man first on their journey; two untoward events which tended to abate the joy which now presided in his heart.

The Macaras had completed about two miles of the journey when they perceived Colonel Claude Gloster and his coachman turning into the public road just in front of them. They, too, were going to Limerick, still a good dozen miles away. The coachman was driving a pair of dapple grey horses attached to a two-wheeled carriage, trotting abreast.

The Colonel, who was a long, lean-visaged, hook-nosed, grog-blossomed man, had spent much of his life in the British army. He had an income of about five thousand a year and farmed a small tract of land at present, in the centre of which stood a large Georgian mansion approached by a very long lime tree-lined avenue. The hexagon-shaped lodge which stood at the entrance to the public road was now untenanted and forlorn looking. It was frowned down upon by pine trees, a fact which enhanced its gloom. One of the horses he drove had won a prize at a trotting competition at the Dublin Horse Show the previous month. The Colonel's pride in these high-stepping horses was very great indeed.

They had entered upon the road at a slowed-down pace so as to negotiate the lodge gates with safety. In a trice, Finola caught up with them and passed them out, grazing the carriage by a few inches. Her father, who was thinking about his approaching meeting with the bank manager about a substantial overdraft, did not notice the daring challenge to the crabbed Colonel and his blooded horses until it was too late to intervene. Then he recollected that more than half his land was held on a mere copyhold lease from him, now on the point of expiry.

The Colonel, who sat on a blue-cushioned seat lower than his coachman, seemed to give a start, sit up and take notice. Then he adjusted his monocle in order to sum up the situation more clearly. Haughty resentment seemed to feature his face. It seemed to say: 'The idea of a mere one-horse tenant farmer with a scrub horse attempting to take the road from prize animals.' It appealed to his risible faculties at first for he was not destitute of a sense of humour, especially when certain of his ability to prevail over an opponent. The fact that a mere plebeian farmer should dare to whip past a patrician landlord and lose him on the road was the very apex of assurance. Then, he remembered that there had been a big political change lately; in fact a sort of revolution well calculated to lend a spirit of audacity to the lower orders. Still, there were limits beyond which they ought not to dare and this was surely one of them. Yes, he agreed he was living through an ugly period of transition, unparalleled since his ancestors, as petty officers, took service under Cromwell and won much landed property by the law of the sword. Here, surely, was a case of castles falling and dunghills rising.

The Macaras continued about two hundred yards ahead all the time.

"I say, my man, flick up these horses when they warm up to their work; don't let us get lost by a mere farmer's nag."

"Never fear, sir," replied the coachman. "I'm keeping a sharp eye on 'em. Let the nag tire a bit first after another league or less. We are having a bit of fun out of them so far. This is the champion joke of the season and one I won't forget for quite a time, your honour."

"That's Macara and his daughter, isn't it?"

"Yes, to be sure, sir. I knew by the gleam of that girl's eye as she sped past us that she was up to some kind of mischief. Isn't it little they pretend to think of prize-winning horses, not to talk of their betters?"

"This is upstart insolence indeed," agreed the Colonel. "They cannot be ignorant of the performances of my horses of late because they were reported in the *Weekly Recorder* and, even apart from that, they ought to show more respect for their landlord. What a brazen hussy of a daughter Macara must have."

The rearward horses, without any stimulation, instinctively felt that they were expected to keep up to the fast-trotting animal up front. The pace was already fairly brisk and the occupants of both vehicles pretended so far to appear as unconcerned as possible, in fact to be unaware of one another's presence. They easily overtook and passed every kind of horse-drawn vehicle on the road except the one they felt most concerned to overhaul.

More than half of the journey had now been covered and the relative distance between them remained the same. Macara himself would not willingly challenge his landlord to a driving contest of this kind yet once the step had been taken there was no cure for it but to see it out to the end. His daring daughter now looked very alert, tense and efficient and he knew that she was all out for victory. He suggested to Finola that if she thought 'the Black', as they all called the mare, was going to be outpaced they could turn up a side road or drop something out of the car, accidentally as it were, as a pretext for falling out of the race.

"I could drop my hat," he suggested.

"That would be hats off to the Cromwellians. Hold on to your hat and your self-respect while you can," she counselled.

The Black had now found its second wind and was perspiring freely, yet still showed reserves of strength and speed. The last league of the road still lay before them and the Colonel's crescendo of choler with the farmer was mingled with rising respect for the horse that he drove. Still, it seemed incredible that a mere farmer-owned nag should be able to show a clean set of heels to his own carefully-bred animals, one of which showed it was the best at the Show while the other was not, he had reason to believe, a whit inferior. It was a gruelling pace all the way so far.

"Lash out and dash out," he ordered. "We must head this procession to the city. This is surely the very apex of bravado."

The coachman then whipped up his charges and at the same time he sounded a blast on his sonorous horn that he was going to take the lead. Then the carriage took the right side of the cambered road, an additional sign that it was going out. They were now within two miles of the town and the road widened out so as to accommodate the greater pressure of traffic. Both vehicles were now level, racing side-by-side for the next mile or so. The carriage horses were reeking with perspiration, and showed signs of distress to a certain extent.

"These horses have just got to win," said the now irate-excited Colonel.

"Yessir," came the staccato, tense voice of the coachman. His horses now broke into a gallop in spite of their driver and he lost speed in the effort to restore them to a trot.

"Better gallop them altogether if there is no other way," commanded the Colonel.

"Yessir."

Finola, equally determined not to be beaten in the last lap, now forged ahead by half-a-dozen yards.

The Colonel, seeing that his horses were fairly beaten in a trotting contest over a distance of a dozen miles, ordered them to be lashed into a gallop and Finola, thus challenged, did likewise and, in fact, widened the distance between them to nearly double what it had been before. They were now in the suburbs of the city and their gallopading antics were attracting an increase of attention every moment.

A somnolent-looking policeman, regarding the phenomenon from the safety of the footpath, had a brainwave that it was not alone a case of fast but even of dangerous driving. He saw a crest on the carriage and a case for the court – but whose carriage. Then he looked the other way and by the time he had uplifted a minatory hand and stepped gravely on to the road as only a practiced policeman can do it, the racers had sped on, heedless of his presence.

In another minute, a traffic block ended the race.

In spite of himself, the worsted Colonel flung a hurried glance of admiration at the blonde driver of a superior bit of horse flesh.

Then he resolved that he would buy that horse.

This incident served to convince him that the gentry were no longer the power in the country that they used to be. Nobody seemed to quail as they should before them now. Unless Macara sold him that horse, he vowed, he would cause him to remember this calculated insolence towards his betters.

CHAPTER XVI

CROSSING THE RUBICON

WHEN Marley Swanton's signed article appeared proclaiming *urbi et orbi* that he had definitely catalogued himself among the time-stricken denizens of the earth, he wilted for a week beneath the blow. He was made aware in various ways that such an uncalled-for and wanton advertisement of his age caused all the tongues in the three parishes to wag both caustically and crucially at his expense. It would lower his stock in the marriage mart for one thing; that is, if it could be averred that he was in such a market at all. He was nevertheless aware himself of his sentiments towards Finola Macara but she did not seem to be in any hurry to reciprocate them. He felt convinced that they were a most unusual family and not to be judged by the usual standards.

There was a certain amount of loss and gain in his candid confession. The age of youth had been considerably prolonged since the advent of the present century. In mediaeval times, man was claimed either by violence or disease in or about forty; nowadays, they were not too old to launch the marital barque at that age. Why should he not follow the fashion in this respect, if he felt so inclined? Then, it was, after all, consolatory to know that he was capable of making money by his pen, and two guineas for such a small piece of writing was not a bad beginning at all. At least his pen, he reckoned, was a good crutch. He had only accidentally discovered a gift that had lain dormant because unsuspected all those years. Now that he had realised himself in that direction, it might behove him to make up for lost time as much as possible. He extracted a greater thrill from this cheque than from many times the amount received from any other quarter; he postponed the cashing of it until it was almost out of date but he did not seem to mind about that aspect of the matter in the least. This was really creative work in a way that teaching wasn't. The shopkeeper, he reasoned, made money by storing something made perhaps in Germany until wanted piecemeal by the public and parting with it at a higher price. There could be little or no artistic pleasure in that kind of human endeavour. At best, it was just a matter of store-keeping and book-keeping. They were what the scene shifter is to the operatic star in theatricals. It must be a dull-as-ditchwater business. The coal-monger caused an ugly, gaping hole to be left in the ground after him; useless for any purpose and a source of danger to man and beast. Yet, he had quarried a striking and lucrative collocation of words out of his own brain and so, far from causing any sense of deprivation, the process had actually burnished up the mental mine. That surely must be art in its highest form. To him it seemed that the difference between art and commerce is the difference between creation and destruction. The poet and the publican as wage earners were antithetical types and he felt that already he must be at least at the foothills of Parnassus. Strange that one newspaper article should bring him more fame than a year's teaching and cause him to be more widely known. Then it occurred to him that he had missed his real *metier*.

The ready acceptance of a few more articles, but mostly in local journals where the rate of pay was small, confirmed him in this opinion. But his joy in one direction was cancelled out by his sorrow in another. The attendance at his school was falling off steadily of late, due to a variety of reasons over which he thought he could exercise little or no control. There seemed to be no immediate prospect of an improvement. If the attendance dwindled a little more he would inevitably lose his average and his school. Besides, a litigious and vindictive parent had prosecuted him lately for caning his boy and, although the case was dismissed, it prejudiced his prestige with the powers-that-be. Then about ten children in the outer rims of his district had forsaken him for the neighbouring school although more remote. The teacher in this school had offered his nubile daughter to him about a year ago and as his heart was engaged elsewhere he unhesitatingly turned her down. Then an estrangement, which developed into a mild form of hostility, began to operate between them. He knew that he was expected to marry a teacher in accordance with the caste system now prevailing in the profession. In any case, the population of the parish had been falling of late because in recent years the people were emigrating at the rate of 30,000 a year. Emigration had practically ceased now, due to the great trade slump in the United States, but that would scarcely operate in time to save the situation for him. There were too many large farmers in the parish, elderly bachelors and spinsters, and they, as a more-or-less leisured class, were becoming increasingly addicted to gossip for want of having their time and attention more fully occupied. He reflected that he had withal made no real or lasting friendships in Menavia, except perhaps with James Macara whose wife was now inimical to him in a quiet sort of way since she had begun to suspect his designs on her daughter. The Macaras, although suffering from a chronic lack of capital, were, he knew, a very proud family; they made a special parade of their pride towards bigger farmers and the gentry wherever they came into contact with them. It occurred to him that all the people hereabouts were possessed of a kink unshared by folk of their status elsewhere. They were a sort of law unto themselves. Mrs Macara, in her last conversation with him, had spoken as if she expected a veritable Prince Charming to come along to claim her only daughter and, of course, her auditor did not appear to be in the reckoning. It was clear that his claims in that direction were not seriously considered at all. In fact, a good deal of the celibacy that was so rampant in the parish was the result of an amalgam of pride and snobbery. These egoistic, pedigreed people would not wed where they could, and where they would, they couldn't, because the other party to the contract refused to take them at their own estimation.

Then there were a number of people reading history for the sole purpose of making out that they were directly descended from ancient kings and chieftains, as a result of which a certain halo still hung round them. That kind of boasting and gasconade generated a good deal of envy in the parish and estrangement between neighbours. Here was abundant evidence that the true Celt still continues to dwell a good deal in the past. His mind is ever harking back to the twilight of fable and pre-history.

He reflected that wherever he had met Finola of late he found her, if anything, more elusive and baffling than ever. She did not seem to take his overtures seriously, or at least in the light of love. Perhaps it was his own fault. Was he only playing the part of an amateur lover after all? He had had no practise in the art of love making like others and it could not be taught in any school. Then again, he reflected that love was an impalpable thing that met one round the corner, at the playhouse, at the pictures, at dances and, in fact, wherever people congregated. Life in all its aspects was leavened with love. Yet, Menavia with all its shortcomings was Ireland in little; of that, he was certain. Another thing about it, too, was that it was the most monarchical country in the world; and given a republic in the morning it would be crying for a kingdom in the evening. Up till a decade ago, teachers were badly paid and then they were only graded in the same level as policemen and petty shopkeepers. Even yet, they were not placed in the same social level as large farmers, doctors and the like. Of course, snobbery was as old as our fallen nature but there was more of it to the square mile in Ireland than anywhere else, because it was a very old, almost worn-out country, and the tradition of kingship was in our blood. At one time, the country, with a population of a million or so, had 300 bishops and almost as many petty kings and princes. That would go far to explain the royalty of the race down to the present time. He had seen a lot of snobbery and empty boasting while living with the farmers of late, so much of it that he had now gone into lodgings in the village as a paying guest. Yet, all this snobbery did not prevent the ingrained love of gossip from having its full fling among the people. Those who were too proud to stand at the crossroads frequent the forge or the pub where all the news of the day was doled out or would tolerate one or two confirmed gossips at their own firesides a few times a week for the sake of the news. The lowly gossip, on the other hand, knowing why he was being given house shelter, developed soon into a garrulous, slanderous and, at times, malicious entertainer. He was more than equal to feeding the demand that he had created. Where life is a grim struggle with the forces of nature, snobbery hides its diminished head, but life was free and easy here. There were, he felt, social climbers everywhere and it was at best a mind-racking, soul-destroying form of endeavour. The climber, if he is to climb, must run after people, toady to them and fuss about them if he is to be taken into their little circle. They will be sneered at and mocked all the time, yet all is well with them if they do not consider it too high a price to pay.

The teacher felt more than ever that the social atmosphere that exuded from Menavia was beginning to suffocate him. He had a good deal of time on his hands and he would lose himself more than ever in his literary pursuits. Then it occurred to him to write a lively account of the great road race between the landlord and his tenant for the *Weekly Recorder*. Since he had blossomed out as an authority on age, its owner had accepted a few contributions from him. That was, he knew, the sort of thing that would be avidly read locally. It would help to illustrate the new-found fearlessness of our farmers and the landslide of our landlords more than anything else. To this end he decided to cycle to Thomond, the county town, and see what journalism was like at close quarters. He called on Noel Clare the following Saturday evening. As he had given everybody but himself a half-day, he was alone in the office brooding over ledgers and the like. The teacher, on making himself known, was warmly received and told to sit down for a chat. On account of his writings he was now well-known to the owner-editor. On being told that the race in question was fairly stale as it was nearly a month old, he was assured that it made no difference as it had not appeared in print before. It would, he was told, be a great "scoop" on the rival paper and that in itself was a matter of some moment. Enquiring what a "scoop" was, he was told that it was an exclusive item of news of the first importance before one's rivals. That was one of the most exciting and gratifying features of journalism.

"Make your description of this race as spicy as possible, old chap," he was told. "Draw, within reason, a large draft on the bank of your imagination. Bring out the pedigree of the owners as well as their respective horses."

"Yes, I shall do my little utmost, sir, to spin an intriguing yarn," his head shaking with narrative as it seemed while he spoke.

Mr Clare then touched a bell and a white-aproned maid appeared through a door which gave from the two-roomed office to the culinary part of the house.

"Tea for two and two for tea, Peggy," said he without consulting the wishes of his friend. She appeared a few minutes later, bearing a large tray laden with a most inviting meal. The front door, which gave to the street, was closed and the tea was partaken of by both. Mr Clare then departed, telling his visitor that he would be back in about two hours, turning the key in the door after him. He came back again to say that it was very easy to get the Irish people to talk but it was almost impossible to get them to put their thoughts on paper. Although a nation of talkers, they were not addicted to either reading or writing. The clergy and teachers should be great writers but they seemed to be muscle-bound even more than the plain people. They were all, he said, under the chronic operation of a form of literary dyspepsia. Then he departed.

Left to himself, the teacher took stock of the editorial sanctum where so many provoking, thought-compelling articles were written. The table at which he sat was covered with well-frayed, moth-eaten, green-coloured cloth. The office contained one solidly fashioned chair and two crazy looking cheap ones. A pile of dust-laden books, out-of-date calendars for the most part, and rubbishy stuff of all kinds freighted the shelves. Even the dictionary was a small, closely-printed, dog-eared volume. He had expected to find quantities of imposing, costly, up-to-date books on all manner of subjects. Next, he pulled aside a curtain and the shelf revealed a few attractive volumes. He took out one book. Who does not like to turn over the leaves of a favour-ite book and appraise its type, size and format before seriously dipping into it? The keys in all the presses were rusty and had long since ceased to function as such. These books were also dust laden. It was, he thought, very strange that the journalist was able to dispense with every book in the place but then, he supposed, he was able to evolve any and every sort of tale out of his head.

Then he recollected that he was there to spin a yarn himself and time was flying. He would like to procrastinate but there was no escape now. Mr Clare had gone to a Farmers' Union meeting and these were prosy affairs that may last for hours. Yes, talking and speechifying was the great popular art in Ireland, the temporary solvent of all our ills. Of course, there was the possibility that a great tide of talk may ultimately lead to action of some kind but what kind of action and when? Yet, thought had to precede speech just as speech had to precede action.

The editor had taken the precaution to place a wad of loosely-bound paper and a pencil before him and mentioned to write on the one side of the paper only, and to number each sheet. He ran his fingers through his hair at the thought of his coming travail and resolutely subsided on one of the rickety chairs. It gave way beneath him as he did not know how to balance its loose legs and he found himself sprawling on the floor. "I don't seem to be too popular here," he thought. "Even the chairs cannot bear with me." Then he grabbed at a pen, only to find that a quantity of ink had coagulated round it rendering it almost impossible as an instrument of calligraphy. Indeed, for that matter, there was nothing much in the whole place calculated to cause anybody to write, but then the urge must come from within. Yes, that must be why Mr Clare was so very careless about the adventitious aids to writing, they were not the concomitants to any real inspiration. Although writing was a form of talking, yet what a divorce there was between them in actual practice, and he was there to find a formula. He knew that Homer had described some equine events in his *Iliad* but that did not help him very much. Then, after revising the opening sentence half-a-dozen times, he wrote steadily on to the end. He had found that the beginning was half the battle.

When Mr Clare returned after an absence of three hours duration, he was pleased to see his friend so occupied in his work. He scanned the opening pages and patted their author heartily on the back, stating that it would be the sensation of the week in his paper.

"It's a thousand pities, old chap, that you did not engage in the noble profession of journalism," said he, "but it's never too late to mend. You are the very type of man who would go far because you are a writer to the manner born. I am ageing and failing of late and I feel the want of a man like you, a man who is neither too old nor too young, with a due sense of responsibility and decorum. As a teacher of book-keeping, you could give me great help right away here. You have proved yourself as a writer, so in no time you would be my literary and commercial crutch. I could even give you a financial interest in the place. A man of your aptitude would learn a lot in a few months all the routine work."

"I'm afraid you're too optimistic, Mr Clare. It took me hours to write a column of fustian that you would dash off in as many minutes. Besides, it takes a lot out of me – the effort, I mean."

"Oh, writers are not so fast as you think. It took the great Gibbon 18 years to write his history of the Roman Empire. Besides, there is such a thing as a fatal facility, especially in the matter of original work."

"What do you mean by original work, sir?"

"Well, I mean anything that is not mere reporting, for instance. That is the lowest form of journalism, though the most important, and gives little scope for a man's literary ability. For all that it is the backbone of newspaperdom, its *raison d'être*, so to speak. Reporting the windbags of our time is not unlike the task of the thresher; the separation of the grain from the straw. When you go to a public meeting where men wrap up a kernel of thought in sheaves, aye, even whole stooks of verbiage, you have to be more of an interpreter than a recorder or reporter. There is where you exhibit whatever art there is. You winnow the chaff from the grain and dress his sloppy talk and woolly thought into crisp attractive form. A reporter, my dear sir, is a species of midwife who simply delivers everyman of his reluctant, cloudy thought. He is the *accoucheur* of other people's thoughts, such as they are."

"I see. That's a very apt illustration indeed, sir. Faith, I thought reporting was more or less mechanical once you had acquired a knowledge of shorthand?"

"Well, it is and it isn't. Every good reporter projects something of his own personality in what he reports. He still has sufficient room to be an artist in selection and rejection. He assists at the birth of everyman's thoughts but he must have none of his own – just then."

"I see. He can exercise a sort of esoteric art?"

"Quite so. Word-for-word reporting is rapidly dying out. You see, the average speaker is not an artist in words. And he has to flounder about in a mass of verbiage in his efforts to release himself of a few banal, paltry ideas. Then all the ambages of speech, all the circumlocution has to be cut out and the thought, such as it, is presented. The ordinary County Council meeting is just like a gaggle of geese and the doleful Dail is just like a glorified County Council meeting. It is right here that reporting ceases to be an artifice and becomes an art. The headings and descriptive touches by which a reporter seeks to enhance his report are all his own, conditioned by the kind of a meeting it is. Shorthand is the curse of the country because it ruins a man's memory and eats up his intellect."

"A gaggle of geese or worse? Oh, hell, how you frighten and amuse me. The man in the street thinks that shorthand is the whole bag of tricks. Well, I'm glad it isn't, after all. As it happens, Mr Clare, I am supposed to have a very tenacious memory. I wish to goodness that I could rid my brain of half the rubbish that encumbers it. I have read a lot in a desultory kind of way and the result is that I find myself quoting, unknown to myself at times. I drifted into teaching by accident and it cannot be my real calling in life because I feel very irritable at times."

"Oh, you're the man for me, my dear sir; you're the man for me. The really great journalist always sets out by intending to become something else; he just drifts into it. He misses his way and finds journalism. Of course, it has not the dulling respect-ability of, say, banking or doctoring. No conscientious parent deliberately launches his son into it any more than he does into poetry or painting. It is filled by the deserter from all the other callings or professions. Every successful journalist has been a failure at something else. The powers-that-be have to spoil a good businessman or possibly a poet so that a journalist may be evolved from the wreck. You have all the qualities in cold storage of a pressman of the first eminence."

"You surprise me, sir. You are the type of person that could talk a man into anything."

"Not at all, old man. What I mean by the word 'old' is that you are already well advanced in my regard."

"Thank you, sir. It appears to me that your precious profes-sion is just the dustbin of all the other professions."

"But it is nothing the worse for that."

"It's a case of when all fruit fails, welcome blackberries, isn't it sir?"

"Not exactly, old chap, not exactly. The door of entry is not wide enough for that to happen. There is room for only a few of us in every county as compared with scores of teachers and clergymen. Most people are inclined to forget all about it as a career and it cannot be taught in the classroom. The disturbing split infinitives can be guarded against, but that is all. Science is the arithmetic of the known but art is concerned with the in-calculable and the born journalist is an artist. He must be able to sense in advance the temper of the times. What he thinks today, the populace must begin to think about tomorrow. He is a seer and you cannot manufacture seership."

"You have a splendid enthusiasm for your work. I wish I had half as much for mine."

"It's a true sign that you are a misfit at it and you ought to chuck it. You must be well-munitioned with zeal for any profession to be a success at it because they all have special snags of their own attached to them. It is very consoling at times to know that you are moulding public opinion and that the public is only so much putty in your hands. I have canalled public opinion along many straight and crooked courses in my time."

"I'm sure they were straight according to your lights?"

"Yes, but sometimes my lights were very dim."

"Well, I'll think about the generous offer you have made to sir and I'll let you know in a week or two. I feel that I am at the cross-roads of life lately in many ways and I could do worse than throw in my lot with you."

"Oh, you'd be a decided success. I copied that article of yours into my own paper I liked it so much. Our life is a bit irregular to be sure but there is a good deal of glamour attached to it while we are young. How soul-deadening it must be for the assistant tied to his master's shop day after day where there is much or little to do. The greatest open-air events happen but they happen in vain for him. The draper is as great a slave to his yardstick as every young hussy is to her lipstick. He drapes his eyes to all when the journalist is in the midst of life as it is really lived. I've kept you here all day. Will you drop into the Diamond bar and we'll have a taiskaun of malt before you strike for the road?"

"Never touch the bally stuff, sir, and I'm not going to begin now."

"Well, it can't be helped, I suppose. My father willed that I should be a draper but I did not see the good of being a counter-jumper measuring out bits of tape and things. Serving the fair sex with camisoles was not a very heroic occupation for a hefty fellow like me. No man beyond the size of the counter and the weight of a jockey should be a draper. It's a most effeminate occupation."

"And yet, look at all the drapers who fought for freedom a

few years ago."

"That was the form of revolt against their job that it took at the time."

"Well, if men shouldn't sell drapery, women shouldn't sell drink."

"I agree with you there and for a purely personal reason. When I was a young fellow, asses' years ago it is now, I was a regular man with irregular lapses. I would be on a loose end for a week or two a few times a year. Then I was a rabid teetotaller for the other fifty weeks during which I would ballyhooley against the evils of drink in the paper. I would only draw a part of my salary weekly and leave the rest with the boss to act as banker for me. One day I went over to Roscrea to the annual meeting of the now-defunct Board of Guardians and District Council at which all the chairmen were elected. Then they all returned to one of the big hotels and started drinking like fishes to celebrate the event. I was only drinking lemonade but unknown to me the barmaid-manageress laced it with whiskey and soon I was shouting and bawling with the best of them. When I returned to the office I drew nearly a hundred pounds and fled to Dublin. I was back in a week a mere wreck and stony broke. I had a wait of an hour at Roscrea and I walked down to this precious barmaid, the cause of all my misery, for a half-wan on tick. I told her I was in a state of temporary impecuniosity. She took back the drink and the want of a stimulant of some kind till I got home two hours later nearly put me in the rats again. A drink at the time would have steadied my nerves. Many a toper ultimately dies as much from the want of as because of drink and I nearly died that day; and she'd have killed me in the double so to speak. Since that day out, I nourish an undying prejudice against women as barmaids or publicans. When I go into a strange town I go to the meanest bung shop rather than face any hotel with its inevitable barmaid."

151

CHAPTER XVII

HOW QUINBURN AMASSED A FORTUNE

A S Peadar Blanche became more addicted to beer, he tended to be more talkative and shed some of that self-respect so inherent in him. Under the influence of a few pints of porter, a comparatively dull man would blaze suddenly into a bright, breezy, entertaining gossip. The trebled price of drink in recent years had done more for temperance than mere moral suasion could ever hope to do.

It was Sunday evening and he felt for once disinclined to wend his way towards the parish pub where as a rule, despite the licensing laws, he would manage to consume about a gallon of beer in a few hours. He did not know how he would be received by the Yankee gentleman who had replaced Paddy Quinburn as owner of the pub and he was now fully aware of the shady part he had played himself in the transaction. He had aided and abetted the designing Paddy in the selling of his custom-shrunken business at a great premium by resorting to a novel device. He reckoned that the new publican might have discovered the truth already; and then it was unlikely that he would do any Sunday business, the same as his more astute crafty predecessor. It was not everybody liked to engage in this surreptitious Sunday business. The Yankee seemed a straight-dealing man but the question was how would he deal with him when he would meet him face to face. Suppose he had been a rum runner in the United States, he would as an angry man be a force to be reckoned with. He might be reckless enough to pull a gun on him and Peadar was not a bellicose man.

Yes, all things considered, he felt that the pub was out of bounds for him this evening and yet he was up against the problem of having to while away a few hours somehow or other. Then, all of a sudden, he perceived that for all his frolicsome and amusing ways he was a lone, isolated atom. Away from his favourite background with a pint in his hand and a few cronies to sharpen his wits upon, what a deadly dull dependent clod he could be. Brilliant, *brilliantine persiflage* was alright in its way, but if it could be superinduced only by the lavish consuming of liquor, time, money and health, then it was a dearly-bought acquirement indeed. Blanche was already acquiring the gravid, flushed appearance of a beer-swiller and an occasional back ache of late would remind him that his liver and kidneys were beginning to revolt against having to do so much overtime work. If you are in good health you are unaware of the existence of these things, as he had been until recently. It would be quite unthinkable to spend all the day and half the night under the same roof as his aged, cranky, exacting mother and, besides, he would excite her surprise more than ever if he did a thing now that he had not done for many years. His mother, who was a dark, distant woman, neither visited anybody nor tolerated any visits in turn for some years past. She lived the life more-or-less of a hermit crab, as many women do in the country when things are not to their liking.

Blanche felt more than ever now that he should in alignment with the old rut he had made for himself do what was expected of him. He decided, at last, to go over to Rahora and drop into the kitchen and engage man and maid in talk of a desultory kind for an hour or two. He knew that he was rapidly out-wearing his welcome there of late. On the other hand, he knew that he had a most interesting, almost sensational budget of news of which to unburden himself. The news-bringer was ever a man of moment in Menavia. Then, for want of anything better to do, he gravitated towards the Macara *ménage* where he could, without much ceremony, subside into a soogaun chair. Then, after the lapse of a decent interval, some of the Macaras would surely condescend to emerge from the parlour or drawing room, engage him in a conversation and offer him a well-prepared cup of tea.

He noted that they were becoming very capricious of late. The way he would succeed in worming himself into the sunshine of their favour would, of course, depend a good deal on what he had to confide in the way of news. It was no easy matter to sustain this role but he was a man of ready re-source. Much of what he had to tell now was, he knew, against himself, but he could distort that part of the story and sup-press unsavoury details. He may even be able to show himself in the light of a mere victim of another man's cupidity and money-grubbing ingenuity. In any case, what was news for but to disseminate it and, by so doing, to extract the last scin-tilla of pleasure from it. Why should he remain silent while such work remained to be done? When in a quandary, he in-variably filled his massive pipe and smoked deliberately; it was a soporific for all his ills. In fact, it did more; it aided the flow of his ideas, soothed his nerves and resolved his doubts. Then, it suddenly occurred to him that one of the greatest drawbacks of rural life is the want of anything in the nature of a club, or even parish hall which can be frequented by all on equal terms. Such a place would be a boon during the long, weary, winter nights and on Sundays when time hangs very heavy on the unoccupied country man's hands. Pubs were now too costly as places of entertainment except at rare intervals for most people. Their day's work over and supper taken, men like to ramble away from the scene of their labours for an hour or two nightly after which they return with renewed zest. The swopping of a bit of gossip with their neighbours in pleas-ant surroundings is as the breath of their nostrils to them. He decided that he would talk to the teacher about providing a hall of some kind where men could smoke, talk, play cards and so, without being under the necessity of having to go into one another's houses, apart from the compliment that this involved. At present, half-a-dozen men would converge on the slightest encouragement on some house at night. They would enter shyly enough with a "God save all here" and the reply to this would be "And you too".

Then, the self-invited visitor, stroller, interloper or whatever he is, is told to sit down and take the weight off his limbs. In turn, he sheepishly remarks that it is cheaper to be sitting than standing. He is keenly feeling his way and the depth of his welcome all the time, and he crowds on his best manners which dry up the wells of his spontaneity. No meals are expected or given and the stroller is never invited beyond the kitchen and its homely comforts of coal or turf fire, paraffin lamps and twisted-hay-covered chairs. The visitor presently begins to chat with more confidence and assumption. In exchange for the boon conferred upon him, he feels obliged to be as chatty as possible and tell everything that he thinks his hosts would like to hear. In response to his host his conversational powers are quickly kindled and nobody can talk for any length of time without giving himself away and giving many others away as well. He does. It is the doings of some neighbour. He develops as a talker and debater and, in time, becomes a sort of entertainer, a host in himself, a card, a character. That is the role he is expected to play, the tribute he must pay for being admitted to the house of his equals or superiors. This is how great gossips are evolved and why the country is such a hot-bed of speculation, criticism and analysis. The broad-acred farmer and the refined lady will tolerate these licensed gossips at regular intervals for the sake of the news they have to impart and their spicy way of serving it up. They fill the lacuna to some extent left by the strolling poets and musicians of bygone times.

Women are not under the same necessity to blossom out as

story-tellers and yarners as men, because they do not ramble about at night. Few women can compete with the accustomed yarner and gossip, and they are only to be found in the country, where he practices his art sitting in his neighbour's chimney corner year after year.

Sunday is especially deadening in rural districts and the cross-roads as a meeting place is at best only a summer resort. Huxter shops are made to do duty as clubs and labourers' houses are frequented by small farmers. But these improvised clubs are being continually broken up. The housewife suddenly discovers that the house is no longer her own from sundown till bed time. Over the cards, her visitors gradually betray their manifold defects of character at first carefully tucked away. Her manner becomes more frigid and formal and they are made to interpret that as a notice to quit; and, shrewd yokels that they are, they swarm elsewhere afresh.

Peadar Blanche was now by way of being the champion gossip of the parish. When drink was cheap, much of the gossip used to be done in pubs because men could afford to frequent them. There was a more manly spirit exhibited therein and besides, the more fuddled state of the bar-loungers precluded that penetrating probing into character and motives that takes place around the fireside.

Blanche was able to find *entree* into many a house because of his yarning proficiency but then, suddenly, its doors would be closed against him. He wasn't as discreet as some of his competitors and, besides, he was much given to exaggeration and purely malicious gossip of late. His rivals were more veiled, cryptic and subtle. Yet in most cases it was enough for his auditors if his inventions contained a working germ of fact. It served its purpose at the time of providing them with a piquant subject of conversation on which they could hang a smug complacent philosophy of life. No story, no matter how unlikely it might seem, would be altogether doubted; the knowing ones would shake their heads and say that there was no smoke without fire. It may not be a big blaze but at least their imaginations would be kindled. Recently, a few young ladies had left the parish on a prolonged visit to their friends in Dublin and Peadar boldly mooted that they had gone away to hide their shame. This was proclaiming too loudly that Menavia was no longer the haunt of innocence that it used to be and the result was he was slowly but surely getting into bad odour as an out-and-out scandalmonger. There were limits, even in Menavia.

It was in this tortured frame of mind that the man, only a year ago the idol of the parish and now recruited to the ranks of the most chronic gossips and tale-bearers, wended his way to Rahora. Ambling along, he reflected on the time when he was *persona grata* in every house in the parish. It occurred to him for the first time that he could do worse than to look out for a life partner for himself; he had lived the life of a gay bachelor to the full and he was not extracting much satisfaction from it of late. But soon he would not have anywhere left to go.

He was feeling the reaction from the heavy bout of drinking that had been forced upon him for the past three days, that is to say, a severe fit of depression. If he could only get a drink or two now to tone up the system.

His five acres of land supported a few sheep and pigs together with a cow and he left the profits from all this to his mother who was a shrewd managing woman. Then, as a small contractor, he had been doing well till lately and spending more freely than anybody else. He began to drink at first for the sake of good fellowship but latterly he was doing so in order to dispel that carking care which he felt was creeping upon him. His drink bill was over two pounds a week and that was too much merely for the satisfaction of one bodily want in bad times. Recently, he had haggled for over an hour about a few shillings and lost a good job of work over a little sum that he would spend in the pub in an hour or so. The publican, he reflected, gets a lot of easy money and all who enter his den seem to leave their economic principles at the door. Why all this sudden display of lavishness and generosity in a pub on the part of people who are really misers when met anywhere else? What a distorted view of life the average publican must have as it is presented to him across the counter. Although Quinburn himself would drink at times, he was cuter in his cups than most people. Yes, those sequestered pubs were a greater evil than town or city bars. What a boon a club would be in Menavia as an offset to all this; and he had drunk the price of one every few years, he reckoned. Now at the end of it all, he has practically nowhere to go; even his doubtful friend Quinburn was gone. Such a club would kill that demoralising habit of cabin-hunting and there men would be under no necessity to gossip for house shelter and for its sake alone as they have to do at present. Here, they could all meet on perfectly equalitarian terms. His short experience of town clubs told him that a certain standard of dignity and decorum ever prevails therein because nobody is under the necessity to gossip mainly about people merely in exchange for a seat and a heat of the fire at another person's house.

These reflections at last brought him to his destination. Near the house he saw what appeared to be the top of a trilby hat moving along a low wall away from the house. He stooped on a stone and let fly at it. It was a glancing blow, however, and the next sound from the stricken object was "Oh, hell". It then assumed a perpendicular position and the figure of Tommy Cooley stood revealed fully two feet above the wall.

"Playing hide and seek, Tommy, eh?" he queried.

"No reason why you should strike an old man, you know, Peadar. I had my day and if you did that then I'd make an old battered half-gallon of you. To strike an innocent man."

Then the pair of them walked towards the kitchen, Cooley feeling irritated that he was not able to elude his friend.

A few minutes later, James Macara and Fergus entered the kitchen and the former said: "Hello, Blanche; here again."

He interpreted it as an unfriendly salute but he pretended to ignore it as he came determined to deliver his message. Better tell the story himself before others could distort the facts to his detriment.

"I suppose you didn't hear the strange news?" he began.

"What news?" queried Macara, laconically.

"Our mutual friend, the publican, has sold out and cleared out bag and baggage."

"Well, he was no friend of mine but it does not matter now. Speaking of baggage reminds me that I lent him some bags some time ago and he had a right to return them, the mean hoofler, before he left. He had no call to sell them anyway."

"Well, he has sold out now whatever, lock, stock and barrel, also his ten-acre plot, as a going concern. He has already cleared away to Thomond, himself and his baggage, as Fergy there calls married females. Devil a ha'porth they took with them so far, only what they stood up in."

"A sort of a moonlight flitting, eh?" asked Cooley. "Believe you me, but 'twas nothing of the kind. They were paid a pot of money for going. They got as much and more for their dirty little yard of a counter as you'd get for your big farm if you had it under the hammer in the morning."

"You don't say," said Mrs Macara, who now bustled into the kitchen.

"Indeed and I do, ma'am."

"Why all this secrecy then and flight from the parish like a pair of frightened redshanks?"

"Don't you remember, mother, that I told you some time ago that Mrs Quinburn gave me a hint of that?" said Finola.

159

"Yes, dear, but I thought it was more of her goster and nonsense and so I let the news in through one ear and out through the other. I never knew her to part with so much of the truth and all unasked before, not indeed that I was ever speaking to her but once."

"She was always as divorced from the truth as a dog is from his bark," ventured Fergus.

"Just talking for the sake of showing off, are you Fergy?" asked his sister.

"And they never did better business than for the past few days," said Cooley. "There was a power and all of people drinking and drivelling about the place with the past three days, all the day and half the night. You were very busy yourself, Peadar, mopping up the stuff with all the mugs and mugwumps. Faith, I didn't think you'd have a leg to stand on for the next week or more. That's why I wanted to give you the slip in the avenue."

"While I think of it, would you let me have a mug of buttermilk, if you don't mind, ma'am. It's the only kind of neck oil to be had today and my throat is as dry as a lime kiln."

Then Blanche looked appealingly at the vanithee. Peadar was then given a pint of this liquid, which he avidly drunk.

"That's a great cure for the crapulous," said Fergus.

"As I was saying," resumed Blanche, "we have lost the man that could relieve all our thirsts. He is gone now and it is only right to say that he belonged to a fine old stock."

"A fine old stock of a weed, you mean," said the fearanthee, rather acidly. "It's about time his kind were weeded out of here."

"Would it surprise you to know that all those fellows as were seen skulking about that pub for the last few days were paid and well paid for their attendance. I was told off to give them the hint that the oftener they said 'the same again' the less it was to cost them. Everything they swallowed was paid for by the generous publican himself. He only wanted a fine big crowd about the pub for a few days and if Cooley had to come along he could fill his maw too at a cost of nothing at all. I didn't see the drift of it in time but the upshot of it all was that he made a decoy duck of me, did himself and the wife. Then when I did, it was too late to blow the gaff; and besides, I'm not paid for being a spy."

"By that time you weren't able to blow the froth off a pint, I think, Peadar," said the laconic Cooley.

"Oh, I wouldn't say that," replied Blanche, somewhat abashed. "I wouldn't say that at all now."

"Oh, by all accounts you made a proper beast of yourself and you can't deny it."

"Well, be that as it may, sir, I was told to inveigle a score or two of the most noted topers in the three parishes on one pretext or another such as land and water sports, land lettings, anything and everything that was calculated to bring a crowd and keep them talking and drinking. I was given lashings and leavings of money in half-crowns and less and when anybody was running short of cash I was to slip him a half-dollar on the understanding that he spent it. We were all to keep drinking like a shoal of fishes in the presence of the stranger behind the bar, a broad-faced, fat, poky little man with a half-high tobacco-coloured hat with a wide grin on him."

"Where does he come in?" asked Fergus.

"As the new publican from now on and the man for whose benefit, or cost rather, all this mock drinking was done. The sports organiser, whoever he was, was missing the first day and, of course, we had all to wait for this mythical man. The time was wiled away in the pub. The other organisers never turned up either and the less they turned up the more we turned in to the pub where we were really wanted as customers in the presence of the purchaser-to-be. Quinburn himself would pretend to make a mistake in the change and hand out more than he would receive for a drink so as to keep them flushed with money. One way and another, we managed as fine as ever you saw to keep the bar full. The money was given around in such a way as that one man would not be seen doing all the buying in the presence of the prospective publican and ultimate buyer. He was there by special invitation to see for himself the great volume of business that was being done in the place. He is only newly-returned from Chicago where all the boot-leggers come from. This big, bluff, beefy bowsy was just bubbling over with breezy Yankee slang and guessing and calculating every second at the sight of all this bustle of business. He ran back to Limerick for his cheque book the second day and when he returned I heard Mrs Quinburn telling him that they had received three additional offers for the pub since he left but that he was still in the re-served list. At the end of the third day's drinking, that is to say last night, the Yank could stand the bustle of business no longer; the bar was cleared, the bargain was clenched and I was called in to witness it."

"Did he get £250 for the rookery?" asked Macara. "It would be a rooking price," added his son.

"You can add another nought and then some," said Blanche.

"Holy smoke, the devil in Hell," ejaculated Cooley.

"The hoofler of blazes," exploded Mrs Macara.

"As I was saying," proceeded Blanche, "the Yankee demurred a bit at the mention of five thousand pounds and the publican-that-was shouted out 'Look at the till, man-alive, look at the till'. Then he shot out his fat, soft paw towards the till and said 'Sure you can count the takings for yourself – twenty pounds a day and upwards'. Then he told the Yank that this was the lean time of the year and that he would get his money back in next to no time. The bargain was then clenched at £4,750 to include everything as it stood, including the few bone-shakers of cattle and the wee bit of land. Then Quinburn and his wife ran off in

a motor this morning early, for good and all, leaving his successor in possession and, of course, wishing him every kind of good
luck. When the bank opens in the morning he'll be on the spot
to present the cheque for fear of mishap of any kind, don't you
know. Some business man I should say he is and more power to
him. 'Tisn't everyone as can cod a cute Yank these times. Quinburn is a man after my own heart. He is, so he is."

"'Tis the likes of him would have luck," said Mrs Macara,
"and I always saw it. Still, money got in that way will surely
melt."

"'Twill melt into the bank, ma'am, where 'twill be as safe as
a house," assured Blanche.

"Perhaps 'tis the Yank's money as is melting now," said
Cooley. "Who knows how he got all that money out there in
the wilds of bootlegging, shoot-at-sight America?"

"Quinburn got that old ramshackle place for a shake of the
hat," said Cooley, "and now he can lie up at leisure like a ferret
in a warren for the rest of his life."

"Those old Yanks talk big and look very cute and critical,"
said Macara, "but they seem to lose their wisdom teeth when
they return to the old country. They, as they imagine, return to
a nation of fools only to be fooled in earnest and then they are
guessing and calculating in earnest for the rest of their lives."

"It's the spell cast by the old country," said Blanche, "the
witchery of Ireland."

"My ancestors were aristocrats on the maternal side, landed
autocrats," said Macara, "but they came down in the world, pulled
down by their environment. The fact is that the old native peasant
is, in the long run, too much for everybody. He is more Celtic,
of course, and more imaginative and acquisitive. His respect for
his social superiors is only on the surface. The Irish peasant will
ultimately pull everybody who has a touch of foreign blood in
him down to his own level and then below it. Quinburn, with

his double-barrelled Celtic name, seems to have even a double advantage. He asked the Yank at the psychological moment to look at the till, but I ask you all to look at Quinburn. He is the type of man who will go far. Menavia was really too small for him. He may be the big noise of the county town yet."

CHAPTER XVIII

THE SEVEN RULING POWERS

MARLEY Swanton now lived in lodgings in the village of Margadnua, about a league away from his school but so much nearer to the county town of Thomond he used to walk to the scene of his labours daily as he thought there was nothing like a good, bracing walk to clear the brain and enable a man in a quandary to see things in their proper perspective. It serves the same purpose for men as sewing and knitting does for women; that is to say, it soothes the jangled nerves. Stick in hand, he would walk to the county town eight miles away almost every Saturday for the sake of the exercise it afforded. On account of his predilection for such a snail-like mode of locomotion he was regarded by many as an odd fish. He had toyed with the idea of buying a small motor car, that perquisite of every teacher nowa-days, but the Hatry fiscal crash swallowed up some of the money he had earmarked for this purpose. This reverse made him turn more to the stock and share lists of his own country. How was it, he asked, that nearly everybody with money to invest turned to the sister isle? Having invested it there, their outlook then underwent a subtle change and they became convinced that our native company promoters were only playing with high finance in the most amateurish way. If England is the spiritual home of every Protestant, then, he thought, it was equally true to say that it is the fiscal home of every second Irish Catholic who has a ten-pound note to spare. No wonder, he rather ruefully reflected, that Ireland continues to remain such a *sans* indus-trial country. Still, he had never done anything himself to adjust this lop-sided state of affairs. But who wants Ireland groaning beneath a mass of factories, chimney stacks and mephitic smoke fumes anyway? He didn't. Factory life brought in its train all manner of vice and sin and Ireland would surely lose most of her hallowed time-honoured traditions.

Still, he should ear-mark a few hundred pounds for investment in the *Weekly Recorder* but that would be time enough. Since he saved Finola Macara from the horns, not of a dilemma, but from those of a bull itself, he wondered had he made additional headway in her affections? In the event of his being able to wed her he would get no money, as the Macaras had none; but then, he could easily dispense with filthy lucre. It was strange, he thought, that their chronic financial stringency did not abate that persistent sense of pride in them; it only ministered for some secret reason to their colossal vanity. Simple, struggling, semi-educated farmers, yet to judge from their conversation issuing daily as it did in conduct and behavior, they looked down on almost everything and everybody. But those qualities were shared by many others hereabouts and he must find the clue to it. Finola, and others like her, would prefer to virgin it all the time rather than marry ever so slightly beneath them. This was the kind of pride that was operating so much against marriage, closing his school and depriving him of a living. As regards the border children who were going to the rival school, he was resolved that he would never try to canvass them back despite the fact that they were solicited away from him. He knew that it was bruited about that Colonel Gloster had a rod in pickle for the Macaras and in a way, he thought, they invited his hostile attention and he was the kind of man that would rub it in.

He was looking through the rain-ridden window when he saw the subject of his thoughts, Macara himself, walking by very slowly on the street as if he were waiting for somebody. Speak or think of anybody very much and they are bound to appear. Was it that they were able somehow to project their personalities? He hastened into the street to greet his would-be father-in-law and ask him to stand in from the rain. Macara was looking gloomy and wore a hunted expression, he thought. He accepted the invitation more readily than he thought.

"You have a nice place here, Mr Swanton," said he, throwing a cursory glance around the parlour. "What a pity that potato-eating, beer-swilling sponge wouldn't hurry up with your new house and not have you going about like this, from Billy to Jack. Blanche ate a stone of potatoes the other night and then washed it down with a gallon of beer for a bet. The devil such a man, whatever."

"Oh, he can spare his labour on that house as far as I'm concerned for I'll never want it now. I'm going to live in Thomond, the county town in short, to use a localism. I'll tell you more about my plans later on, sir, but just now I'm more concerned to find out more about that fatal, facile tuber known as the potato."

"What about it, anyway? There will be a great shortage of them soon due to the Eucharistic Congress in Dublin."

"Well it caused the great famine of '47 which carried off over a million of our people. It was only an exotic tuber introduced into Ireland 160 years before and the gift of an Englishman. In its continued absence, people would have cultivated corn for bread instead and that would not have failed. Up till then, the people were given over to the two curses of the country, that is to say, a blind hopefulness and a fatal content. They were a bland, ineffectual people at that particular time, thinking that old spouting Dan O'Connell was a magician that would work miracles for them. People in the past ate a lot of potatoes and while they sated the pangs of hunger they left them weak as a rush and therefore work-shy and inactive."

"Radioactive, did you say?"

"I didn't then. The Irish people down the centuries have been simply cramming themselves with potatoes and this gluttonous indulgence softened and altered their character for the worse. It even altered them bodily and gave them soft potato faces and smaller and less attractive noses. They lost those well-articulated features of the Englishman. Then, these bally tubers created a great craving for drink."

"Buttermilk or creamery milk, I suppose?"

"No, then. Brewed and distilled stuff such as whiskey which is a drug rather than a drink, and porter which is a pig's drink. Just like man's love for woman, certain sorts of food create a craving for certain sorts of drink. Meat-eating people have fine aquiline noses and more energy. Now it's salty pig meat we seem to want – another kink in our character so that we shall have to drink after it."

"Yes, it seems to me, now that I think of it, that our countrymen would never ask anything better than the three Ps, namely potatoes, porter and pork."

"Yes, indeed, Mr Macara, all foods of comparatively recent origin in this country. And now, I trust you will allow me to pour you out a drop of the craythur, as they call malt in Menavia. It's real ten-year-old, or at least, so Mogue Murphy says, and he ought to know."

"Thank you ever so much. I wouldn't give a thraneen for that man's word. He made drink for a house full of people at a wake one night out of a pint of malt. Still, this drop is more to my mind. These publicans are a very rum lot."

"Yes, they belong to the seven ruling powers right enough."

"And who might they be, now?"

"The priest, the parson, the pedagogue, the politician, the pressman, the publican and the policeman. A formidable array and all beginning, like our friend the potato, with the same letter."

The teacher then poured out a naggin of malt for his guest, remarking that there wasn't a headache in a gallon of it. As he had decided to have a long chat with his friend, he rightly reasoned that he was giving him a sufficient dose to free him from all the inhibitions regarding this and kindred subjects.

"It's too generous of you, old chap," acknowledged Macara, sipping it like the epicure that he was and pronouncing it to be really good stuff.

"I've noted some traits about the people about here," resumed the teacher, "which have caused me to think. The Cork people are a witty, gay, laughter-loving lot but you can never plumb the heart of a Kerryman. Look at the perfectly Protean character of the greatest humbug in history, O'Connell, for instance. Kerry is still a *terra incognita*; it was never much invaded and it has very little infusion of foreign blood. But the people of Connacht, and this county is really part of it from a topographical point of view, are a bit of a puzzle to me. They can be, and often are, so very grave and glum. You were very down in the mouth for instance when I called you off the street."

Macara, who was beginning to glow under the influence of the whiskey which he was sipping lovingly, said that was a long story. Ireland, he said, was really conquered by Queen Bess for the first time and then half a century later Cromwell steam-rolled it. "By fire and sword, he created the stillness of death in Ireland and there was nothing after him for a long time but the silence of the unlaboured fields. He turned the country into a cemetery and called it peace. Yes, sir, he drove all the people to this side of the Shannon and called it the Irish Pale. He dealt out impartial devastation, however, for he drove all the old English, irrespective of religion, with them into the wild and barren West. The labourers were left to slave on for the new planters and ex-soldiers. In that way, he fused two races in spite of themselves. Yet what has that got to do with the question that I have posed?

"Everything, my dear sir. That fearful Hegira is the clue to the character of the people about here."

"Well, Spenser wrote his great masterpiece here from borrowed native materials down in Cork where he was squatting down upon three thousand acres of land. He advised Queen Bess that the only way to conquer the country was to kill the cattle and burn the crops and that would solve the Irish problem for ever."

"Oh, the fiend; the Prime Minister of the Devil."

"Yet his own grandson was driven helter-skelter into these here parts by Cromwell and sank down to the level of a labourer. Then this poor, benighted province became a compound for the cream of the Irish and Old English nation from 1649 onwards. Lords, chieftains, poets, judges and gentry, driven from their fine mansions and fertile lands, had to eke out a miserable hand-to-mouth existence among the grim, gaunt moors and stark and sterile mountains, reedy rivers and storm-tossed hills. Faith, 'tis no wonder that some of us wear a lonesome tragical look even to this very day, Mr Swanton."

"Yes, sir, I thought I noted a suspicion of it even in yourself when I called you off the street."

"Never mind me now. But I can assure you that there is more blue-blooded aristocracy to the square mile in the west – and this is part of it in a way – than in all the rest of Ireland put together; but you will now find them under mud cabins disguised as mere peasants and labourers. Anyway, sir, they were driven willy-nilly into the Burren and still more forbidding places to live or die as best they could among the long-settled who pitied yet despised them. Most of them had been rich and well-nurtured and now, as outcasts and pariahs, had to live in dire poverty, crying in the wilderness. Most of them failed to get a foothold there because they were forestalled by the aboriginal population who owned the soil. The West was simply horrible to them after the rich lands of Leinster and Munster. They pined amid the eternal gloom and barrenness of their new prison and they were beggared besides. Many gladly

sentimental and, he thought, slightly lack-humourous. Why this constant harking back to the dead and distant past? Then he remembered that the present is only the child of the past and the parent of the future. It seems, he thought, that at a certain age the minds of people become a sort of rut in which only the things of the past are stored. Doubtless, Macara was a poet of a kind. The only difference between a poet and an ordinary man is that the former can express what the latter feels just as vividly as a poet or nearly so. The ruralist, who lives so close to nature and to mother earth, is more timeless in his outlook than the urbanist. That is why everything that ever happened is, he thought, only an event of yesterday with men like Macara ever boasting of the MacMahon blood that courses in his veins. This man was so full of his past greatness and present potentialities that it would be very hazardous at present to intimate to him that he greatly desired to be affiliated with his family. He was just the type of colossal egoist who would consign his children to a life of celibacy on the altar of his great ancestral pride. In that attitude, however, he would have to reckon with one of the strongest instincts of nature and, as he was fighting vicariously, the dice were heavily loaded against him. In the matter of a proposal for the hand of Finola he would only have to wait and see.

Then he realised, with a pang of alarm and mild regret, that he was no longer a teacher. After nearly 20 years, teaching had become almost second nature with him; he was as rutted in it as Macara was in his memories and his family tree. It was now mid-August and he had been given six weeks holidays on the first of the month, tendering his resignation as a teacher at the same time. He had been just below the school average and that ominous fact would in any case efface him in no long time. He felt that he had never been popular in the parish – except with James Macara; but, then, popularity was a capricious thing, so often bestowed without merit and lost without reason. He was never understood and, as a result, never trusted. There was, for all their pretentions, still a good deal of the primeval about all these people which a smattering of primary education could never refine away. Throughout Thomond they were on the whole, he thought, a dangerous brood when aroused and it did not take too much to kindle them. Slow enough to make friends and quick enough to take umbrage even where no insult is intended, ever on the look-out for hostility and able apparently to discover it around the corner. The people everywhere had become much more touchy and sensitive since the Great War and the two native wars. What was the reason for it? Then he thought of the old man he had seen the previous Sunday, a man named Houlihan. A few children playing ball struck his house with it. He ran out to complain to him. "Look at the way, sir, those beggarly blackguards are crusthin' me dhure."

How vehement, trembling and passion-pale he looked, this old man.

He had a feeling that Mr Noel Clare and himself would get on well together. He was a Protestant but he would be all the better for that in many ways. So many Catholics lack a due sense of respect for one another. Later he would invest some money in the paper and thus consolidate his position. All things considered, he came, he thought, fairly well equipped in respect of his new venture in the uncharted sea of journalism. Was he not fairly well grounded in history, philosophy, economics, politics and, above all, he had the gift of expression on paper.

He decided to join the *Weekly Recorder* the following day, He had been taking part in a play in the village during the past few months and the locally-formed company was to produce it in the county town that night. Yes, he decided, he would write a critique on that as his first serious contribution to the paper to which he now owed his allegiance. He had to make a start somehow in his newly-adopted profession and here was really good material to hand. It would enable him to analyse the life and manners of the countryside up to date and that, in itself, was something.

As a result of about two hours travail, this is what finally appeared in the local newspaper that week-end:

"Sweet & Twenty Up To Date

"There is a tradition that the old playboy played the very devil with his 'da'; the new one is only gallant with the girls. Let us look at this modern Gallio.

"This is a much younger Ireland than that depicted by either Shaw or Synge in social outlook. We no longer go down to the sea in ships, but go motor-biking pillion fashion to the movies, the talkies or the steadies as the case may be.

"The Pegeens have simply become pillion girls; and betting on dogs, dancing, smoking and Sweep-ticket selling have become the amiable vices of the day. There are concertinas and cotillions in the countryside kitchen, and three-valve sets in the parlour. According to the dramatist who cannot be suffering from what GBS would call time-lag, we are evolving at a hectic rate. Soon we shall have nothing to copy from anywhere.

"The dialect now heard in the country is no more the lilting, lyrical lingo of the first Abbey plays; it is leavened with the rags and tatters of American slang with which Hollywood has besprinkled even the hillside houses and cabins. And more is the pity. Yet some of the old witchery and fascination abides. The author is not too expert in developing his plot out of the ordinary story of pastoral polemics, bickering and brawling.

"But what transpires is of little moment; we are avid of the sayings rather than the doings; we are especially concerned with the rascality of the old scamp so vividly portrayed by F Macara, for this actor is clearly to the manner born. He has the grand manner of knavery. Watch him with his head tucked owlishly to one side and a smile that won't come off in a hurry. A veritable smiling, smirking villain. He poses as the guide, philosopher and friend of all humanity, the one selfless, altruistic creature in the entire county, the common benefactor of all and sundry. Here, surely, is the very stuff of humbug in the homespun. Humbugs have ever hung from the peaks of comedy down the ages.

"All the acting of the Margadnua players who presented *The New Gossoon* in the local village this week is endowed with a clarity and vigour that are enormously convincing and refreshing. They are thrown a few sentences just as you would throw a bone to a dog and, with this slender material, they build a whole host of living characters that live in the memory. They waste no words and lose no lines. They are provided with direct, hardhitting stuff to hurl across the table and the tea things and over the lout's bike, he who is the cause of all the trouble. Talk of a tempest in a tea urn; we have it here.

"The pastoral comical is too often made to evolve from tippling, and the fumbling of the rude swain over the publican's porter bottles; Mr Shields needs no such adventitious aids to amusement. The vituperations of family strife are enough and to spare for him and the players cause them to suffice for our needs. We have the choleric uncle, the outraged father, while Delaney of the brindled hair and gushing manner is an ideal incarnation of the new gossoonery that has now infested the country like a plague of locusts. The ladies – God bless 'em – are one and all a splendid incarnation of delicious coquetry. They certainly got their message over the footlights. Such a rare and radiant array of talent has not been assembled in any part of the so-called Banner County for many years. This play is now being produced in London, by the way, under another name because the Gaelic word Gossoon, which simply means 'boy', is caviar to the general in the home of the Cockney... Lastly, you will always recognise a Thomond man anywhere, for the simple reason – that he will never sound his diphthongs."

Mr Clare, who was a keen judge, said it was the best thing in its genre that ever graced the columns of his paper, an uncanny portrayal almost of the spirit of the age and the temper of the times.

Everything was new to Marley Swanton but he entered into his new profession with great zeal and a determination to succeed at all costs. True, the paper was in a somewhat moribund state but he would soon bring about a change for the better.

Soon, he began to instil new life and vigour into it as he had foreseen and it began to win back many readers and advertisers who had gone over to the rival journal. The very worst thing that could happen a paper is the tendency to forget its existence. Better that it be burned in the public square occasionally and execrated by all and sundry than forgiven and forgotten. As an exponent of news and views, it cannot afford to hide its light beneath a bushel.

CHAPTER XIX

NOTICE TO QUIT

WHEN Paddy Quinburn sold out his little shop and ten-acre holding in Menavia on such advantageous terms, he took a fairly large private house in Thomond, not more than ten miles away, and treated himself to what he considered was a good serviceable second-hand motor car. In time, however, he found that he was only taking over another man's cast-off troubles, but he was a mere tyro as yet in such matters and as such would have to pay for his experience.

With a fine suburban house vacated by a bank manager, he also took over his housemaid, an assertive, exacting, self-willed type of girl yet withal a ceaseless worker and considerably self-sufficing. She now began to play her well-deliberated part in that liberal education which the Quinburns were henceforth to receive as suburban dwellers of note. The maid felt it her duty to carry on the unbroken traditions of the house and any time her new mistress would argue with her on the score of economy she would cite her former mistress as an example of how everything should be done. She became the norm set up to coax or compel Mrs Quinburn into a higher standard of life. Little by little, this dominating maid had her way and ere long the quondam publicans found themselves living in the lap of luxury.

There was one aspect of their new mode of life that sorely afflicted them. They resented having to buy their groceries at retail prices. Besides, as Paddy himself took a liberal dose of drink very occasionally, the satisfaction of his alcoholic needs would now cost him very much more. Then, one day, he assured Belinda Mary Anne that the buying of everything in this wasteful way was tantamount to a hole in their pockets which would have to be plugged or bunged up somehow, sooner or later.

They both missed that parade of plenitude which is such a concomitant of shopkeeping, even in a small way. Besides, Quinburn was still slightly at the sunny side of fifty while Belinda Mary Anne was at least a lustrum younger; a trifle too young yet awhile, they thought, to withdraw from the exciting battle of life. The desultory life of a rural pub still had its attractions for them. It occurred to them that they should do a bit of jobbing in shops and houses, more especially as they had made such an auspicious beginning. Was there not the example of the landless cattle jobber who buys and sells livestock at the same fair? They would have to do something or they would die of *ennui*.

They had acquired no hobbies in the country beyond a game of '45' at cards and this crude game was dispensed with in the towns in favour of Bridge and similar games. This added to their sense of loneliness, ignorance and isolation. The maid would have to teach them but then could they ever hope to become proficient at their age? They were cut off from card "parties" as a means of distraction and they would have to turn to something that they could do, especially if they could turn it to profit. This humdrum mode of life was not to their mind. Learning to play any sort of a game now at their time of life would, they felt, reveal to the onlookers their starved and poverty-stricken youth. So much idleness so suddenly sprung upon a pair who used at one time to work from sunny morning till dewy eve was not at all to their liking just now.

In their Ford car, they used to drive through Menavia a few times a week, but not as far as their former pub which was located in a land's end of a place. They would love to alight there, go in and stand a round of drink to their old customers at whose expense they had become enriched, but they were rather afraid of the consequences. A chat now and again with their old cronies would be so pleasant and they could extract a lot of comfort from it in many ways but, then, their successor was a choleric manner of man and he might possibly turn upon them and call them a pack of robbers or worse. Still, they continued to pine for the kind of news that they had been so accustomed to hearing for years and years.

Although they had gained much by their outwitting of the gasconading, prosy Yankee, still they felt that they had lost something. There was a lacuna in their lives; nostalgia in its worst form was upon them; would it pass in time? Menavia, with all its shortcomings, had cast a spell upon them greater than they could ever suspect or desire.

Their fear of a face-to-face meeting with the returned American was well-founded. It did not take him very long to discover that he had been fooled and he was very crestfallen for a variety of reasons. He had thrown away most of his hard-won life's earnings as a bar tender in America before the advent of pussyfootism; and now this business since he took it over had further decayed. That big, bluff manner of speech, so naturally expected of and even becoming to Yankees, had already left him, and even Blanche interpreted this as a certain sign that Paddy Quinburn had plumbed his pockets. It galled him to the quick as a much-travelled man of business to be fooled by a mere clodhopper who, as he himself put it, had "never been a perch from a pigstye".

Paddy felt that he had seen enough of the man he had so cleverly plucked. When an Irishman spends a number of years abroad where every man is free to pull a gun on you, he is an unknown quantity. Yes, the Yankee should be eschewed at all costs. It would be surely inviting trouble to return to the scene of their former labours and final fiscal triumph.

They extracted, however, a large measure of pleasure from touring about Menavia and skirting the pub at a fast pace in their new role as people of independent means. Even a Ford car was more than most people in that parish could acquire without stinting themselves unduly in other directions. If they hadn't their pedigree and their pretentions, at least they had more pelf and pleasure, some of the things that derive from the possession of a substantial bank balance. Who, with any degree of common sense, would give a fig for the faded glories of yesterday? It is not what one was but what he is that really matters in the prosaic practical life of to-day. In any case, all this pretention to past greatness was simply an attempt to live in the reflected glory of others. The borrowed plumes of all these people was really sickening. They could never understand the respect in which certain families were held and this veneration they themselves seemed to think was due, and even overdue, to them.

"A murrain on all such people," he at length ejaculated. In this way he relieved his long-pent-up feelings of resentment against them, at least for the time being.

Quinburn was already launched on a much higher and more costly scheme of living than he had ever intended, but he seemed to be hurried on, in spite of himself, little by little. Town life demanded it. Cora Stamer, the hoity-toity servant, also played her part at this stage in the orientation of the Quinburns by dolling herself out in finely laundered cap and apron at certain times of the day, compelling their admiration and awe. Then she would recite to them the routine in the houses of the well-to-do professional classes and add significantly "Sure you are as good as the best of them".

Her parents lived in the outer edge of Menavia and she knew that they had the money and, as a childless pair, could afford to maintain a decent standard of living; and, besides, it would ameliorate her own condition. She was, at this conjuncture of affairs, a big asset in their social advancement. It was more fatally easy to go forward now than to retrench and, besides, had not Mrs Quinburn fallen in for a legacy of over three thousand pounds since her arrival in the county town, thus serving to show that it never rains but it pours. In her youth, she had spent five or six years house-keeping for an uncle of hers, a small back lane publican in the poverty-stricken district of the Coombe in the city of Dublin. She never dreamt that, dead or alive, he could ever be worth even a tithe of that amount, owing to his stingy, miserable mode of life. Now she was to be suddenly enriched because of this man's avarice. This horde represented the money spent and misspent by the very poor on what they least could afford – drink.

The one-time struggling, lowly-rated publican of Menavia, openly despised by most of the farmers there, henceforth began to attract more than a little attention in his new habitat. Here, he could practically obliterate his sordid and banal past inasmuch as it was a closed book to his new acquaintances, and start afresh on a clean sheet as a man of justly-won property. There would be no longer the suffocating atmosphere of Menavia to contend against, with its crusted and outmoded forms of pride and prejudice. Yes, they both felt that they were finished with their lowly and somewhat humiliating past.

Cora Stamer had now introduced napkins for dinner and shown them how to use them. At first, Paddy was inclined to stuff his napkin under his collar but this *gaucherie* was tactfully corrected. Belinda Mary Anne was next initiated into the mysteries of napkin-folding and soon the bishop's mitre form of the art became her favourite.

There was perhaps a subtle reason for this. Already they had attracted the attention of the bishop of the diocese by reason of a subscription of ten pounds to the funds of the political party to which he adhered at the moment. A quarter of a century before that, His Lordship, in his quality of politician, declared with all the weight of his exalted position that John Redmond and his 74 followers in the British House of Commons were not alone the army but the navy of Ireland and as such stood for everything that the Irish people could ever hope to desiderate. Later, he verted over to Sinn Feinism for a while, only to desert it for a more mild form of politics. How long he would remain wedded to his latest political tenets was a matter for anxious speculation among the wily political wire pullers who flourish in Ireland as thick as blackberries in autumn. His adhesion to any cause, right or wrong, wasn't worth much but, somehow, he always contrived to be on the side of the big or winning battalions, for the nonce at least.

This subscription helped to establish Quinburn as a man of substance, in fact as a plutocrat, in a small way. On the strength of it, he was co-opted a member of the Standing Committee.

Still, he continued to feel a certain not-easily-defined lacuna in his life which his newly-acquired style of living could not supply. He was not averse from a good jorum of malted liquor at intervals of recurring frequency. His wife would not throw a drop of sherry over her shoulder either. Now, they had to buy these beverages at retail prices like the mere man in the street and the vendor's word on trust as to their quality. They had imposed upon people so ably in their time as traders that, the more an article of merchandise was now belauded, the more suspicious they became of its quality and flavour.

After some months of enforced and unaccustomed idleness buying instead of selling, window-gazing instead of window-dressing, drinking liquor instead of doctoring it, talking outside a bar counter instead of dictating behind it, Paddy's spirit was chafing and fretting to the point of exhaustion. He could stand it no longer and so it came to pass that he bought a public house and grocery business on one of the main streets for £470. He heaved a sigh of relief and felt in his true element once more.

It next occurred to the Quinburns that they could usefully attend the auction of the household effects of Colonel Claude

Gloster, who was going to live for the present in Bray where he had bought outright a new bungalow as a result of leasing the big house and lands to a wealthy poultry farmer and greyhound breeder.

The chief auctioneer in Thomond had a fine, bluff, breezy way with him and he was an excellent judge of humanity. Once he caught the eye of a potential purchaser, he took a perfectly paternal interest in him or her. His perfervid interest, while it lasted, was well calculated to magnetise the money out of your pocket, and he did not waste it on wastrels. He concentrated on Paddy and his spouse today and they felt entirely flattered and elated. It was such a welcome change from the barbed wit and veiled sarcasm of Blanche and his circle. The vendor had an arrangement with some of his friends brought from a distance that they were to puff certain things in a judicious way whenever they seemed to be in request. Before they had quite realised it, the Quinburns had bid fifty pounds for a bed that was not worth ten at most. Had they shown less eagerness and bid in a casual kind of way, they would not have elicited the attention of the puffers and the alert-brained auctioneer who saw at once that they were bed-hungry people. Besides, they took a great pride in showing off before the people of Menavia; they felt they were the cynosure of all eyes. They were not to be outbid in anything on which they had set their heart to-day; and they bought quite a lot of things for their pair of houses.

Before the bed was removed, however, it was unfortunately sat upon by a huddle of country women and badly damaged.

Peadar Blanche turned up at the sale, as usual, but he bought nothing. He came to criticise and garner material for cross-road talk and he considered that he was getting good value for his money, because he had to pay half-a-crown entrance fee which was not refunded to him as he had bought nothing. He wanted nothing, and he wanted the wherewithal even if he did. Latterly, Peadar was often merry, simply because he was melancholy. Cooley was there to cart away some things that his master expected to buy.

"Begor, but Paddy Quinburn is throwing his financial weight about today, Cooley," said he.

"I never saw the bate of it, Peadar. Never. The poor old Yank's hard-earned money will get wind today. Fifty pounds for a bally old bed that's not worth a fiver. Ill got, ill gone, as the saying is."

"Who knows by what cut-throat ways that Yank came by such a pile of money either, in a raw, rude class of country noted the world over for such strange happenings and such devious devices."

"Faith, I'm thinking that it's easier to make money betimes than to spend it wisely or well."

"Now you're talking, Tommy. It's easier to buy most things than to get a middling amount of satisfaction out of them afterwards. It's almost impossible for any ignoramus of a man who suddenly comes by a power and all of money to know how to spend it again without making an ass or a beggar of himself or both into the bargain. That fellow will scratch a beggarman's backside yet and that will be his own, if he's not mighty careful entirely. He will, so he will."

"Oh, that's only one slip and he's as cute as a rat, believe you me, taking him all round. Besides, there may be a special virtue in that bed for a childless couple, as they seem to be so far."

"Who would ever dream that such a mere clod as Paddy seemed to be till recently would sleep in such a bed of down? A great landlord's bed."

"And why not," interposed James Macara, joining the accredited tattlers of the parish. "There's only three generations from clogs to clogs, you know. The father lays the foundation of a fortune, the son increases the store, and the grandson scatters the pile to the four winds of Erin and then sinks back again into obscurity. That is what I would call the Great Divide because the third man divides it once more among the people from whom most of it was unjustly wrested for the most part. Only for that law of division, the clutching hands of a few would own the earth."

"All the same, sir," replied Cooley to his master, "people and things should stay more put than they are. I'd rather see a man when he is up staying up and when he is down staying down, somehow or other. As between Quinburn and the old Colonel, it's just a case of castles falling and dunghills rising. I don't like to see the old stock running out of the country at all, at all. They gave more pay and an easier time to their workmen than any butt of a farmer. I hate these mushroom growths. The world is turning upside down too quickly for my taste. I sometimes wish to goodness that I was shut of it altogether. I do, so I do."

"Even where farm hands get no more wages, they prefer to work for the gentry," asserted Blanche, "because they have more company and they can talk the time away better."

"It's the gregarious spirit in man that accounts for it," said Macara. "Country men are much more oppressed with the spirit of loneliness than they will ever let on, especially if they have not a first-class education with all its resources to fall back upon. Labourers prefer to work for a rich man even when less well treated and paid. A breaking-up farmer finds it hard to get labourers if they can get labour elsewhere at less money even. The sense of loneliness of the lone labourer in the land is sometimes simply appalling."

Marley Swanton, now a more-or-less fully-fledged journalist, arid-looking debonair and light-hearted, was hailed by the speaker. "All Menavia is here at this auction today," said the latter. "I came down to render an account of this thing in the paper and I stuck a few notes in my pocket thinking that some things at least would be dirt cheap. You can sometimes save money by spending it and that's a paradox, but not here. Between Quinburn and a few whipper-snappers of strangers, nobody can get anything except at prohibitive prices. He is parading his pelf in a most vulgarian way today. I'd have got several lots of books at taking-away prices but the moment the fellow saw me bidding he butted in and snapped them up. He seems to nourish some undying grudge against me somehow. I followed a sewing machine for Miss Finola to fifteen pounds in vain. However, I got some memento of the auction for her while he was fuming over the broken bed that he bought. I should have got you to bid for me, Blanche, but it's easy to be wise afterwards."

"Delighted, I'm sure, Mr Swanton. What the heck does he want of all these bally books for? They're in your line and your perusal of them would help to brighten up the *Weekly Recorder* for us. We all hang upon its every word now since you have thrown in your lot with it. It's the improved paper, it is now indeed."

"Yes, these people have a private as well as a public house now in the town while other families have to live in lodgings. Two people filling up two houses."

"We are living in a time of great transition," said Macara, "but things will sort themselves out somehow, sometime or other. Look at the way the landlords are fading out of the picture and who would even imagine it a generation ago? Gloster was often threatened and look at the way he is being snuffed out quietly. In its passing away form, landlordism held the field for a long time, didn't it, Mr Swanton?"

"Yes, for about three centuries, ever since the time of Queen Bess and Cromwell, 'The curse of Cromwell on you' is still the favourite malison about here for whatever it is worth as a blighting expletive. 'Twas a great pity that our landlords as a class never identified themselves with the common people and their aspirations, and promoted their material interests. Had they won the hearts of their tenantry by a host of things that they could do at a trifling cost, they would never have been shot at and, later still, legislated out of existence, by a British Parliament, too. They insisted on being a haughty, exclusive and excluding caste and lived like petty kings in their big mansions."

"We are told," said Macara, "that when the Normans came here 750 years ago they became more Irish than ourselves. What prevented these landlords from doing the same, even when many of them were Irish? That is a poser, indeed, beyond any kind of a satisfactory answer."

"Oh, no. It is susceptible of ready explanation. These land-lords were, for the most part, Cromwellian soldiers of a low type, who got large tracts of land in lieu of money for their *sanglant* services in the cause of a brand new medley of religions let loose by the Reformation. The Normans were gentlemen, and they shared the religion of the people among whom they settled, but did not extirpate them. Cromwell hunted everything he saw into Connacht during his nine months stay here, and gave the rest of Ireland to his followers. That is what I would call the Great Divide. Then these landlords vied with one another in building all these mammoth mansions astride of every fertile hilltop in order to overawe the heart-broken peasantry. They contrasted so queerly with the mud hovels all around them and thus helped all the more to emphasise the poverty of the people. Some of those Georgian mansions contained a room for every week in the year. Look at Annamoe, with its forty rooms. The building of such elaborate mansions, halls and castles became a disease under the weight of which they first began to crack up because most of them were mortgaged to money lenders from one gen-eration to another. Then many of them, unable to live in style on their estates, fled abroad and thus remained aliens from first to last. By marrying foreign ladies they completed the process of remaining strangers in a strange land. They made no attempt to conciliate the people on whose vitals they lived, vampires that they were. In turn, they were robbed, as absentees, by their land and law agents. They continued to hate the common people all the time for the simple reason that we always hate those whom we wrong. Look at the fine, massive gates on the Gloster estate. Latterly, he was unwilling, but most of his class were even unable to keep them painted. Land used to be the highest form of property, but it is no longer so."

"It took a whole parish almost, to support these big mansions," said Macara, "by way of rackrents. They were heart-break houses, at first to the peasantry and at last to the landlords themselves."

"And besides, they have grown out of date in many ways. There was no architectural design about most of them, just a huddle of masonry, and less warmth or comfort. It would cost a pile of money today to have them lighted, heated and sanitated."

Just then, Colonel Gloster strode by and, without looking at the quartet or even stopping, exclaimed in his high-pitched voice: "A word with you, Macara. Be so good as to follow me straight to the library presently, please."

Macara, who proceeded to obey, after the lapse of about five minutes to show that his time was his own, nevertheless had an uneasy feeling that this duologue boded no good.

On arrival at the library he found the Colonel smoking a cigar and striding impatiently up and down. Then, fixing the farmer with his monocle, he exclaimed in clear icy tones: "No need to apologise for keeping your betters waiting here on your sweet pleasure, Macara. You have not excused yourself in graver matters than this and you are willing, I'm sure, to take the consequences. I always treated you very handsomely but there is an old saying that when the puckaun goes to the door he does not stop till he goes to the altar."

"What do you mean, Colonel?"

"I mean to tell you to clear out of that part of my estate, and the best part of it too, ninety-five acres that you had for the past forty years and dirt cheap for a mere hundred a year. I am now getting much more from the poultry farmer. You could have it forever but for your own blackguardly behaviour towards me, sir, of late."

Macara visibly wilted beneath this blow and the blood mounted to his head for a moment, but he found words to stammer out: "But wasn't I always a satisfactory tenant, eh, Colonel?"

"You ceased to be acceptable to me the day you passed me on the road. I may possibly have forgiven that colossal impudence but you got Swanton to ridicule me in the public press and turn me into a jest for the entire county. Then, to add insult to injury, you refused to sell me that mare that you drove that day, for a clear hundred pounds, double what it is worth and now I hear it is dead."

"But, sir . . ."

"But me, no more buts. You'll hear from Hunt, my solicitor, in due course. There's the door, Macara, and get thee gone out of my presence."

Before Macara could formulate a defiant challenging reply, the haughty landlord opened a door at his own end of the quadrangular room, passed through it and slammed it heavily behind him.

Macara directed his footsteps homewards, feeling like a man broken on the wheel of fortune. Then he realised that he would have only about twenty acres of poorish land to live upon henceforth and, worse than all, he would have to sink down to the level of the small struggling farmers of the parish whom he lorded it over in his own way for so long, just as the Colonel had lorded it over himself in his heyday. Then he realised the tragedy of lost status with a dull sickening pang of horror and dismay. Whatever, he asked himself, would he do? His love for the land was little less than his love for wife and child. He knew it would be idle to parley further with the red-faced, flaming Colonel; once he came to a decision he held on to it with granite-like inflexibility. His primordial sense of dignity and pride were injured beyond all possibility of repair.

CHAPTER XX

SOULS IN AFFLICTION

NEARLY four months had elapsed since the memorable auction and most traders were looking forward to Christmas, and the trade fillip that it brings, with feelings of pleasurable expectation. Marley Swanton, who had postponed his holidays all along, decided to take just a week off and drop over to London. He grudged even this short absence from the paper as he thought it might lose some of its attractiveness and appeal. The public was a capricious monster, yet he knew that he had his finger on the public pulse and that the withdrawal of his services for a week could not greatly matter. Then it occurred to him that there were certain compensations in journalism that don't extend to other forms of human endeavour. Everything that he wrote was read by a host of people and earnestly canvassed, whereas everything that the accountant or any other class of penman wrote was locked away in a ledger or the like, unseen by all but a few. The teacher, for instance, was seldom thanked and more liable to be heartily hated by his recalcitrant pupils for his efforts to instill some small measure of learning into their passive but mostly resistive minds.

Taking stock of his monetary position, he found that he had some money invested in English industries, and he would now try to sell them and realise some ready money for investment in the paper. Latterly he felt more drawn towards Finola than ever but in the event of an alliance with her in the near future he would want a few hundred pounds to set up house and furnish it. The present he had bought for her at the auction had been highly appreciated and that, in itself, was something in his favour. Then he reasoned that the sad reverse the Macaras had recently sustained at the hands of Colonel Gloster would have a long overdue chastening effect, enough to entertain a proposal of marriage from him in respect of their only daughter. It was a case now or never of taking the rebounding ball on the hop. Of course, the Macaras were an egregiously proud people, but their recent setback should make them more amenable to reason.

As regards the *Weekly Recorder*, he had introduced several new features of late and they seemed to be what the people wanted, judging by the accretion of sales. The machinery, however, was very old and a new lino was badly wanted. When he would realise his investments he would make a concrete proposal to Mr Clare and the investment of some money would give him a stake in the place. He knew that he had long since made himself almost indispensable in the place and now was the time to enter into a deed of partnership with his boss. He would, he felt sure, welcome such an arrangement for the money that it would bring to him.

Then, he hurried over to London and succeeded in realising nearly twelve hundred pounds on his investments, more than enough for his needs. His trip to the sister isle opened up, as he expected and hoped, fresh avenues of thought and speculation which he could turn to good account for the benefit of his readers. He would marshal an array of reasons against the possibility of benefit that would accrue to Ireland, should she ever become a highly industrialised and peopled country. The Shannon Scheme had done little towards that end so far, beyond lighting up the comparative poverty of the country. Still, there was an ever-present straining after wealth and industrial endeavour and all that they connoted. The Irishman of today dreamed and debated as much about material success as any people in Europe. Wasn't he himself urging every week in his paper the clamant need of cement works and bacon factory for the county town. All his incessant talk and clap-trap about factory revival would ultimately issue in some big ventures. Of that, he had no doubt. And then? Big-scale industry and factory life would surely bring in their train all the vices and moral soilure peculiar to such a hectic and crowded mode of life. Ireland had already shown that she would be no exception to the rest of the world. A little more sunshine, factory life and plentitude of money due to it, and Ireland would exhibit daring passional proclivities held in leash just now. Factory life would not be all gain, and every light casts its shadow. Besides, the country would really go sport mad, and it was bad enough already. Excessive love of sport and all that it implied was an oblique form of irreligion.

England, he found, contains above one person to the acre and, on the same basis, Ireland should now have not four-and-a-half millions of people, but about twenty-two. Why, the mere thought of such a crush of people in this lone island appalled him, yet God would provide for them all. Why? Because in the Middle Ages when Europe contained only about twelve millions of people cattle weighed only about two cwt as against five times that weight today. Corn fields now yielded ten times better crops, due to improved methods of cultivation. Yes, it was flying in the face of God to assume that even a doubled population would exhaust the food resources of the earth. It wouldn't. The supply of food would grow automatically with the need for it, the same as manna was rained down to the people in the desert. Yet, what a sardined country England was. Ireland because of her empty spaces, he thought, would be in some danger of a friendly invasion from the densely-peopled nearby isle. Job-seeking young men would flood the labour markets; then the loneliness that has been so pervasive of the countryside from time immemorial would disappear. The country would lose most of its charm and witchery. The large, grass farms would be legislated out of existence and a century hence a fifty-acre farm would be considered the limit. That would be still another aspect of the great Divide. At present, the broad-acred farmer preferred to reserve it for one son, educate the others and send them into the towns and cities. There is an element of pride in this policy; he wants to remain a territorial magnate like Macara, Linnane and the rest of them. The old tribal system under which the farm was divided anew among all his sons accounts for the tiny dry-walled fields that dot the country and make the use of tractors impracticable for farm work. Gone were the days when it was thought well to wall in an acre of land. Our remote ancestors built high walls up along mountain-side and did a lot in the way of hedging and ditching that would never be attempted nowadays. Life, he felt, was largely a food snaring expedition and that was what caused all the wars and invasions in the past. Then the poet and historian came along and flung a halo of romance and high-souled chivalry over the whole sordid blood-letting business and every generation grew up thinking that war was a glorious thing.

Yes, Marley Swanton was returning from London in great good humour; he would make the paper hum with what he had seen and felt. He was the sight-seer, thought provider, and prophet for the amorphous more-or-less heedless unthinking public. His life in the paper so far had been a glorious adventure and still fraught with undreamt-of possibilities. Until recently he was teaching only a score or two of the undeveloped minds of a parish; now he was moulding the adult thought of an entire far-flung county along sane, healthy, orthodox lines. So far, he had been given a free hand in the development of the paper and he had not betrayed his trust. True, his salary was only five guineas a week, but that would improve with the progress of the paper. His patience and perseverance had filled the despairing staff with new life and hope for the future; working so earnestly night and day as he did, he had made things hum.

He arrived home in a state of great, yet well-masked,

elation. He was met at the railway station half-a-mile from the town by the junior reporter, who acted also as accountant in his spare time. He thought he presented a very doleful, crestfallen appearance and he resolved to buy him a present when he got to town. It was so good of him to come to meet him.

Then he was told there were strange happenings in the office all the week and still stranger rumours about the town. The gist of his information, conveyed with a gloom that clings like a sea mist, was that Quinburn, the new publican and grocer, who lived only half-a-dozen doors away, had been into the office several times during the week. Asked if he were sure of his man, he described him as a medium-sized, middle-aged, red-faced, sturdily-built, square-headed, gruff-voiced man. That was Paddy, to be sure. He was, he said, companioned by Father Hamill twice. The first time they were closeted with the boss for half a day, at the end of which he showed them the machinery during the absence of the printers at dinner.

Father Hamill he knew well under a heavy, ever-smiling, highly-coloured visage and rotund exterior. He had the name of being a deft political wirepuller and sound man of business. He had taken a keen interest in Quinburn since his fat subscription to the political league to which he adhered. Now he would shepherd him into another form of endeavour. Brains needed bullion if the best results were to be obtained, and Paddy had the money to which His Reverence would unite the mentality. His sunny manner and close connection with sport and athletics also made him a force to be reckoned with.

Dame Rumour had it that the publican had been induced to buy the *Recorder* and run it as a narrow party organ, being assured of much support from certain advertising shopkeepers.

" 'Tis all over the blinking town anyway," continued Marley Swanton's informant, "and what is more, it is believed. The price he paid for it is said to be £2,000, half the money down and the remainder spread over a period of three years at a low rate of interest."

"That is very precise information to be bruited about," said Swanton, "too much so to be merely rumourous."

"I may tell you, but that is strictly *entre nous,* that the statistical part of my information is straight from the stable, because the boss's tall hairpin of a slavey who told me, and who knows everything, had her ear to the keyhole, as usual. Our new boss is said to have lashings and leavings of money. He'll be the hell of a change from the old boss, a Protestant and perfect gentleman to his finger tips. I told the printer's devil and he said he'd join the police force only that they are fed up with recruits now."

"Yes, the police force is the cure for many young men's ills at present. Of course, Quinburn knows nothing about the business but precisely for that reason he'll be all the more difficult to deal with. I never take a holiday but it is taken out of me in the double soon after. There seems to be no pleasure without pain. I must give up this trouble-bringing practice of holidays. I'd prefer anybody to this purse-proud upstart publican as a boss, because I happen to know more than a little about his antecedents. When he finds his sea legs. . ."

". . . there will be wigs on the green," added the junior reporter.

"Well, that's a fine type of a mixed metaphor, yet your meaning is clear enough. This man is evolving at a rapid rate. I first knew him as a purely parochial publican and now he is straddling across the whole town, or will, before long. He has the money and he is being run by the right crowd in whose hands he will be putty for some little time yet. He is a head-strong, pig-headed man and he will kick over the traces but not for the present. I wonder is he travelling too fast?"

"Devil a bit, by all accounts. He is moving into Mr Clare's

house as soon as he spends a few hundred pounds on repair, and a fine house it is."

"Then he'll be eternally on tap on the premises."

It was now well advanced in the afternoon and as Marley Swanton's holidays would not wane to a close until that night he decided to give the office a wide berth as long as possible in view of the disturbing news. He suddenly conceived a kind of loathing for it and he felt dismayed at the prospect of the publican as his master.

They had never liked each other.

He decided that he would crowd all the movement and thrill that he could into the few free hours that remained to him. Whenever he felt perplexed he would always go for a long walk; he was a born hiker, even before hiking became fashionable. As he entered his rather shabby-looking lodgings in a narrow, decayed back street, he perceived that the kind-hearted but prosy old landlady was simply consumed with curiosity; but he would give her no conversational openings. He intimated that he was going into the country soon again and that time was of the essence of the matter. She retired in order to fry a chop and prepare a small pot of tea for him and he breathed a sigh of relief. So sympathetic, yet so boring and inquisitive at all times, but he was in no mood for that kind of attention just now. He paid thirty shillings a week for his lodgings, and could do better elsewhere, but he knew that she needed the money.

He would like to walk to Rahora, over ten miles away, but he was pressed for time so he mounted his bicycle and set out, covering the distance in an hour.

He found the Macara family in a much more forlorn mood than he had expected. So, far from recovering from their reverse, they seemed to be brooding and moping more than ever under the stress of it. Still they were heartily glad to see him, gladder than they had ever been before. His own carking cares slipped away from him in the presence of greater grief, the great deprivation that gnawed at their hearts day and night. He had always perceived that there was an indefinable something about this family that attracted him and he felt more than ever drawn towards it today because of the great affliction beneath which they were visibly wilting. He entered the big house through the kitchen so that his visit would seem more casual, friendly, informal. Finola was making an apple cake and, despite her anguish or perhaps because of it, she looked more wistful, dreamy and pretty than ever. His heart yearned towards her. He silently noted that she was a true type of blonde and the nature of the work she was now engaged in seemed so becoming to her. How frail, fresh, feminine and clean she looked. Any he-man's fancy.

Her mother was pottering about in the fussy, futile way of worldly old women. As it was supper time, he noted the absence of Tommy Cooley and the maid of all work, servants who had become such a fixture in the place, and was told that they had gone to service with the poultry farmer to whom the Colonel had let his estate as a tenant at will for the present.

"We have no use for servants any more, alanna," said the vanithee, dolefully. "We'll soon be too poor to be our own servants. Twenty acres of poorish land wouldn't pay much wages. We have had a big topple down in the world since you used to stay with us. Oh, wirrasthrue."

"Gloster's dying kick has put the kybosh on us," added her husband. "It's the broken destroyed people we are this day, but sure welcome be the will of God, if it be his will, avickyo. God permits misfortunes to fall upon the erring which he would ward off if they had not departed in some way from the path of rectitude. Between Gloster's sense of outraged pride and our own foolish challenge to his pair of nags on the road that day and still more unfortunate victory, we are paying the price in poverty this day. If we only had had the good luck to sell him the mare itself afterwards when he offered a good price for her, all might be well, and now it is dead."

"I always heard," said Swanton, "that it is most unlucky to refuse a good price for anything. Then something nearly always happens to it."

"Yes, it was in a lather of sweat the other morning when I went out to see it, like as if somebody had been riding it all the night. That poor mare must have been taken by the fairies I suppose. They only take the best."

"We must thank you all the same, Mr Swanton," said the vanithee, "for coming to see us in our double trouble. We are left pretty much alone in the world since this blow fell on us. I used to hear my poor father, God rest him, talking of fair weather friends but, faith, now I know what he meant. I now know all about the loneliness of the poor. We thank you from the bottom of our hearts for your thoughtfulness towards us this day, sir."

"Not at all, ma'am, not all. I am more concerned about your welfare now than ever, and why not. Besides, your temporary reverse gives me a chance to make a few proposals that would be otherwise out of the question."

"And what would they be now?"

"Later on, madam, later on. We have all our own peculiar type of skeleton in the cupboard and we try to keep it hidden away."

"And why reserve such a fine piece of furniture for such a plaguey thing as a skeleton anyway?" queried Finola. "Wouldn't the dunghill be the proper place for such a grisly thing?"

"Oh, don't be silly," rebuked her mother, irritably.

"Don't suppress originality of thought, ma'am," protested Swanton. "It's a devilishly clever question to pose and one that I shall consign to the tables of my memory for all time." Then he shot a glance of admiration at Finola which, he was glad to know, was returned with interest.

"Yes, she often punctuates our deepening spirit of gloom of late with her puckish flashes of drollery," said her father.

"The very time to laugh away your troubles, sir," pleaded Swanton. "If some people had no trouble, that is to say, no family skeleton, they'd soon manufacture one."

"As I was saying," pursued the vanithee like a lady luxuriating in the narration of her troubles, "we are now only wee craggy farmers since that stony-hearted villain ruined us – but we'll leave him to God. Many is the cut and rebuff we have got since we came down in the world. 'Tis a terrible thing to be poor."

"Not if you were never rich or, at least, in a biggish way of business," corrected her husband.

"I wouldn't mind our fall so much," said Finola, "only that small farmers who used to address father as Mr Macara now call him James and soon it will be Jim and even the still more familiar Shamus. The labouring element have dropped the word 'sir' when answering him. It seems so trifling in a way but really it is the most galling part of it all. It brings our downfall home to us more vividly than anything else. Such rude and calculated familiarity on the part of the common people. It is really shocking."

Then she applied the corner of her check apron to her tear-dimmed eyes, an action which wrung the hearts of her hearers, especially her lover who had not seen a woman in tears for years.

"Father is keeping out of the way of being insulted by these rude yokels from now on," she added.

"Hadn't that codraulin' old beer-swiller, Peadar Blanche, the cheek to propose to our poor girl the other night," whined her mother. "This old lout of a mason, and next to no education or breeding on him. Indeed then, I could stick him for it and when the outrage came to my ears I told him never to darken the door again. We may have lost most of our property, our pride or our pedigree or sight of that sense of respect that is due to us even still."

"You cannot imagine what the new poor have to put up with, Mr Swanton," added Finola. "I hate this place now and I will go away from it as soon as I can"

"Come with me, Miss Macara," he blurted out on the spur of the moment. "All I have is yours and your parents, if you will become Mrs Swanton."

The intimation about Blanche had given him the courage to say what he had been yearning to express for a long time, and yet he feared a rebuff.

"That is what I miss too, lately," she continued, "the prefix Miss to my name and I appreciate your way of putting it."

"Sure you won't be wanting it any longer if you will honour me by saying yes. I won't take no for an answer now that I have gone so far."

Then turning to her parents, he said in a voice filled with emotion: "Your difficulty, much as I deplore it, is so-to-speak my opportunity. Otherwise perhaps I wouldn't have the spunk to speak to you so soon on a subject that has been nearest to my heart for years. As a member of your highly-respected, in fact I may say blue-blooded family, I could do much to build up your broken fortunes. I could let you have a thousand pounds here and now to help to restore what you have lost. This help is contingent upon one short word from yourselves and that is the word 'yes' in respect of my proposal to the hand of your beloved daughter."

"You overwhelm us with kindness, sir," said Macara. "Really we didn't think there was so much goodness left in the world. My answer is in the affirmative, speaking for myself at all events."

"But you know, James, that Finola isn't yet twenty and she

doesn't yet know her own mind," objected her mother. "And besides . . ."

"Faith she wasn't too young to outrace old Gloster and bring all this poverty upon us. She raced us all to ruin that day and I knew that harm would come of it. You weren't too young yourself to marry me at the age of nineteen, and my own mother was married still younger. The devil a bit, whatever, but you're the funny old woman,"

"But you boasted of what she did, you know, James, at the time, and apparently egged her on to it, and now you have another tune. Are you forgetting Murty Linnane now James, up at the National University. He's a boy of her own age and you know that they correspond. He'll be a doctor for certain in next to no time. Finola will know her own mind by then and, besides, he will be more to her mind. What Mr Swanton wants would be the mating of Spring with Summer."

"They used to correspond before we came down in the world, but not now, as far as I can see. Beggars like us can't be choosers. What a fool old Linnane is to let his brilliant young son, worth a thousand pounds fortune, marry a decayed farmer's daughter with nothing except what she stands up in. Bare as a hand stick. Put that out of your old foolish head, once and for all. You were always a proud beldame but there is a stop to your gallop now."

"We can shake hands on the pride part of it, I think at any rate, James, if you ask me."

"Here is the best of good fortune knocking at our door in our hour of dire need and you would like to spurn it away, you would. There is a reason for everything and it is no wonder at all that the Macara family are tumbling down in the world. For the love of Mike, put your filthy pride in your pocket before we are all in the County Home. Stop your castle-building on the sands of your imagination. I always had a kind of a rough and ready liking for the ex-teacher here. He never let himself down in any way or at any time worshipped at the shrine of Bacchus. That tripe hound Quinburn always hated him and his hatred is about the best testimonial that a man could possibly have. It is a veritable Prince Charming we expect should step out of the lying pages of romance to wed the daughter of a pair of paupers?"

"Thank you ever so much sir," replied Swanton. "I knew that I always had one friend in the family, at all events."

"Now that you talk about pride and vanity, James," said his spouse, determined to have the last word, "it is only since our downfall that humility has overtaken you. We are all tarred with the brush of pride."

"A tincture of family pride is no harm at all," palliated Swanton. "It keeps one's courage up and saves them from sinking into low and unworthy company. People with mere pelf would exchange a lot of it for a bit of pedigree and people with pedigree, as a rule, are destitute of pelf. Fortune never comes with both hands full. It's the way you carried yourselves that always caused me to admire you above any family in the parish, although my attention was often invited elsewhere."

"Put it there, young man," said Macara, extending his hand towards him, "and I'll shake it myself. You can rely upon me to do my little for you in the matter of your emotions, but the acceptance of any money from you is out of the question at present.

"And now, Sephora, said he, turning to his wife, "we will adjourn to the parlour with our joint son-in-law-to-be for a taiskawn of tea. Women will be women, Mr Swanton, women will be women."

"And men will be old fools," called out his wife as he was passing into the parlour. "See the way he let the cat out of the bag with regard to young Linnane. You want a bit of rivalry in those things, and he has made away with it."

CHAPTER XXI

MR CLARE'S SWAN SONG

OVER the tea things, Macara told his guest that in addition to the mare, he had also lost four well-conditioned cattle and a few calves during the past few months. Black quarter and murrain had levied a heavy toll. When he withdrew the live-stock from the lands he had forfeited, he had to put them in grass elsewhere and the change did not agree with them. Then, to make matters still worse, he had to sell off a number of stores at the wrong time at a big discount. "It never rains but it pours," said he, meaning that misfortunes never come singly.

Then Sephora ruefully reminded him that he should not be broadcasting their troubles in this reckless fashion, that it did no good. He countered by stating that it took the load of grief off his heart to talk about it and in any case it was time to look upon their guest as a member of the family. "Our spinsterish daughter and our crusted bachelor will have to come to some kind of an understanding sooner or later," said he. "Losses at my time of life affect a man's nerves and really terrorise him much more than any form of physical violence. I haven't the resilience to stand up to that kind of thing any longer."

Tea over, Swanton said he should be getting back to town and, as he was shaking hands with Finola who looked coy and sphinx-like as ever, her father said to her: "I hope you will come to no decision regarding your future without the approval of your da."

"Obedience is said to be better than sacrifice, sire," she replied demurely.

On his return journey, Swanton passed the evening's events in review and felt tolerably satisfied with the result. He likened his growing friendship with Macara to that between David and

Jonathan and the Biblical phrase sprang to his lips: "Nothing can be compared to the faithful friend and no weight of gold or silver is able to countervail the goodness of his fidelity."

Despite her reverse of fortune, he felt that Mrs Macara was still a vain type of woman and nursed strange illusions. He would have to reckon with her active opposition in the winning of her 'correctly cold and regularly slow' daughter. The chronic tenacious pride of this family caused him to exclaim almost aloud between the handlebars of his bike: "Humiliation followeth the proud, and glory shall uphold the humble of spirit".

Still, he was rather puzzled by Finola's somewhat negative demeanour during the evening. What an adornment she would be in any home, he reflected, and how trusting and confiding she could be where her love was engaged. In the light of recent events, her mother's hostility to him would be a weakening force.

He resumed work in the *Weekly Recorder* the following morning with a heavy, apprehensive heart, at ten o'clock. He suffered from a feeling of deprivation and impending disaster. If it had been anybody else had bought the paper but the pugnacious publican with whose life history he was alas only too familiar to hope for a happy time henceforth, all would be well, he thought.

A letter lay on his desk and a glance at the superscription told him that it was from his former employer, while the postmark showed that it had been posted three days previously from Salthill. Proceeding to open it, he noticed that it showed signs of having been opened before. There was a certain amount of soilure about the flap and it came away easily. Who, he wondered, was the culprit?

The letter ran:- "My dear Sir, - You will be surprised to know that I have parted with my interest in the second oldest newspaper in Ireland but where needs must, the devil drives. My life love now goes to a mere grocer who will, I daresay, run it as an appendage to his pigs and porter. Therein he can display his prices gratis. Our thought-freighted paper will now be run as the creature of a certain blundering political camarilla with an outlook on everything as narrow as a razor edge. Its crusading aspect will be forgotten and it will be run on shop-till lines. I was rushed into this sale and now when the deal is closed a host of big traders such as the MacMahons, Roughans, Duggans and Tierneys tell me that they would have rushed to my rescue had they known that it was a case of financial stringency. My action looks like a great betrayal but it is easy to be wise after the event. I did my best to invest a few hundred in the paper on your behalf but the purchaser would not hear of it. It would have given you a stake in the place. I feel like Oisin after the Fenians, just now. It's a terrible thing to feel that you have out-lived your utility, as my deracinated self has done. At such a distance as this from the scene of my first and last love, I hope to be able to forget all the more readily.

"As the friends of your youth daily drop into their graves or the emigrant ship, you become by way of solace more wrapped up in your work for the sake of company, as you make no new friends after a certain age. When that remaining solace of lethean work is torn away from you, then you have no more to live for and you pass from time into eternity.

"The abolition of a score of corporate bodies in this county, by the poachers now turned gamekeepers and doing duty as a Government and centralising every blessed thing in Dublin where all the playboys themselves live, has deprived county papers of most of their advertising revenue. Under you and me the *Recorder* was wedded to principle and probity but from now onwards it will surely exhibit all the buffoonish qualities of the quick-change artist.

"I trust, however, that you will try for the sake of your job to trim your sails to every strange and capricious wind of doctrine. Henceforth, it will be the kept mistress of a lost and lost-souled party, steaming for nowhere and getting there."

When the absorbed reader regarded about him, his new master, who had entered unheard because of his rubber-soled shoes, was standing partly behind him. Swanton still preserved a good deal of the dominating manner of a teacher and his spirit inly revolted at the sight of his new boss standing so ominously and silently near him. However, he contrived to jerk out a "Good morning to you".

"The same to you," replied Quinburn. It was ever so slight a variation on "the same again" so fondly heard by publicans.

Swanton, so as not to appear idle, reached out for some writing materials but he felt in a state of unspoken, unacted revolt at the cruel blow of fate. Quinburn continued to glower upon him.

"Look here, Swanton," he growled at last, "I am now the sole boss of this here show and nobody else owns a stick in it. I bought out old Clare and it was about time. You will carry on for the present. I'm a bit new to the business but I'm more wide awake than you think and I mean to make things hum here. The first thing that I've found in you, sir, already is a lie on your lips."

Swanton stiffened and said: "But I've only said good morning so far. It does not happen to be either wet or windy so it is by inference a good morning."

"You don't mean to tell a man of business, sir, do you, that it is still morning at half past ten o'clock. It will be midday in next to no time. You have already spent a precious half-hour of the time that rightly belongs to me poring over your private correspondence when you should be about your master's business. I will dock you for it. See here now, and don't have me to have to tell you again, that you'll be in here afore nine o'clock every other morning to see in turn that the printers at the back are in to their work at nine o'clock to the second. Every second of your time here, sir, from nine to seven, save an hour for dinner, belongs to me, do you hear and don't forget it or I'll not be forgetting to dock you on Saturday night. I'm, above all, a business man and I'll have business methods or every man jack of ye will have the sack. Understand that from the first air and it will save a whole sea of trouble, mind you. No more half-dead-and-alive ways here for the future. You see I bought this here show in the nick of time and ye should be all devilishly thankful to me."

"Why, sir?"

"Because," he thundered, "the bally show would have gone smash and ye'd be all abroad there at the street corner, polishing the Bank of Ireland with yer backsides. Wouldn't that be a nice how-do-ye-do? I have saved the counter boys from being corner boys and ye should be all very thankful to me; that is, if there is any gratitude at all left in the world nowadays."

"The paper would have been bought by others, as far as I know."

Swanton saw that a jarring note had been struck from the outset and he was determined, much against his will, to return to more friendly relations. That they should antagonise each other thus so early boded badly for both. He realised that Quinburn was now releasing a quantity of pent-up venom against him now that he was at last in a position to do so.

"I can assure you that I'll continue to work with the same will and energy as before," he added.

"You'll have to do much better than that, sir, if we are to rub along here together in double harness for any length of time. I'm a self-made man; I started from scratch and even behind it and let nobody try to stick their finger in my eye."

"Alright. Will you dry up for the present, please, as the printers are clamouring for copy and they must be attended to."

"Did you order me out, sir?"

209

"No, sir."

"Because if you did, sir, you could be taking a walk for yourself to the aforesaid bank. That will be your destination any day now, sir, if you are not very careful. It's not brat-walloping down in Menavia you are now, do you hear."

"Yes, but I want a certain amount of peace to concentrate my thoughts upon what I am doing. You can vegetate where you are if you like so long as I can get on with my work."

"Fire away then, but look here…"

Quinburn continued to stand at right angles to his manager and gaze morosely into the street through the glass-panelled door. He continued to stand and stare for nearly an hour but he remained wedded to taciturnity, however, which was all that the other man demanded. His brooding presence generated an uneasy feeling and neither Swanton nor his assistant was able to give of his best. They now knew that in future they would have to contend against a very suspicious, querulous man. They were caught in the web of fate.

During the next few weeks, tradesmen were busy renovating the house, two rooms in the ground floor of which formed the offices of the paper. Then Quinburn moved in, giving a "house warmer" to about a score of merchants and would-be advertisers, but ignoring his manager. He used the telephone to promote his grocery business. This brought him into the office a dozen times a day where his presence was an additional source of annoyance to Swanton and his two assistants. At such times he would hang about, prying into everything and generally fault-finding on one pretext or another.

Then he got a lay teacher in from the local college twice a week to brush up his knowledge of book-keeping. He got a door-way broken between the kitchen and the office; then his tutor and himself would go through the account books about twice a week at night, unknown to anybody. He did a nice grocery business at first and even attracted a number of customers from Menavia, including Peadar Blanche. He cultivated Blanche for the sake of the tidings he still desired from that parish.

On hearing that his successor, the Yank, was a custom-shrunken man, he rubbed his red, soft, fat, pudgy hands gleefully together and said: "Peadar, I'm a business man. I sucked that old lemon down there bone dry and I got out while the going was good and can you blame me? Business is business and everything is fair in love, war and business, do you know."

Quinburn did not trust anybody in the matter of money. He adopted certain devices to see if he could catch either Swanton or his clerk napping. He would give cronies of his own, including Blanche, small sums of money to go into the office in the ordinary way of business to insert small notices in the paper about one thing or another. Then he would go through the secret door of which he held the key and peruse the cash receipts book at night to ascertain if these little sums were all entered up. They invariably were, however; otherwise somebody would be ignominiously dismissed and summarily so too, and his fault told with gusto throughout the town.

In the beginning, Quinburn devoted all his attention to the commercial side of the business and Swanton found that he had to do the same. The result was that the literary side of the paper, which was what really concerned the public, began to suffer and the paper to deteriorate and lose its appeal. One penny of a mistake in the account books was enough to cause a first-class crisis lasting for days of recriminations and frayed nerves in the office. The account books, and how they should be kept, soon became an obsession with both sides. Swanton and his assistant poured over them by day and Quinburn and his tutor by night, the former fighting for their probity, the latter straining after any kind of a discrepancy that would land them in the dock.

As Quinburn became more proficient at the books, he would rush in to the office from his pub a few doors away, demand the keys of the cash boxes, count the money therein and compare it with the entries in the books.

Swanton began to grow nervous, and so did his clerk. He would count the money after a while, several times a day. Then he kept a week's salary stowed away in a corner of the press so that he could balance the books in the event of a deficiency on the spur of the moment. The lock in the press that contained the money was very defective and easily opened. Then he began to fear that Quinburn, in order to ruin him, would sneak out at night and abstract some of the money. Gradually an all-pervasive atmosphere of suspicion began to grow up and Swanton would look like a nervous wreck at times.

Then, one day in the midst of it all, Swanton ventured a day in the Margadnua district, fixing up new agents and collecting accounts and soliciting job printing orders. By good luck, he finished sooner than he had expected so he decided to pay another visit to the Macaras who lived about a league away. He felt that he was at last getting a move on with regard to his love affair. But, on the other hand, it would be more dangerous than ever to marry now because the office had become a cauldron of contending factions and he had no security of tenure. Then he remembered that he had given one hundred pounds a few years before that in respect of a daily paper that would be published from Dublin sometime or other. He had drawn no interest on his money ever since but he did not mind that as he would secure a position on the staff on the strength of his investment – perhaps. Anyway, he felt buoyed up with this hope for the time being.

He was as stiff as Quinburn was stout and this daily clash of strong wills and proud personalities would eventuate in a serious final crisis in the near future. He heartily despised Quinburn and Quinburn hated him, so there was no love lost between them. He felt that, despite all he could do, Quinburn would put him in pillory sooner or later and then he would be disgraced. It was a battle of nerves, but the publican could always select his time and the *casus belli* and besides, he could take a certain amount of drink to sustain him at the appropriate time as a shield for his nerves, while Swanton was a rechabite.

A small exclusive item of news or a longer report in the rival paper which could afford more space to everything because of its greater size was enough to set Quinburn off at a tangent. A paper printed in long primer could not hold as much as one set in brevier.

Yes, he decided that, come what would, he would go full steam ahead in his fight with Paddy and in his fight for Finola. This review of the position brought him to the Macara farmstead, such as it now was.

It was a glorious evening and the weather for the past week or so seemed to be working overtime in an attempt to make amends for an atrociously wet July. Despite the sunshine, there were evident signs that the year was on the wane; these days seemed to be lingering and loitering by the wayside, waiting on the order of their going, but not gone.

He noticed a shop sign over the lodge door which stood sentinel, as it were, to the big house. It was now functioning as a hucksters' shop and some candy and oranges adorned the little mullion-shaped window. Is there anything more incongruous than a shop in a lodge? It seemed to be an outrage on all the accepted traditions. This change, more than anything else, showed the declension of the Macaras and brought it home to his mind. Tommy Cooley, who lives there, was now working for the new poultry farmer and owed no further allegiance to the Macaras who no longer owned his habitat. Gloster even subscribed five pounds towards the idea, as he knew it would minister to the humiliation of the proud Macaras. It was a subtle touch of desecration.

Near the house, he noticed the Macara family at work on their few paternal acres. As he came nearer he found Macara, despite his advanced years, mowing corn with a scythe. A "God bless the work" broke the rhythm of the swish of the scythe. Fergus and another youth were sheaving the corn and binding it after him. The old man gladly laid aside his old-fashioned implement and subsided on a few corn sheaves.

"I fear I'm interrupting the good work," protested Swanton, "interloper that I am. It's no joke to interrupt the hook in the harvest."

"It's not as bad as all that, asthore," palliated the mower. "Besides, the women folk will be here in a moment with a cup of tea, the 'four o'clock' as we call it in the country, so that we can afford to rest a bit."

"It's rather strenuous work, mowing, isn't it, for a man of your time of life, sir?"

"Well, it is and it isn't. It's one of the few things, mind you, that I'm nearly as good at as ever. Much of the corn is lodged as a result of the recent rains so that a machine, even if we had one, would be useless. We are giving up tillage now as it would be uneconomic to keep horses and a stock of implements in such a wee farm. That's one of the drawbacks of small holdings, not enough to do in them for machinery and horses. The weather is so uncertain now that a man must watch for a fine day to lash down his bit of hay or corn as a cat would watch a mouse. And borrowing implements is out of the question as we are all mowing or mourning, cutting or cursing together. So few can use a scythe now that I had to resume the labour of my youth or lose the crop."

"I believe the use of the scythe is now a lost art in Ireland."

"In the plains, yes, but not in mountainy and craggy

places. The scythe yields a much bigger crop of hay and the grass grows faster after it. When I was a gorsoon there used to be mowing contests and a champion mower used to be looked up to like a champion boxer today. Many a man could knock an Irish acre of hay or corn a day. Mowing used to be a great art. The set of the blade to the mower will determine the width of the swathe between six and eight feet. Some fellows can mow in a kind of a way but they cannot whet or sharpen."

"It's like being able to play the fiddle if somebody else tunes it for you."

"Quite so. Excessive speed will leave uncut grass so the mower must steal along, scarce lifting his feet. If you watch the heel of the scythe, the point will take care of itself. Edge goes a long way and the born mower has his blade as sharp as a razor. Short men near the ground make better mowers and it's dogged as does it. A minute lost would not be made up in an hour."

"It's all very interesting, indeed. A farmer must be able to turn his hand to a great many things. Farming is both a science and an art combined."

"It is a great worry and disappointment combined. Some parts of a scythe wear out long before others but that is the trouble with all machinery, including the human machine itself."

"A very apt analogy indeed, sir. Men, like machinery, wear out unevenly and that is why a man with a good liver is very often killed by a bad heart. Some organs wear out twenty or thirty years before the others; it's he whose internal machinery wears out evenly who sees seventy. Various diseases lie in wait along the road of life for us and the man who just dodges consumption by a hairsbreadth is caught by cancer a bit farther on in the road, and so on and so forth. Mechanics and medical men are posed with the same problem, the one with the machine, the other with the man."

"Seemingly. There is too much chopping and changing in farming nowadays for real comfort, and prices and climate are more uncertain than ever. Rents have gone down a bit but rates have been trebled in my time. People were much happier and contented long ago and they sang merrily through their work the whole day long."

"But we are all too disposed to praise the past at the expense of the present. We throw a halo of romance over everything after the lapse of time to which it is not entitled. When I was a youngster I used to hear the old men romancing about their youth; according to them, the young fellows then growing up would never be worth a groat. One day, I took one of these old fellows unawares. I asked him were the old fellows in his young days running down the youth of their time and lauding themselves up to the skies. He said they were and that he was often called a raffish ruffian. They did the same in every generation, and what is more, I'm already inclined to do the same myself, which goes to show that I'm in the sere and yellow stage of life. It is an inevitable sign that we have finished with youth. Human nature is much the same from one generation to another and the quality of the human intellect does not change. We may seem more clever today but that is because we are the heirs of all the ages, with a tremendous deposit of knowledge that was not available to our ancestors in the dim and distant past."

"We'd be better off without the half of it," said Fergus. "We have so much knowledge now that it is beginning to cumber the earth. The barbarian Danes burned all the books they could lay hands upon for a century-and-a-half after coming to Ireland and so did away with a lot of rubbish and romance then doing duty for fact and reality. We are being suffocated under a great weight of dead learning and hoary-crusted tradition. We are all becoming fossilised in spite of ourselves and growing old long before our time. Everything that we eat, think, wear is now standardised. What we want is an end of all that has been, and a fresh start. About every two thousand years, something like that happens. There was the Deluge, which made an end of all but a few. Two thousand years later, there was the coming of Our Lord, and he killed off the worship of false gods and the bowing down to wood and stone. Seventy years hence, we will have the end of the world as we now know it."

Swanton puckered his brow and cleared his throat as a sign that he was keenly aroused, but ere he had time to give vent to his kindled feelings, Finola Macara was seen tripping lightly towards them, armed with a large hot-water jug full of tea, home-made buttered bread and some tomatoes. The company glowed with pleasure and Swanton ejaculated "'Tis an angel appears".

He noted that the food-bringer looked as demure as a violet and as fresh as a rose; he feasted his eyes on her blonde and brindled hair anew. Something like the desire of possession kindled within him but his sensuous feelings were, withal, far from being as red as sin or as crimsoned as a field of poppies.

"Mr Swanton, you here too?" she queried.

It appeared to him that she, too, was flushed with pleasure because of his presence.

"Yes, indeed," he replied. "I come without asking, like the bad weather. There is something that magnetises me to Menavia. Is there anything more ideal than an *al fresco* meal, and in such a setting as this and from such hands as yours?"

"Oh, you're a fine old word-spinner," she countered, "but sure that's your business isn't it, yarning in print for the public for a living. You must be hungry, but your name isn't in the teapot because I didn't know you were in it. How was I to know that you'd drink tea with a sheaf of corn for a chair and another for a table?"

"It's really a delectable way to dine, Miss Macara, in these all too sophisticated times. It is the very essence of the simple life, the elusive spirit of which we are forever trying to recapture."

"Oh, you'd soon tire of eating in the open if you had to do it daily in all samples of weather. Father and Fergy enjoy it in very fine weather for a change, but they pretend they don't have time to come to the house for it. You will have to come back to the house with me and then there will be two for tea and tea for two, as the song has it."

"Delighted, I'm sure."

"Yes," said Macara, "this is the most exhilarating and exciting part of farming, the saving of the haysel and the garnering of the corn crop. It appeals even to a hard-bitten old fogey like me."

"Because you are a bit of a poet and a sentimentalist, sir," said Swanton.

Then Finola suddenly sang out:

I sits with my feet in the brook
And if anyone axes me why
I hits 'em a whack of me hook
'Tis sentiment kills me, says I.

Then she turned on her father and said: "You were never cut out for a grubby worm-cutting old farmer. So mother says, and she knows. It's something in the city you should be, like Mr Swanton there."

"Yes," he concurred. "I'm beginning to think that it's a bit of a square peg in a round hole that I am this day."

"Yes and every other day, da," added his daughter.

"Look at me now in the evening of my life and only twenty mangy acres of land with me, and my forefathers owned thousands of acres hereabouts."

"Wielding a pen instead of a plough has its own vexatious drawbacks, too," said Swanton, "and besides, the farmer is the most independent man on earth."

"The most dependent man, you mean," said Macara. He

218

simply scratches a bit of ground chicken-deep, flings down a bit of seed on it and waits, cap in hand, to see what nature will do. He is simply a sneaking parasite upon the plough, the cow and the sow. What they give him over and above his own wants, he passes on to the town toiler. Civilisation is, for all that, founded on the farm, such as it is, but these lowly foundations are hidden away and the more showy things in the towns come in for all the admiration. Despite its basic importance, farming is and will ever remain the Cinderella of all the trades or professions. We hear a lot of twaddle about knocking machine guns into mowing machines. Let a general dangling his sword, and myself staggering beneath a harrow, parade together in any town in any clime at any time, and just think of the opposite feelings we would arouse in the public mind. He would be a hero and I would be a joke. It would be a harrowing sight. There is a lot of praise, but it is only from the lips out, beslavered upon the farmer, but that is the acid test. Then we had a Farmers' Party in our native parliament and it sold itself to the ruling powers for a mess of pottage did the representatives of our 70 per cent industry."

"For all that, farming is the fulcrum round which everything else turns," said Swanton.

"A worthless advantage, for all that."

"We are the most reviled, rebuked, belectured and legislated against tribe on earth," added Fergus.

"And yet you are sticking to farming after your college education," twitted Swanton.

"I'm changing my mind because I have only twenty acres to stick to now. Can you suggest what I should do out in the world? Every finger-wagging wiseacre has a fling at the farmer nowadays."

"Tiny farms such as we have now have no attraction for me, at all events. I must clear out too. I will not rusticate here much longer. We are at the parting of the ways." This was Finola's contribution to the debate.

"And then we have the awful silence of the unlaboured fields of Rahora," said Swanton.

"Nursing or millinery is more in my line," added Finola.

"I see," said Swanton. "The destiny that makes a Grafton Street mannequin by spoiling the mistress of a farm and the mother of a family. So that's your myopic outlook in life, is it?"

"But surely we cannot all remain wedded to twenty miserable acres of land simply because we were born here under much happier conditions.

"Yes, it's the virile country recruits the towns, otherwise their populations would die out in a few generations."

"Come, come, lads and lasses," said Macara, jumping to his feet having done ample justice to an edible meal. "An ounce of work is worth a ton of talk. This kind of thing will never save the corn crop. One of the most awful sights is corn lying, either uncut or unbound."

The trio then resumed their work in a vain attempt to make up for an hour-and-a-half devoted to tea and talk, which is everywhere such a concomitant of it.

Finola and Swanton gravitated towards the house where they had tea alone in the absence of Mrs Macara who had not yet returned from town where she had gone to do a little shopping.

They got on very well together, Swanton telling her that she need not worry about farms or the future if she put her trust in him. "I will provide you with the oldest and noblest profession on earth," said he, "and you will never rue the day."

He was then informed that Cora Stamer was very interested in Peadar Blanche of late and was even on visiting terms with his dour mother who never entertained anybody before. "She spends most of weekly half-holiday down here now," said Finola.

"Yes, I believe I saw her out of the corner of my eye," said he, "as I was coming along here but I don't think she saw me."

Swanton returned back to town feeling that he had made some progress in his perfervid siege of Finola's heart.

CHAPTER XXII

AN ABNORMAL SITUATION

WHILE Swanton was spending a pleasant evening in Rahora condoling with the Macara family and thinking out schemes for their amelioration, he was unaware that quite a peck of trouble was brewing for himself.

Quinburn, as an afterthought, decided that the kitchen floor required to be tiled and a new range installed, so he sent for Blanche and entrusted him with the job. Here Blanche came into close contact with Cora Stamer, the house maid, and they got on remarkably well together in a short space of time. In the course of three weeks, she served up more edible dinners and teas to him than he had ever eaten before and he began to think how nice it would be if that posture of affairs would only endure. Although this excellent cook was beginning to look a bit scraggy and faded, he greatly admired her charm of manner and managing qualities. He had often seen her before, because her parents lived not more than a mile away from Menavia, but she had aroused no amatory feelings in his breast. Here, however, was propinquity and all that it implies, and Cora was set like a jewel against her proper background.

Lest by any chance he should lose a most efficient housemaid – a remote possibility, he thought – Quinburn told her in his most casual manner in advance that Blanche would drink the Shannon dry if it contained porter. He was, he said, not alone a rake but a muckrake. Even as regards whiskey he was, he said, a two-bottle man and no purse could stand that strain in these times of dear drink.

Pottering daily about the kitchen together, she began to admire his rude strength and his hearty manner and it occurred to her that she could reform him in the fullness of time. It was a bit funny, she thought, for her master to be preaching against drink and he so fond of it himself. Besides, wasn't he squeezed out of it, so to speak? Besides, she felt that in her own case she was beginning to look a bit time-ravaged and had little time to lose if she intended to wed. Speed was of the essence of the matter and she was now ready to risk more than ever. She was not going to be intimidated by a sup of drink in a man. That would be, she thought, her last chance of a man and, as if to show that Providence itself had a hand in it, hadn't it come into the very kitchen to her. As day succeeded day, he was more to her mind than ever. Yes, all things considered, she decided that Blanche's overtures were not to be spurned at her age and, besides, he was a fine, upstanding figure of a man.

On his side, Blanche reflected that she would make a splendid successor to his poor aged mother. Well-cooked food was, after all, a great antidote to the public house.

The result of all this mutual admiration was that Cora Stamer, who had availed of her weekly half-holiday to spy out the land for herself, was returning from a visit to old Mrs Blanche when she saw Swanton cycling in the opposite direction. She casually mentioned this irrelevant fact to her mistress on her return, who retailed the fact to her husband.

Next morning when Swanton entered the office, Quinburn rushed in and asked him was he paying him to be spending half his time down with the Macaras when he should be doing his master's business?

Swanton, who was flabbergasted at this sordid display of sharpness, said he had finished his business in the village much sooner than he had either desired or expected and, as the day was far advanced, he decided to look up a few old friends. In any case, a manager was not supposed to be timed like a labourer.

"Manager, did you say?" taunted Quinburn. "Mismanager would be much more like it. I'll tot up your work-shy lapse to half a day and you'll find yourself 8/11 short in your pay sheet, sir, on Saturday night. You may just as well put your hand down into my pocket and take so much money as to do what you have done – a man like you, preaching morals in my paper every week for the public, moryah. You ought to put your own house in order first."

"On the other hand, sir, when we were working against time I often stayed in this office till nine and ten at night. One thing should balance another. It's not the loss of a few shillings that I mind if it will appease your unjust anger, but it is scurvy treatment on your part."

"Faith, I'll have a bigger crow than that to pluck with you, as you'll know before long, sir."

This kind of contention would have gone on for hours, as it so often did before over smaller issues, when a gentleman from a well-known firm of Dublin auditors announced himself. Quinburn at once escorted him into the inner office, slammed the door and remained closeted with him for an hour during which he was heard, when he raised his voice, airing numerous suspicions against the staff. Then, the door was thrown open and Swanton was told to yield up all the account books.

The auditor was a blend of formality and freeziness. His attitude was begotten of the conviction as a result of what he had heard already, that the office staff was utterly destitute of both principle and probity.

Then, Quinburn departed, feeling highly elated, and helped himself to a glass of whiskey, followed by a few cloves in order to take the smell away from his breath. He always carried cloves and arrowroot about in his pockets for this purpose.

The dignified auditor then started on the cash receipts book, running with amazing rapidity through a pile of figures and already showing a great familiarity with everything. Taking a double row of figures in his stride, he was really a puzzle and a pleasure to contemplate and Swanton stood in awe of him. After ten minutes, he announced that in respect of one week the book owed the book-keeper a sum of ten shillings and three pence.

Swanton heaved a sigh of relief and stated that the cash was handed over every Saturday night. He mistakenly thought he was short that amount and supplied the deficit out of his own pocket as he was always prepared to do in the event of a shortage.

His young, tall, pallid assistant stood by, trembling like an aspen leaf. He conjured up a vision of mistakes in the books which would be interpreted by the boss as so many acts of dishonesty. Before long they would be the talk of the town. Even the cool, calculating Swanton was not, he thought, too sure of himself; and, in any case, even the best in the world would make a slip of the pen or a whole series of them in the hurried, exciting conditions under which they were working. Quinburn would only see one meaning to it all.

The auditor continued to remain as frozen and glacial as ever and preserved that atmosphere of cold aloofness best shown by a court official to a culprit. The clerk already imagined himself in the dock.

Meanwhile, the keen, crime-expectant auditor would boom out enquiry after enquiry without troubling to raise his head or look at anybody. Both Swanton and himself were, he thought, only ciphers, too, for the time being.

At six o'clock that evening, Quinburn strode into the inner office where the auditor sat buried in books and as deeply engrossed in their contents as ever. He shot a malicious glance at Swanton, and the clerk expected revelations soon to follow of a nerve -shattering nature.

"Have you found out a lot, sir?" queried the publican. "'Twas about time to clean up the mess left by these fellows."

Then the door closed with a bang. Half-an-hour later, the

sturdy figure of Quinburn passed out but his face revealed nothing.

"That man would love to disgrace us," said Swanton to his assistant, "so long as it wouldn't cost him above a fiver or so. It would be great fun, wouldn't it, posing as a victim throughout the town of our embezzling propensities."

"Yes. Indeed. A missing tenner would be exaggerated into a thousand in no time. I can know by the faces of the people that they are on the tip-toe of expectation. Sitting in his pub like the spider in his web, he hears every tittle of gossip. A gossipy, well-doing publican can scatter news almost as fast as a moribund newspaper, such as this was before you came along."

"Oh, he has his ears to the ground and he hears every blessed thing that happens and much that doesn't. He revels in that kind of gossip that no paper could print."

"Yes, he gives big parties now and he won't give us a pebble of coal for the fire in the winter time, even when it is below freezing point."

"They are fast developing as social climbers, you know, and what they spend on them they must stint on us. Belinda Mary Anne is running after her betters, toadying to them, bowing and scraping to them and fussing over them so as to be taken onto their circle. They bow down to their betters and make a doormat of their inferiors. They're the worst class of people to deal with, because they are neither fish nor flesh."

Towards the end of his fourth and final day's labours, the auditor relaxed in manner even to the extent of asking a match from Swanton and tendering a cigarette by way of exchange and friendship.

Swanton readily interpreted that as a clean bill of character. Then he had to explain about a second-hand typewriter got on the instalment system. At first the staff were expected – and actually did for a while – pay half the instalments in respect of it. He was told that that was a very strange arrangement.

"But you don't know the awful boss that we have to deal with," he replied. "If I paid out nine pounds all at once for what he still thinks is a mere bauble, it would mean more warfare and, dear knows, it is bad enough as it is. There is a clash of tempers, tongues, temperaments almost daily as it is. It is largely a war of nerves and he stands a chance to win, and a good one, because he can always invoke the aid of drink to fight for him. After a few hours of this kind of thing, he rushes out for a swig of Dutch courage, as it is called, and returns to the fray like a lion refreshed or, if you like, like a dog to his vomit."

"Really. He doesn't look such a terrible tartar as all that now, does he?"

"The man is still developing and showing some hitherto unsuspected fearful side to his character day by day. Now the woes of a childless man are crowding upon him too, to make matters worse. There is an old Gaelic proverb to the effect that a childless couple seem to have the care of nine upon them. They have the care of ninety-nine."

"And Rachel, crying for her children, and would not be comforted because they were not."

"The situation is not normal here at all since that man got hold of this place. His financial and social elevation was too sudden. Then, there was no cultural background there either."

"Yes, I can sense strained relations certainly. The atmosphere is a bit tense. I'm glad you have emerged from this audit of mine with a plenary degree of credit because, I may tell you, I was led to believe otherwise."

"Thank you, sir. It is a very small slip, either intentional or otherwise, that would not bring disgrace upon us all. He is all out to humble us to the dust by fair means or by foul. There was a mysterious fire at the back lately after-hours, seen and put out by himself, and I know the strange culprit. Every letter that comes here must first be brought down to the shop where it is perused. My private letters, marked personal, are opened and read. Even a cablegram sent to me from New York, addressed to my lodgings and sent on here, was opened and read by him. When he comes in here, well nourished and chewing arrowroot, how am I to know whether he is normal or otherwise."

The sturdy figure of the person under discussion then strode in to the office, overhearing some of the last sentence. Here he remained with the auditor, telling Swanton that he would lock up the premises himself.

Three months later, Swanton wrote to the former newspaper proprietor, who still continued to live in Salthill, as follows:-

"My dear sir, In accordance with my promise to drop you an occasional line and thus let you know how we are all faring here, I am scratching a hurried note outside of office hours. I trust you will condone my execrable calligraphy but the typewriter is out of order and Paddy says that pens were made before clickers. He is, by the way, becoming daily more impossible and the more he is frustrated in his designs to catch us napping, the more eager he is to return to the fray. He is now suffering from a dose of swelled head. He turned fiercely on a Mr Macara lately when he came in to put in a notice about a stray sheep, just because he addressed him as Paddy. If somebody would only get a Papal title conferred upon him, then his Christian name would be more palatable. He sprung an auditor all the way from Dublin on me recently but I weathered that storm. There were a few pounds of a loss on the year's trading due to repairs and replacements and his own interfering policy, by which we cannot give the news that the public want. Progress has been held up and we are slipping back in many respects. He rushed in one evening and asked me could I do any better? In the heat of the moment I said no.

" 'This is Saturday, here is your unearned pay and you need not come back,' said he.

"I told him to forget for the moment that he was in his little pub now and that he could not do the chucker out with me in a moment as if I were a drunken man. As a professional man, I said, I was entitled to at least six months notice. That riled him and he made a grab at me, pulling a button off my overcoat. I turned in on Monday, thinking that he had spoken in bibulous haste, but he was more adamant in his facinorous frenzy than before. My solicitor then dropped a bill upon him for a year's salary and he sent for me. I sometimes feel that under the strain of it all I am losing my perspective and sense of proportion.

"Last week, I asked him to motor the reporter to Coolfin, ten miles away, to an important District Court on publication morning, promising to have the papers for that town ready at ten o'clock for him so that we would get there before the rival organ. His maid used to hand out the key of the printery to the foreman on the morning of publication at seven o'clock but she happened to be away getting married to Peadar Blanche. The foreman knocked in vain for the key for an hour-and-a-half because Paddy, who gave a party the night before, overslept himself. He was an hour late as a result in starting for his objective and in his great speed in order to make up for lost time he cannoned from a car into a cow, killing it.

"Thinking that I knew nothing about the real cause of the delay as I wasn't supposed to be too friendly with the foreman, he comes in next day like a man bereaved of his senses and bellows out much louder than the cow that he killed: "See here, you pay for that cow, £18 worth, or clear out. You were the real murderer because you broke your bally promise and kept me that hour late on the road that would have enabled me to have missed that blinking beast. Here's the blithering bill; will you pay now, will I stop it out of your salary at the rate of a pound a week or will you clear out to Hell out of my sight for good and all? Look at what your rotten promise has resulted in, you blackguard. You're not fit to manage a mousetrap.

"My tenure of this intolerable job can be only a matter of a few months at most. If it was the presidency of the country, it would not be worth it under such nerve-shattering conditions. They are both in the doldrums about the loss of their maid, the girl who bestowed upon them a liberal education.

"We miss your genial and gentlemanly presence more than ever, and no wonder, when we contrast you with the type of human shoddy that has replaced you, alas and alackaday."

CHAPTER XXIII

A DOUBLE DISAPPOINTMENT

THE Macaras continued to wilt and wither and shed their courage under their reverse of fortune. Ever land-hungry people, they luxuriated in a big spread of it more for the prestige than the profit that it elicited. Given a choice, they would rather be extensive, semi-solvent farmers – what they had been, in fact, in their heyday – than small, solvent, even wealthy farmers as, in a way, they were at present. When they lost the Gloster lands, they had to sell off a number of cattle at a discount and the money thus realised enabled them to liquidate most of their debts.

Following the recent crash, their younger son, Wilfred, was adopted by his childless uncle, so that Fergus was now the only male claimant to their twenty-acre farm. He had become morose and somewhat silent of late; he no longer took rank with the first-class farmers' sons in the district, he felt that he was being ostracised by them. On the other hand, the sons of the smaller-acres men rallied around him and began to treat him with a hail-fellow-well-met sort of familiarity which he chafed under silently. He was resolved to get away from all that, but where to? He felt *déclassé*.

The twenty acres that remained to them was the worst of the land, too, and it exacted constant attention in the way of manuring and draining; it was arable rather than pasture land. As small farmers, they were not expected to pay any wages except for a week or two in the harvest time. For that reason, the small farmer has to be a sort of jack-of-all-trades as he has to do everything for himself in the absence of paid labour. James Macara was now disabled by years from adapting himself successfully to these altered conditions, and his son from the lack of them. Besides, Fergus had had a fairly good school and college education which, he thought, he might be able to turn to account as a way of escape from the cramping conditions with which he was now confronted. Living in such a big house with such a small parcel of land to sustain it, he compared to the condition of a man whose barn is bigger than his corn haggard.

His father, too, began recently to feel that he was becoming physically used up; the recent mowing had taken quite a lot out of him. A hard-working man all his life, he was now sinking beneath the fardel of his years. He had been advised that soon he could resign the land to his children and seek the old-age pension, but his proud spirit revolted from the idea, stating that it was a form of bribery and boodle of which a Macara would never be guilty.

On hearing of his son's resolve to quit the hand, he said that too much education only unfitted a farmer for his work, distracted him and filled him with yearnings that he could not hope to satisfy. So long as a farmer could read the market prices in the newspaper and reckon the price of a few stone of oats, that was about all he needed. He now asked himself why did he not think of that in time in respect of Fergus. Instead, he had supplied him with wings with which to fly away, although not very high. Yes, that was yet another form that his pride took at the time, hydra-headed monster that it is. Again, he reacted to that idea. It was, he thought, alright to love the voiceless, inarticulate music of oxen if one had a big farm, and his own little patch was not much of a magnet for anybody just now. Then he reflected on the non-industrial state of the country and concluded that it would be ever thus. Ireland, destitute of either coal fields or gold fields, would never have many factories to blow dingy desolation in the form of smoke like the sister isle.

In the midst of these meditations by the kitchen fireside, Fergus and Marley Swanton burst in upon him. It was Sunday afternoon and the latter could not be penalised for being absent from the office on that day. Quinburn now watched his every action with grave suspicion and drew fantastic conclusions from it. The result was that the thoughts that Swanton should be devoting to paper were withdrawn inwards and fixed upon himself. The animus between them had narrowed the issue down to that, and the paper was losing its attractiveness and appeal. Self-preservation is the first law of nature. The most trifling thing nowadays was enough to cause a rumpus and keep Quinburn stamping and rampaging around the office for hours at a time.

Recently, he complained that his managing editor was overpaid and threatened to reduce his salary by a pound a week. Swanton retorted that he was only getting the pay of a policeman and that Quinburn himself was getting three and even four times more for his beer and spirits than formerly. Swanton was glad to get away from this kind of nagging and whining for one day in the week.

After being shown into the parlour, Swanton told Mr and Mrs Macara that Fergus had been talking to him about entering an agricultural college for a year at the end of which he would be eligible for a post in a creamery. When a salaried man dies, everything dies with him, but a farmer cannot take the land with him; all that he wants of it is six feet by three. Everything was the product of labour but the land, which was eternal.

"I don't see much in your point of view," said Macara. "Labour, as such, creates nothing either. Seeding the ground for a crop of oats or potatoes is not creation; neither is creation the feeding of a piglet till it grows into a fat pig. Labour never created anything; it only modifies the material upon which it works and which nature so lavishly provides. Land, as such, is the material upon which the farmer works and on which he expends his labour, but it is not its product."

"Yes, sir, but you forget that in farming the forces of nature labour in the fields side by side with the farmer, as it so clearly declines to do for anybody else. He just scrapes the surface of the soil, throws down a few fistfuls of seed on it and bountiful nature multiplies it fifty-fold. If I write an article in the *Weekly Recorder*, will any good fairy come along and increase it even five-fold for me? The aid given to the farmer by nature cannot be less than half of what he supplies himself. If a tailor cuts out a suit of clothes, will the forces of nature sew it together for him? Talk about our fairy godmother, she exists only for the farmer, and Fergus should remember that before he so recklessly runs away from the boons and blessings of mother nature. Land is still the supreme form of property and those who have it should stick to it like a limpet to a rock."

"Well, it didn't stick to me, sir," retorted Fergus hotly, "except twenty acres of bad stuff that's not worth bothering about. In any case, land is only raw material upon which a fellow has to expend every ounce of his sweat in order to extract any kind of a living. I'll get away from here anyway, even if I have to work my passage to America."

"Yes," supplemented his father, "and what man supplies to the land, such as buildings, drainage, manure and so on, has only a strictly limited life. I did work on the land that would not be recouped to me for the next ten successive years. There are too many grand ranches and bullocks in this parish and too few small farms and children. That's what closed the school."

"Even the blessed grass grows and the bullocks fatten while the farmer is sleeping. Does anything multiply in my line of business while I am sleeping? That is a great argument in favour of farming. Besides, Fergus cannot emigrate now, because America has ceased to be the home of opportunity and the movement of our exiles is homeward. During the Great War years, our young men were compelled to remain at home as they grew into manhood, and these young hot-heads caused two wars in this country. The same is happening once again and we may look out for squalls very soon. A large body of young and fairly well-educated men at a loose end because of unemployment is a certain menace to the peace of the country. The Government is now trying to turn the thoughts of our youth away from war and towards a manner of sport so that they will not embarrass them unduly. If the population continues to grow, the big ranches hereabouts will have to be broken up and Fergus will get his share of what is going."

"Oh, that is a live-horse-and-you'll-get-grass sort of argument," said Fergus and it does not appeal to me in the least. What you say will inevitably happen, but I will be growing grass myself by that time, as a corpse."

Ireland is, in some respects, living way back in the early ages of tribalism almost. The five stages of evolution are hunting, pastoral, agricultural, manufacturing and commercial. Ireland is still 75 per cent agricultural and fifty per cent pastoral, stages that have been left behind by all progressive countries such as England, France and Germany centuries ago. We are still way back in the Middle Ages in Ireland, and that's that."

"As for ourselves," said his father, "we may now have just enough to keep us from becoming wage earners but too little to be able to pay wages, as of yore."

"And worse than all, we have lost our social milieu," added Fergus.

"Then, why not stay at home and head up a great divide-the-land movement and recover some of your Gloster property?" asked Swanton.

"That would be politics," said Macara, "and politics are the curse of the country. Look at what happened during the past decade or two. All our young men were ardent, orating, altruistic, walk-over-my-dead-body style of patriots. Then, they suddenly sobered up at twenty-five or so, settled down, took wives and all the jobs and property that they could lay hands on unto themselves. It's guns and young men these fellows fear today and want out of the country, for fear of trouble. 'Tis the old, old story. Save me from the ranting Irish patriot of twenty. Politics and patriotism are the greatest nest-feathering industries in Ireland to-day. In the name of God, Fergus, go anywhere, do anything but don't engage in the dirty low-down game of politics. As between Bill Cosgrave's party and Dev's party today, it's the same old worm cut in two. They are both out for the spoils and the fat of office, power and all that it implies, at the expense of the common people. The average Irishman is now the most money-grubbing wretch on earth. Whoever said he was a sentimentalist was an ass. The German is the first sentimentalist in Europe and the Englishman comes a good second while Paddy is down the field."

"Paddy Quinburn, you mean, sir?" enquired Fergus,

"If you like. He is the most typical Irishman I know."

The good vanithee then bustled into the parlour to prepare some tea for the men and to welcome Swanton, none too effusively as he thought. As she moved about the dumb-waiter, he took stock of her as a possible mother-in-law. He noted that she was even still a fairly plump little woman with the remains of what was once a pleasant face, and hair more silver than sable. Her voluminous dress became her well. When she liked, she could be full of unvarnished kindness. Just now, she looked the embodiment of sweet expansiveness.

She explained that Finola was staying with an aunt of hers at Stonepark, near Limerick, for a few weeks and he felt a pang of disappointment. She was, she added, on the waiting list of a Dublin hospital and expected to be called to the nursing profession any day now.

"There is nothing much for any of us here now," said Fergus, "and the sooner that we realise it, the better."

"Well, I came here, ma'am, to renew my offer of financial help," said Swanton. "If you want any more land, I will back you as far as four figures will go."

"A friend in need is a friend indeed, but your kind offer is out of the question, at present anyway. Besides, there is no land offering hereabouts. Why should we take your hard-earned money?"

"Well, as I seem to be doing my little utmost to be affiliated to your remarkable family, it is up to me to try to rebuild its fallen fortunes as far as lies in my power."

"Sephora and I contended about you a good deal of late and I think I am winning, but you never can tell with the women. It's really a war of the sexes. I told them to give up all idea of young Murty Linnane now that we have toppled down in the world. I don't see many letters from him or hear about them either."

"You're a fool, James, you're a fool and I always thought you were," said his wife, looking rather peeved.

"Well, I'm a truthful man at all events, if that's what you mean. I don't want that young Dublin jackeen as a string to our Finola's bow, and besides, there is no need of a show of rivalry where Mr Swanton is concerned."

"No, indeed, sir," replied the latter.

"Well, I'm not staying here any longer, father," said Fergus. "You can do what you like with the farm, such as it is. Give it to Finola or whoever she mates with. All I want is a year or two at an agricultural college and then I'll paddle my own canoe, but that's a matter of money."

"So is my affair, too," added Swanton, "matrimony."

They all laughed heartily at the play upon words, except the vanithee.

"That poor guessing and calculating Yankee who was pauperised by the crafty Quinburn," said Macara, "is returning to

America and he offered me the pub and the ten-acre bit of land that's going with it for £250. He now wants, as he says, 'a quick getaway'. We could sell this place and buy it."

"It would be from the frying pan into the fire entirely with us then, da," said Fergus.

"Wisha, I suppose so, avickyo."

"Although I'm not a drinking man, I have seen one publican at close quarters for some time past and I wouldn't advise anybody to join the order of the Knights of the Spigot. They are a strange and subtle, greedy tribe. They seem to be possessed of a queer indefinable species of cunning unshared by most other traders. There's Quinburn, for instance, but I seem to have that man on the brain."

"Yes, there is a lot of talk lately about yourself and himself. Blanche's wife and others are yarning and, mind you, she is no friend of yours."

"I can't help that. Paddy is monkeying with the works more and more. It's himself will be the loser in the long run because I won't be there to keep him in check."

"Well, as to Fergus, we can fit him out to raid a farming college for a year for a share of its learning. That is, I think, scarcely beyond our slender resources so far. He would never do much in this little parcel of land, and he could never keep the big house in repair from the profits of twenty acres of scraggy land. He is right to take some other twist out of himself. In his absence we will have to abandon tillage and it's anything but a pasture farm. As for Finola, she is a bit troubled, too, lately. She feels that by out-racing old Gloster on the road that day she has brought all this trouble upon us. As far as a match for her goes, she would defer to our wishes even against her will if she thought that by so doing she was making things easier for the old woman and myself, do you understand?"

"Quite, sir."

238

"She thinks she has killed our happiness. She is very grateful to you for your more than generous offer and I have reminded her more than once that you are all out for a sleeping partner, do you know?"

"Yessir."

"You have stuck to us through thick and thin while all our fair-weather friends have long since deserted us. Whatever about forgiving Gloster – and we will have to forgive if we expect forgiveness in the next world – there are two things I can never forget and one of them is your kindness since the loss of our land. I have not much else to think of now and although I keep an eye on eternity, which is peeping at me round the corner so to speak, I'll keep the other eye on the wrongs that have been heaped upon us. I don't suffer from the two curses of Ireland any longer, that is to say a blind hopefulness and a fatal content."

"Well, I'm clearing out, anyway, as soon as possible," said Fergus. "Once a small farmer, always a small farmer, because there is nothing fluent about the business the same as shopkeeping. One exists rather than lives on a tiny bit of a farm. On the other hand, you have some chance of getting on out in the world."

"And every danger of demotion, too," said Swanton.

"As for Sephora and myself," continued Macara, "we are almost broken on the wheels of life and we won't be long an encumbrance to anybody, I hope. If it's God's will that you should become our son-in-law, you could live here."

"Never, sir."

"What do you mean, sir? Do you hear that Sephora?"

"You're right, Mr Swanton," added the latter, smiling for the first time.

"I mean, sir, that I'm only too willing to fall in with the first part of your wish," replied Swanton, "but not the second."

"Oh, that's different, sir, that's different," replied Macara. "You did give me a bit of a shock, the way you put it, believe you me."

"What I mean, sir, is that people setting up house should live to themselves. Newly-wed people should start out with an empty house, and that house I mean to provide myself. Three generations trying to live together has caused a lot of bickering from time to time in rural Ireland, but they know better in the town."

Returning to town that evening, Swanton made up his mind to sever his connection with Quinburn as soon as possible as their daily, almost-hourly bickering was becoming the talk of the town. People were beginning to look at him askance. He was, he felt, finished with teaching forever, and besides, an artist never repeats himself. He would have to look out for something to do in Dublin. Yes, he would have to strain every nerve to get there so as to be near Finola and watch over her in her new surroundings. Then the rest would be comparatively plain sailing.

A few weeks later, he was attending the funeral of Canon Law, who had died as a result of an operation. He met Peadar Blanche, who told him that Murty Linnane had been home for a few days and that Finola Macara, who was going nursing in Dublin, had returned with him. She had written home too, he added meaningly, to her mother that they were fast friends in Dublin.

He did not like this news, but then he thought it was the kind of story Blanche would like to have for him. The latter, since he got married, had been compelled by his alert managing wife to give up drink and the public house knew him no more. To Swanton, he seemed quiet in himself and, in fact, rather henpecked-looking. His old camaraderie manner had left him.

Owing to Quinburn's ravening tactics, Swanton found that he had to fight for his own reputation rather than that of the paper. The paper's progress under such nightmarish ownership was no longer possible and the sooner that he parted company with a declining concern the better. He was often tempted to turn on Quinburn as if he were a schoolboy and give him the father of a hiding, but he held himself in leash. Quinburn now directed all his thoughts to one point and pointed them to one purpose – his own disgrace, whenever he could accomplish it. On the other hand, Quinburn now felt convinced that Swanton was grossly overpaid and was staying on for a whole six months or a year in spite of him. Why could he not get rid of an employee, he asked, as readily as he could chuck a tipsy man out of his beer shop? It was monstrous. Why should he give Swanton six months notice in order to get rid of him?

For the first time in his career, Swanton felt that he was under the operation of something like ill-defined phobia, because he was dealing daily with a desperate man. He felt that just now the reputation of a lifetime could be lost in an hour. He decided to clear out while his reputation was whole. He returned to the village of Margadnua where he could live on his money for the present.

Then he remembered that a new paper was starting in Dublin. He knew the managing director well and had often befriended him in the past when he was a poor struggling politician. He even addressed meetings on his behalf at general election times in backward parts of the county where he was not known. Besides, he had a hundred pounds worth of stock in the new daily paper. He wrote to the rising politician for a post, but got back an evasive reply that he could on no account interfere with the discretion of his editor.

"Nothing doing there," thought he. "Macara is perfectly right in his estimate of politics and politicians. A perfectly raffish crew."

Had he got this position, he was determined to give a few hundred pounds towards a movement to convert the teacher's house in Menavia, now built at last, but no longer required, into

241

a parochial club where chess, draughts and billiards could be played. Here all could meet on terms of equality; it would end, once and for all, that obnoxious cabin-hunting habit among men, the cause of most of that idle gossip and backbiting for which the parish was noted.

To add to the over-flowing bowl of his sorrows, Finola wrote to him a short curt note that she could not entertain for a moment any matrimonial intentions he may entertain in respect of her.

Then he subsided into a chair and said aloud: "Life up to the present has been an unbroken series of disappointment and inhibitions for me." For want of something better to do, he jumped up, made a grab at a pen and a wad of paper and proceeded to write his first novel, making it partially autobiographical.

Quinburn – now known as the Gilla Dacker, or difficult boy – continues to pursue the turbulent tenor of his bibulous ways, a strange portent of the spirit of the age and the temper of the times.

– ENDS –